The Amendment

THE AMENDMENT

A Novel

Sue Robinson

A Carol Paperbacks Book
Published by Carol Publishing Group

First Carol Paperbacks Edition 1991

Copyright © 1990 by Sue Robinson

A Carol Paperbacks Book
Published by Carol Publishing Group

Editorial Offices	Sales & Distribution Offices
600 Madison Avenue	120 Enterprise Avenue
New York, NY 10022	Secaucus, NJ 07094

In Canada: Musson Book Company
A Division of General Publishing Co. Limited
Don Mills, Ontario

Carol Paperbacks is a registered trademark of
Carol Communications, Inc.

Manufactured in the United States of America
ISBN 0-8216-2501-2

10 9 8 7 6 5 4 3 2 1

Carol Publishing Group books are available at special discounts
for bulk purchases, for sales promotions, fund raising, or
educational purposes. Special editions can also be created to
specifications. For details contact: Special Sales Department,
Carol Publishing Group, 120 Enterprise Ave., Secaucus, NJ 07094

Grateful acknowledgments to a courageous publisher, Steven Schragis, and to a superb mentor, editor and friend, Stewart Richardson.

ARTICLE XXVII

Section 1. With respect to the right to life, the word 'person' as used in this article and in the fifth and fourteenth Articles of Amendment to the Constitution of the United States applies to all human beings irrespective of age, health, function, or condition of dependency, including their unborn offspring at every stage of biological development.

Section 2. No unborn person shall be deprived of life by any person: *Provided, however,* That nothing in this article shall prohibit a law permitting only those medical procedures required to prevent the death of the mother.

Section 3. The Congress and the several states shall have power to enforce this article by appropriate legislation.

The Amendment

Chapter One

"When we began our struggle to protect the Unborn, to protect tiny, helpless babies from wanton destruction, we were so very few upon the barricades! Only fifteen states had ratified the Human Life Amendment; we were belittled and scorned and spat upon! But five more states ratified. And then seven more. And ten more. And this year, on Valentine's Day, the last one. Number thirty-eight!" First Lady Mary Holt Morgan's voice vibrated to a high fever pitch, soaring on hot fevered wings across the high golden ceiling of the New Orleans Superdome, reaching out to the multitudes gathered there, their sweat-streaked bodies jammed tightly into every high-backed bleacher seat and onto every square inch of "Mardi Gras" artificial turf on the New Orleans stadium floor. Their hot shining eyes were fastened on the podium, on the ramrod-straight, triumphant figure of the First Lady of the United States. Together they had stormed the very gates of Hell to rescue Unborn children in abortion clinics; again and again and again they had borne witness to the murder, to the slaughter, to the genocide of the Unborn. Now they were together in victory, together in triumph, together at last in celebration of the ratification of Article Twenty-Seven, the Human Life Amendment. The air inside the vast Superdome was heavy

1

with heat and sweat; but the sweat of this exultant capacity crowd reeked not of the sour salted crust of fatted perspiration, it ran sweet instead, sweet and pure as only the mother's milk of the righteous is sweet and pure; sweet as milk and honey and the Rose of Sharon.

First Lady Morgan reached out to them with her slender white hands, reaching out to each one of them, to each delegate of the Rights for the Unborn League gathered tonight at the Louisiana Superdome in New Orleans. "When we formed the Rights for the Unborn League, twenty-five million American children already were dead. A generation had been lost. This must never happen again!"

The crowd rose to its feet with a deafening roar that rolled like thunder across the high, wide expanse of the Superdome; like heat lightning, it cracked across the soaring concrete dome, and the glittering constellation of lights on the domed ceiling shone down on them as if from Heaven itself.

"We will wipe the evil of abortion from the face of this country. We will prosecute illegal abortionists who defy the Human Life Amendment to the full extent of the law!" Mary Morgan, First Lady and President of the Rights for the Unborn League, was the impassioned general of their armies of light. Saint Mary of the terrible swift sword of righteousness; Saint Mary, the glorious blonde Madonna of the forces for Life. Sweet trails of perspiration ran down Mary Holt Morgan's face as she stood alone at the podium on this hot New Orleans night, her hands clenched into fists raised high above her glistening blonde head, her full red mouth thrown open, her pink throat open to them. Behind her, a giant screen replicated her image, and she appeared again on eighty-five video monitors scattered throughout the glistening Superdome. She was Mary the Madonna of the Glory Road.

"Now the Human Life Amendment is ours! We have saved the children at long last. Praise the *LORD!*"

Across the wide and muddy Mississippi River, and almost within sight of the Superdome, host tonight to the Rights for the Unborn League's annual National Conclave and its celebration of the recent and final passage of Article Twenty-Seven, the Human Life Amendment to the United States Constitution which gave full citizenship to the unborn, Dr. Michael Green closed and locked a faded wooden shutter in the old front parlor of a dilapidated rowhouse. He fiddled with the latch, which had eroded with rust, pressing it downward until it slid into place. This was not a night of celebration for Michael Green; it was another hot and fetid night given over to the careful and secret carrying out of the wishes of anonymous women who did not want the fetuses within them to be born.

Michael Green was a graduate of Tulane University School of Medicine, and he had interned in obstetrics at Charity Hospital, where in addition to delivering live babies, he had on occasion, performed abortions. After the passage of various state statutes restricting abortions, Michael Green had ceased performing them at Charity Hospital. The Human Life Amendment had become part of the U.S. Constitution just after young Dr. Green finished his residency in obstetrics at Charity Hospital. Then something happened to Michael Green, M.D.; something that shredded the short blocky obstetrician's finely drawn decision to leave abortions alone into a heap of dust at his feet.

The incident involved a child with a fetus in her, with her abdomen stretched hard over her expanding uterus and her blackened eyes dull and watering. Michael Green, assisted by Nora O'Brien, Registered Nurse in the Sexual Assault Unit at Charity Hospital, had performed a dilation and curettage on the child, scraping from her uterus the tiny white pieces of tissue until they were all gone. He performed the abortion in his nineteenth century cottage in the old Garden District. Nora O'Brien had anesthetized the child for him, using a small and steady drip of sodium-pentathol in a vein. When it was over, and while she still slept, Michael Green tore the sleeve from one of his old shirts and knotted it into the shape of a rabbit head with long ears and a round faded-blue chambray rabbit face. Emerging from the anesthetic, the child clutched the rabbit to her chest. She took the toy rabbit with her when she left Green's apartment with her grandmother. He thought about the child now; he wondered where she was, if she were with her grandmother; he hoped she was with her grandmother.

So it went on from the child, to other women and sometimes to other children. Green turned from the closed shutter. "How many do we have tonight, Nora?"

"Four without drop-ins." Nora O'Brien was four inches taller than the five-foot-six Green. "No D & Cs tonight. All suctions," she said. She liked Michael Green. Mike Green is not arrogant like a lot of doctors, Nora thought, and he has small fingers. She believed all OBs should have small fingers. They had been working together for six months now, working in the evenings three or four times a week, carrying out the wishes of women who found them, of women who came fearful and trembling in the night to them, some tight-lipped and defiant, some beaten and in despair, and the saddest with a false cheer that rang sharp and off-key and lonely and alone.

Dr. Michael Green, M.D. and abortionist, pulled on his wrinkled green surgical smock. "All four confirmed by telephone?"

"Yes," Nora O'Brien said.

"Let's get to work, then," he said.

"The anti-abortionists are in New Orleans tonight, you know," Nora O'Brien said. She jerked her head in the direction of the Mississippi River. The rowhouse was close to the Algiers ferry dock. The ferry ran from Algiers to Canal Street on the New Orleans side; the Superdome was a few blocks from Canal and the borders of the old French Quarter. "They're at the Superdome for their frigging prayer meeting. Taking up all the parking spaces, getting drunk all over town."

Michael Green had never been inside the Louisiana Superdome; he had never been to the Sugar Bowl Classic, and he had never attended a New Orleans Saints National Football League game. With his thick and stocky body, he resembled a wrestler or a boxer, and in fact he worked out four mornings a week with weights. But the fingertips of his small, slender hands were calloused and hardened from playing the cello, the mandolin and the dulcimer, which he had learned in undergraduate school.

"We'll have one drop-in tonight," Michael Green said. "A woman I know from the Conservatory of Music."

"OK," Nora said. She wiped one hand across her forehead and pushed her thick brown hair away from her face. It was hot; the old rowhouse bricks had stored up heat all through the hot day; now the bricks were radiating heat like a thousand tiny furnaces, radiating it through the thin old walls of the rowhouse.

On the New Orleans side of the Mississippi, and just over a mile from the Superdome, Rights for the Unborn League Special Security Assistant Jack Riley was just finishing a pre-operative briefing of a New Orleans Police Tactical Unit. Riley and members of the Unit were about to depart from the Tactical Unit headquarters. They were to load onto the Canal Street ferry and cross to Algiers, where certain members of the Unit already were in place. Jack Riley, leading remaining members of the Tactical Unit, hoped to crush yet another underground abortion clinic, one of dozens of such small, clandestine outfits that Riley was assigned to find and destroy. The New Orleans Police Department had cooperated fully in this; the Louisiana Parish prided itself on its commitment to protect the rights of the unborn and Riley, with the aid of Rights for the Unborn League computers, had provided a wealth of information on illegal abortion clinic operations in the South.

"All right. We expect two clinic staff, perhaps three," Riley said. "It's a small operation. But they're efficient. We estimate this outfit has performed at least twenty abortions a week for the past eighteen months."

"Murdering pigs," Morris West said. Morris West was the Sergeant in nominal charge of the Unit. He was a big man and Riley had observed that West himself had the appearance of an overweight boar; flat cheekbones, a thick heavily veined nose shaped like a snout, watery blue eyes disappearing into folds of pasty flesh.

Jack Riley ignored West; Riley had reservations on a flight out of New Orleans in the morning. He wanted to finish this job tonight.

Chapter Two

The crowd in the New Orleans Superdome was on its feet, swaying as if to music; the heat and light of its Righteousness beating an endless sea across the brightly-lit stadium; the sea ran toward First Lady Mary Holt Morgan, toward the President of the Rights for the Unborn League.

"I love you all!" Mary Holt Morgan bent her head toward them and closed her eyes. The ocean of heat and applause rolled on and on; onward in the white hot purity of Truth. "We were soldiers, marching to a battle to save our nation! This was a long struggle for the very soul of our country; it is not over yet!" She raised her head still higher, lifting her strong chin, clenching her white, even teeth. Her voice dropped, pitching lower. "Every state must ratify the Human Life Amendment; in every state, we must have this unshakable commitment. For even now, even as we gather in prayer and Thanksgiving, the evil threatens." Her chest heaved as she gathered her strength once again. "Yes. Even now. Even with the Amendment, even with the Right to Life written into our Constitution, there are those who are misguided, and there are those who would try to profit, who would traffic in illegal abortion." She paused. Her anger welled up, welled up in a hot, hard knot in her chest. The murderers, she thought. Murdering the innocents. God will punish them; we are God's instrument, she thought. The League is His instrument; I am His Instrument. Be with me, Father. Bless me.

"There are those who would break the laws of our country; break them in vile evil. Abortionists." She spat out the word, spitting it like poison from her mouth. "Traitors. Murderers. Preying on young mothers like vermin. The League has joined law enforcement agencies across this nation to stop them!" Her shoulders began to shake with rage; her voice cracked and dropped to a whisper. "We will stop them," she said. Her voice hissed from her throat, borne across the Superdome as if on the flapping black robes of an executioner.

And across the Mississippi River, away from the Superdome, away from the bright lights of the Vieux Carré and the French Quarter's giddy mobs of tourists and jazz aficionados, Jack Riley, Special Security Assistant for the Rights for the Unborn League, along with members of the New Orleans Police Tactical Unit, moved into position.

Jack Riley sucked in a breath. The odor of rotten eggs was drifting up the Mississippi Delta. The smell and the July heat in the Louisiana Parish was suffocating. He wiped one hand across his mouth. His hand tasted of salt. Riley turned to his driver, Sergeant Morris West, and pointed toward a ferry dock. The unmarked police car moved slowly past the dock and stopped.

The ferry was on its 9:00 P.M. run from the Canal Street station on the New Orleans side to the gritty waterfront neighborhood of Algiers. The ferry moved sluggishly toward the slip.

Riley opened his transmitter. "Number Two, are you in position?" Riley could see the outlines of an abandoned rowhouse two hundred yards ahead. An adjacent building had been gutted by fire.

"Number Two in position."

"Get the doorway in focus," Riley said into the transmitter. He looked down the street at the rowhouse. A slit of yellow light sliced beneath a shuttered front window. They were there. He guessed maybe eight or nine people were in the rowhouse. It was a small clinic. One doctor, one nurse, maybe an assistant. Maybe not. This clinic had been elusive. Small and mobile, it had escaped three other attempted raids, vanishing like a ghost, leaving nothing behind. Then a break. A father, enraged at a teenage daughter's abortion, gave it to them. The father forced a confession from the girl, forced her to spill out the details. They left the girl alone and moved fast on the clinic. Now they were closing in.

Riley squinted through the darkness, searching for a particular window in the building across the street. It was an old paint factory. The Tactical Unit had been in the building for three days. "Number Two, how many pictures do we have, please?"

"Twenty-seven rolls." The receiver sputtered. "I have the doorway."

"Thank you, Number Two." Riley coughed and wiped the perspiration from his forehead. Fucking Amendment, he thought. Six months into it and all hell was breaking loose. Underground clinics were fucking everywhere. I should be home in Miami, he thought. It stinks here. The job stinks. But Jackie my boy, he thought, think of the money; the wonderful money you are hauling in on this job. Money, money, money, he thought. What was the song? He couldn't remember. Ah. The musical about Berlin; Joel Grey singing "Money, Money, Money!" Except that it wasn't just the money; it was the other part, the seductive adrenalin rush of the hunt, the addiction to it. Riley had the addiction; like war lovers and mercenaries had it, except that he was not in Asia or Central America. No, no, he was not in some jungle, rotting with the fungus that always reappeared on his hands and feet when he was in the tropics; this was the United States in

1998, and Jack Riley was on the side of the Righteous, a soldier for the Rights for the Unborn League.

Riley watched a stray cat, fur matted and scarred with mange, pick its way over a pile of newspapers near the end of the street. The animal leaped onto a garbage can and turned to look back at the unmarked car. Its yellow eyes glittered. The creature turned and streaked into the darkness, leaving them behind on the dark street, leaving them to their night's work.

"Smart cat. Knows when to get out," Morris West said. He turned to Riley and chuckled. The police sergeant drummed sweating fingers on the steering wheel. The lower edge of the wheel pressed against his protruding belly.

"Shut up," Riley said. He reopened the transmitter. "Listen up. We will move in on the Redline signal. And we will be careful," he added. The receiver rattled with assents. Riley would have no more stinking incidents like the one that made the papers in Dallas. Three women got hurt in that one. Women, hell, he thought. One of them had been fifteen. No. Jack Riley liked them quick and clean; clean as a whistle. In fast, out fast; slam bang, thank you ma'am, he thought. No lingering sticky threads, no stinking messes.

Riley closed the transmitter. He pulled a crumpled pack of Camels from his damp shirt pocket and punched in the cigarette lighter. Riley's grandfather had smoked Camel cigarettes until the day of his death at 87. His grandfather had run a shrimp boat on the Texas gulf coast. The old barometer from the Louisa V was on the wall in Riley's Miami apartment. Riley took a long drag on his cigarette and turned to watch the ferry from New Orleans maneuver into the slip.

At 9:03, the ferry secured its moorings and began disgorging passengers. A line of cars moved off and swept away from the dock area, red taillights arcing north toward the Naval Air Station at the tip of the Mississippi Delta. Foot passengers moved rapidly toward a parking lot a block distant.

One, a woman wearing a light khaki raincoat, turned south at the dock, walking toward the line of abandoned tenements.

"Number Two." Riley cracked open the transmitter.

"I've got her. '' Riley heard the click of a lens shutter. Then the soft whoosh of the film advance. Click whoosh. Click, whoosh. He wondered who she was. It didn't matter. She sure wasn't a virgin. He took another drag on the Camel.

Hillary Foster's fine blonde hair was damp and lank in the stifling heat. She felt a rivulet of perspiration roll between her breasts. Her shoe heels clicked on the pavement. The sound echoed. A few cars were parked along the street. One stood stripped of its wheels, hubs on wooden blocks, already going to rust. She scanned the street, saw nothing, and turned toward the rowhouse. Fifteen seconds later, she reached the steps of the wooden structure.

She pushed a metal buzzer and waited, tapping one shoe against wood plank steps.

A peephole opened. "Yes?" A woman's voice came thinly through the opening.

In the warehouse above, the camera clicked again. Click, whoosh.

"My name is Hillary. I have an appointment with Mike Green."

The peephole closed. A dead bolt ground. Then a chainlock rattled and the door opened. A shaft of bright light slanted over the steps.

"Inside. Quickly." A hand reached out, grabbed Hillary's arm, and pulled her through the doorway. The door slammed behind her.

A woman with thick brown hair and the big, open face of an Irish peasant greeted Hillary Foster. "Hillary, my name is Nora O'Brien. I'm a Registered Nurse, and in spite of what this looks like, this is a safe, clean facility," she said. Nora O'Brien was thirty-five years old. She was tall; her large-boned features were softened by extra flesh and her face was pockmarked with old acne scars. She wore black trousers and a light green surgical smock. "Did you bring your things? I'm sure Mike filled you in. And if you can afford it, we'll need your payment now," Nora added. "If you can't pay, that's OK. This place is not exactly a profit center." She laughed a booming, deep laugh.

"No. I can pay. I know you need the money." Hillary pulled a small plastic bag from her purse. Then a white envelope. Five hundred dollars in cash, in twenties, was in an envelope.

"Good." Nora slipped the envelope into a gray canvas bag. "I'm sorry we have to collect like this, but our expenses are high. We've already moved the clinic three times this year."

"I understand." Hillary Reed Foster was standing in an entry hall. The parquet floor was blackened with age and layers of wax. Wallpaper with pink roses entwined in strands of green ivy wound up the walls and across the high ceiling. A lightbulb fastened to an extension cord hung from the ceiling. The hallway smelled powerfully of disinfectant. Hillary could hear a low hum of conversation coming from a room to her left. It was screened from view by bedsheets nailed to the wood molding.

"Well, let's get started." Nora said. "Come along this way."

A few moments later, they were crowded into what had been a butler's pantry. The wood shelves were lined with glass jars. A metal sink, newly installed, held several coffee mugs, dregs of coffee long since cold.

From one of the shelves, Nora extracted a vial of yellow capsules. "Take one of these now." she said. "It will help you relax. There's a dressing room over there," she added, pointing to a narrow door. "Just slip into one of the gowns. Be sure to bring your things with you."

It was unbearably hot in the windowless dressing room. The rough fabric of the gown rubbed against her shoulders. Hillary tied the strings on her gown, finished folding her clothes, and stepped back into the hallway. She had made the last of a dozen calls to her oldest and best friend, Elizabeth McKinley, in Washington, D.C., just before leaving her apartment. But there still was no answer; she left a long message on Elizabeth McKinley's answering machine, trying to explain to a tape recorder what had happened. It was difficult, talking to a machine. How could she explain that she was pregnant because student piano player Oliver Quinn had flushed an apple down the toilet in the boys' lavatory two and a half months ago, flooding the third floor of the New Orleans Conservatory of Music, and that she, his teacher Hillary, had gone to a jazz spot in the Vieux Carré to recover from Oliver, and that a combination of music and cognac—remember the Courvoisier her mother served at Christmas?—and the charms of a man from New York had lulled and seduced her into making this big dumb mistake? How could she call him in New York? Well hi, and guess what? No. Elizabeth, I'm paying for my mistake, she thought. She brushed her damp hair back from her forehead. Will a little ghost be there now, tapping me on the shoulder, tap tap tap, it's me, Hillary? Hello, Hillary.

Hillary Reed Foster looked down the hallway. The gown was so thin. She felt naked in it. Maybe Elizabeth was home by now; maybe she got the message on her tape recorder. Maybe Elizabeth was on a flight to New Orleans right now.

Morris West scratched at his belly. "When are we gonna move? Two of them got away already!"

Riley glanced over at West. Fucking greaseball, he thought. West's sweat smelled like pig sweat. "We want the clinic operators," he said. He scanned the darkened street. One small figure, a woman, had emerged from the front of the rowhouse. A second woman had exited from the rear of the building. She had been carrying a parcel wrapped in newspaper and secured with adhesive tape. We were right, Riley thought. The clinic is a small operation, a backyard outfit.

Hillary followed Nora O'Brien to a room at the rear of the rowhouse. The floor was covered in pockmarked green plaid linoleum. A window in the rear was covered with dark green cloth.

An examining table was in the center of the room. There was an aspirator beside it, half covered by a white cloth.

"Hillary?" Dr. Michael Green took her hand. "How are you doing? Any nausea? Fainting spells?"

She had been healthy, full of health, even lush with a pink blooming. "No," she said. Would it have been better to be sick? To be sick unto death? She smiled a sad little smile at Michael Green, physician and cello, mandolin and dulcimer player, who came often to the New Orleans Conservatory of Music, where Hillary was a teacher. When Hillary Foster discovered she was pregnant, she went to Michael Green. She felt safe with him, utterly safe.

He squeezed her hand. "We'll take good care of you. This won't take long. I'm just going to give you a shot to numb the nerves around your cervix. Then you can relax for a few minutes."

The table was hard, the obstetrical stirrups cold. Hillary watched as Michael Green pulled a speculum from a stainless steel bowl filled with disinfectant.

He slipped a sheet over Hillary's thighs.

"Just relax," he said. "That's good. That's fine," he added. "Um hm. You have a nice, healthy cervix, Hillary. Nice and pink. Have you seen your cervix? It looks like a bright pink doughnut. And, you're about ten weeks along. We can do a suction, no problem. I'm just going to take a look here, and then I'm going to numb your cervix," he said. "You'll feel a little pinch. Breathe deeply. Good. Almost finished. OK." He removed the speculum and tossed his surgical gloves into a metal wastebasket. "You'll need to relax for a few minutes so that the local can take effect," he said helping her up. "Nora will take you along to our ward. It's not that great, but it's all we've got right now," he added.

"It will be fine," Hillary said. "Just fine."

The old parlor was another high-ceilinged room filled with the same ancient wallpaper as the foyer. The floor had recently been painted white. It already was streaked with scuff marks.

Lying on a cot, Hillary began to feel drowsy. The medication was beginning to take effect. She wished she could go to sleep. Wake me when it's over, she thought. Like a line from a song. She stared up at the high ceiling. Maybe I should have gone to Mexico for this, she thought. Or Sweden. Lots of people are going to Sweden for them. But Mike Green is right here. I'm safe with Mike, she thought. Please Lizzie, be at my house. The thought was like a little prayer. Mike Green is an OB and he's clean and nice.

Hillary Foster was not alone in the room. Other women, she counted three of them, were on cots nearby. She could hear snatches of whispered conversation from two women on cots across from her. She didn't want to talk to anyone. She sat up and fumbled in her bag for a cigarette.

Hillary lit her cigarette, leaned back on the cot, and turned toward the wall. She began to count the wallpaper roses, counting row after row of roses entwined in strands of paper ivy. Was it too late to turn back? There was no going back; there was nothing back there. The curtains that shielded the room from the hallway parted.

Nora stood in the doorway. "Hillary, we're ready for you."

"Sure. Well. Here I go." She stubbed out her cigarette in a battered aluminum cannister beside the cot. Yes. Too late now, she thought. God help me.

Jack Riley looked at his watch again. He opened his transmitter. "All right, gentlemen, we are three minutes from Redline." He clicked off the transmitter. Stinking New Orleans, he thought. It smelled like a tropical hellhole; it smelled like some other places he had been, places with a particular odor, a sickly sweet odor that pinched the nostrils. He felt the beginnings of an adrenalin surge.

The obstetrical stirrups felt cold and hard on the soft flesh beneath Hillary Foster's feet. She watched as Dr. Michael Green slipped on a clean pair of surgical gloves.

"How are you feeling," he said.

"Fine. OK." So will there be a little ghost tap tapping me on the shoulder? She couldn't think about it now. Someday I will have children, she thought. This isn't the end.

"Hillary, I can put you under if you want. It would just be a drip of sodium pentathol."

"Will it hurt much without it?" Not the end, she thought.

"You'll feel some pulling and tugging. Some feelings like cramps," he said. "I just thought—well, if you're asleep for a few minutes, you won't have anything to remember."

"There's a little more risk with anesthetic, though." Nothing to remember. Nothing at all?

"There is a very small additional risk," Michael Green said. "Would you like the sodium pentathol?"

ʏ "No. It's OK like this," she said. I don't want to forget, she thought. I don't want a gray blank space where this would have been. How will I remember if it's all covered over with gray? She looked up at Dr. Michael Green, who was waiting for her. "No," she said. "I'll be fine." She turned her face to the ceiling as Michael Green bent over her.

"Hillary, just try to relax." he said. "You may feel some cramping and pulling. The more relaxed you are, the less discomfort you will feel. OK?"

"OK."

He opened her vagina with the speculum and began gently dilating her cervix. The cervix was strong and tight. Very slowly, the cervix opened. There, he thought. Right about there. He reached for the suction aspirator.

Jack Riley's glance swept over the dark street. "All right. Ready at the front. Let's go!" He shoved the car door open. "Move! Now!"

Doors slammed in three unmarked cars as men rushed toward the rowhouse. Above the street, the camera operator dropped a roll of spent film into the metal box and finished reloading the camera. He ground out his Panatella and brought the focus tighter on the rowhouse entrance.

Riley pulled a police service revolver from his shoulder holster, hesitated, and flipped off the safety. He could hear Morris West's labored breathing just behind him. Oh Christ, he thought. Here we go.

The thick wooden door splintered from the force of a blow from the blunt end of an axe.

"Police! Stand clear!" Riley shoved a woman in a surgical smock against a wall in the foyer. West and three other men pushed by, ripped the sheets from the entrance to the parlor and burst into the ward.

"Bastards!" Nora O'Brien struggled against the brute force of his arms.

Riley grabbed her by the shoulders. His gray eyes bored into her. "Where's the surgical suite?"

"There is no surgical suite here."

"Where is the O.R.?" He pressed harder.

"Find it yourself." Nora spit at him.

OK. Fuck her. He wiped the spittle from his face and motioned to one of the men. "Hold her. Start getting a statement. Make sure the exits are sealed off." He turned toward the parlor. Then he saw a staircase off to the left. Maybe the surgery was on the second floor. He bounded up the stairs.

Hillary Foster heard screams, scuffling sounds, the crack of iron against wood. "What's going on out there? Oh Jesus!"

Dr. Michael Green stopped. So it had happened after all. They were here; the police were here and Michael Green was finished. But not quite yet. "Be still," he said harshly. "Don't move." He stood and walked quickly to the door. He bolted it, then shoved a kitchen chair against it and returned to Hillary.

"Just a few more seconds now. We're almost through." He turned to the aspirator controls and increased the force of the suction. Then be bent over her, working rapidly, aspirator tube slicing back and forth across her uterus, searching for the remaining pieces of tissue.

"It hurts!" Oh my God. She tried to struggle up. Let me go!

"Just be still. I know it hurts," he snapped.

She heard footsteps pounding across the floor above. The footsteps moved toward a staircase that led to a third floor. Michael Green swore under his breath.

"Oh, God," Hillary panted. Cramping pain flooded her abdominal cavity and vibrated toward her chest. Someone was pounding on the door. The hinges rattled.

The lock snapped. The wooden chair splintered as the door crashed open.

Morris West stood in the doorway holding an axe. Beads of sweat dotted the flesh above his upper lip. He slammed the door shut, threw the axe to the floor and pulled a short hardwood truncheon from his belt. "Doc, get that thing out of her, you sonofabitch!"

The physician looked over at West. "Go to hell." He turned back to Hillary. "We'll finish."

"Do as I say, you fucker!" The hardwood swung to and fro.

Hillary heard the sickening crunch of wood on bone. Dr. Michael Green's muscled body crumpled to the floor. The blow had struck him along the back of his neck and across his left shoulder, breaking his neck and incidentally shattering his collar bone. Michael Green's last thought was that he should have given her the sodium pentathol; he should have insisted on it.

She clutched the bed sheet that was drawn over her thighs, fevered hands gripping the cloth like iron. Help me, God. Still, she thought. Be still.

West looked at her. The aspirator churned.

"Abortion is illegal, you know. The Amendment made it against the law."

"Go away."

He reached over and turned off the suction.

"Please."

West blinked, curled his fingers around the aspirator tube, and pulled.

She screamed. Her uterus ruptured just above her cervix. The room began to swim. White into gray. Cloudy. Lizzie? Mother. No time. The room turned black.

West lifted a cloth cover that covered the aspirator and looked inside. A small pool of blood and tissue was there. "Not much to see," he murmured. "Well." He turned back to Hillary.

The door to the surgery burst open.

"What the hell is going on here?" Jack Riley saw the physician lying inert on the floor, saw the woman on the table. "The surgery," he muttered.

"They were right in the middle of one," West said, turning to Riley. "Midway through one. I stopped 'em."

Riley pushed past him and pulled his transmitter from his pocket. "Get an aid team to the rear! Two casualties at the back of the building."

The transmitter sputtered an affirmative. Riley turned back to West. "Get out of here! Out you bastard! You sonofabitch!" Riley saw the angle of the doctor's head and neck and he knew even before he reached for a pulse that the abortionist was dead. He turned to the woman on the table and felt for a heartbeat. It was weak. Shallow and going down. Well, shit. Christ on a crutch.

"Nations around the world are watching us. We are an inspiration to them, an example to follow, a bright light on a dark sea!" First Lady Mary Holt Morgan clasped her hands together, cupping them before her, reaching out to the crowd in the New Orleans Superdome. Her full red lips quavered and her eyes glistened in the blaze of klieg lights. Oh Lord, they love me! It's all been worth it, she thought fiercely. All the speeches and the meetings and the plane trips without her husband and the endless political battles had been worth it. She wished fervently that her husband were at her side tonight. But President Edward Morgan, who did not play second fiddle for anyone, not even for his dear wife, was at home at the White House, having a late dinner on a tray in the family quarters, preparing for a meeting with the Prime Minister of Japan in the morning. In New Orleans, the Rights for the Unborn League's annual National Conclave was nearing an end.

"We have been sustained by our faith. Will you pray with me?" She stretched out her arms to them. "I love you! Let's say the Lord's Prayer together," she whispered to them. "Let's all rise for the Lord!" She spread her arms out wider and lifted her palms, and across the vast stadium the audience of Rights for the Unborn League delegates rose as one, their glowing faces raised up to her, lifted up to Mary Holt Morgan as to a bright and shining star.

Chapter Three

The body of Hillary Reed Foster, borne on a flat reinforced steel drawer built into the refrigerated wall of the morgue examining room, slid feet first into the bright fluorescent light. Her body was covered, except for her ankles and feet, by a white poly-cotton sheet. Bending over her, as if to a lover, as if for the first time, was the morgue attendant, Hilton Montgomery, who was a medical student at Tulane University. Montgomery delicately lifted the sheet from the dead Miss Foster's face. She had been dead for nearly ten hours, since shortly after midnight, and already her fine features were colored with the faint but unmistakable yellow pallor of death. Montgomery straightened and stepped back respectfully, his running shoes scuffling gently against the concrete floor of the New Orleans morgue. Hilton Montgomery was exceedingly respectful of bodies as young and fine as this one. He participated in autopsies at the New Orleans morgue, and later this morning, he would participate in this one, a rare opportunity indeed to examine young and healthy tissue in a white woman.

Frances Reed Foster stepped in front of Montgomery and bent over her daughter's body, her hand trembling slightly as she reached out to touch Hillary's face. There was a mark on Hillary's cheek, a long scratch that extended from just below her left eye almost to her ear; droplets of dried blood had congealed

22

along the scratch and some of the blood was smeared on her earlobe. But when Frances touched her, the droplets were hard against Hillary's skin; Hillary's flesh was cold to her mother's touch, cold as marble is cold, cold as only the icy water of death is cold. Behind her, Frances Foster heard someone clearing their throat. It was the detective who had brought her down the long elevator ride to the morgue, and she remembered that he wanted her to tell him that yes, this was Hillary Reed Foster, her only child Hillary, because the police wanted to go forward now with the investigation and would she mind, please, to just go ahead and formally identify her, and thank you, uh, Mrs. Foster ma'am. And Frances Reed Foster summoned all the strength of her sixty-three years, all the muscle and sinew of time and fortune and hard experience, gathering all this within her as if she were poised on a high platform, poised for a very high and complicated dive into dark waters far below her: "Yes. This is my daughter Hillary," Francis Reed Foster said. She said this to the wall of steel drawers, speaking over the head of her daughter, who could not hear her. The detective, who could, scribbled something on his clipboard and rocked back on his heels, waiting.

Frances bent again over Hillary's body, bent to caress the cold, still face once again. My darling. Oh God help me. Hillary. Frances Reed Foster had traveled all night, flying in the dark from New York to New Orleans, flying into the hot hell of the Southern July morning, to claim her daughter. The phone call that started this journey had come shortly after midnight in New York and now she was here with Hillary, with what was left of Hillary; a slender naked body under a poly-cotton sheet, a body cold as marble. Frances reached out and smoothed Hillary's hair across her forehead, smoothing the fine blonde hair that was so unlike her own thick and wiry brown hair. My hair isn't brown at all anymore, Frances thought. Why do I still think it's brown when it's almost white? I can see in the mirror that my hair is white. I'm old, Frances thought suddenly. I'll get even older without her unless I die soon. And Frances knew she would not die soon; that she would go on and on, day after day, month after month, year after year, and each day and month and year would be without her daughter, without her only child. So I am the last of the Reed Fosters after all, Frances thought; I am the last of us.

How did this happen? Frances Foster stood erect and still over her daughter's body, one hand on Hillary's fine blonde hair. She remembered the sketchy details police had given her. An abortion clinic raid, Hillary there, the abortionist operating on her, an accident, the police officer said. A terrible incident and the abortionist is dead, the police officer said. Of course she didn't believe them. For Frances Foster knew in the cold hard part of her heart that still was beating, beating like a muffled drum, that Hillary had been murdered in the police raid; she knew that. On the long plane ride, sitting in the empty First Class Section of a Delta Airlines red-eye flight to Atlanta, and changing planes for the flight to New Orleans, Frances Foster had gone over this in her mind, disjointed piece by disjointed piece, and while there were many pieces missing, she could see Hillary's murder in the fragments. Murdered, she thought. Murdered by her government, by the police, by the Right to Life amendment, by the Rights for the Unborn League and their Righteousness.

Frances Foster had come by taxicab to the police station in downtown New Orleans, but her cab had been forced to take the long way around, north from the airport and then east over Interstate 10 and through the backside of the city, because First Lady Mary Holt Morgan's motorcade had been enroute to the airport just then, and police had blocked off the entire reach of the Airport Highway for the long black motorcade carrying the First Lady. *DAMN* her! Frances thought. Damn the Bitch! *SHE* did this! And now the anger welled up in Frances, welled up like a volcano, a hot red anger from hell threatening to spill out of her in an explosion of rage. She lifted her hand from her daughter's face and spun on her heel to face the police detective: "I will make arrangements to take her home," she said to him. She lifted her chin, holding her head high, staring down at him with half-closed eyes, her mouth closed in a flat line.

The detective took a step backward. It was an involuntary step back, the step a man takes when instinct impels him to regroup, to gather his forces to withstand an assault. "Uh, an autopsy—"

"Yes. Someone upstairs informed me," Frances Foster said to the detective. "Will it be over by tomorrow morning?" Her half-closed eyes bored into him and her mouth closed again into a hard straight line.

Now Hilton Montgomery, medical student and this morning's morgue attendant, stepped between them. It was not for nothing that his parents had named him Hilton, hoping that the famous name would rub into him and shine him like gold instead of like brass, where he really came from. "The autopsy will be completed this afternoon, Mrs. Foster. We can release the body to you in the morning," Hilton said smoothly. Oh, she was a cold-looking old battle-axe, he thought. But her suit was worth a grand if it was worth a penny. Hilton tilted his head deferentially to her. "We'll be very careful with, ah, with your daughter," he said.

Frances nodded and turned away from them once again, turning back to Hillary's face once again, gently running her hand over the soft mouth. Hillary's mouth was closed, her marbled face expressionless. Did she know? Was it a quick death? Frances burned now, burned for every detail of Hillary's last night on this earth. A woman had been arrested in the raid on the underground clinic and she was somewhere in the New Orleans police complex. Frances Reed Foster determined that she would talk to that woman. Without warning, she turned on her heel and walked swiftly out of the morgue. The startled detective caught up with her at the elevator.

In the morgue, Hilton Montgomery gently covered Hillary's face with the poly-cotton sheet and slid the long reinforced steel drawer back into its slot in the wall.

Three reinforced steel drawers away, in another fully refrigerated metal slot in the wall, the body of Michael Green, M.D. and abortionist, lay entombed, awaiting final identification; no immediate family members had been found for Michael Green, and in another hour or so, an autopsy would proceed to determine exact cause of death even though it was obvious that death was a result of a severe trauma to the neck by a heavy blunt instrument.

Hilton Montgomery had already examined the body of Michael Green, and he looked forward to participating in the autopsy on this young male. Hilton already had gleaned, via the old reliable rumor mill, that members of the New Orleans Tactical Unit were saying that Michael Green died when he fell against his own examining table as he struggled with a member of the Unit, who was trying to stop him from aborting the unborn child of a woman who at that same moment was drugged and unconscious on the examining table. Unit members were saying that abortionist Michael Green's clumsy attempt at the hurried and dangerous abortion had caused the young woman's death, and the death of her unborn child. Hilton Montgomery, in his earlier examination of Michael Green's finely conditioned, compact body, had not found signs of such a struggle; in fact, Hilton found nothing at all to indicate a struggle. There was just the trauma to the back of the neck and one shoulder, and the only unusual feature Hilton found on Michael Green's body were the round and hard callouses on the tips of each of his fingers and on the thumbs of both hands. Although Hilton Montgomery did not know this, the callouses were from Michael Green's soft and expert playing of the cello, the mandolin and the dulcimer, musical instruments which the abortionist would play no more.

In the fluorescent cool of the New Orleans morgue, Hilton Montgomery began to prepare a table for the autopsy on Hillary Reed Foster, humming tunelessly as he stripped down the long, brightly lit examining table in the center of the room and laid out freshly sterilized instruments on a white poly-cotton cloth.

Directly east of New Orleans, in the Kenner District, First Lady Mary Holt Morgan and her small contingent of United States Secret Service agents had arrived at New Orleans International Airport and they were about to depart for Washington, D.C. The First Lady, wearing a white linen suit, her golden hair swept away from her face in a smooth and glowing chignon, was standing on the short flight of metal steps leading up to the cabin of Air Force Two. A pre-selected crowd had gathered on the roped-off tarmac to see her off, and the tarmac was a hot blizzard of small American flags, each one clutched in the hand of a member of the Rights for the Unborn League. Mary Holt Morgan stood tall and rigid on the gray metal steps, raising one hand up high to quiet the crowd as they pressed forward.

"Last night, as we renewed our commitment to the Human Life Amendment, the brave men of the New Orleans Police Department were carrying out their difficult and dangerous duty. They stopped the operation of an illegal abortion clinic here in Louisiana," she said. Her upraised hand dropped to her side. "Regrettably, there was bloodshed. Five unborn children were not saved. One young mother—a lost, misguided soul—was also lost. The abortionist who murdered these children was killed." She raised her head and closed her eyes before the hushed crowd, their tiny American flags drooping in the hot and humid morning air. Her chest heaved with rage. "I am filled with anger at the

death of those innocent babies. And the young mother." Tears
sprang to her eyes; they glistened with tears, glistening like
bright lights before the still crowd. First Lady Mary Holt Morgan raised her hands once again, raised them high above her
head, clenching them into tight white fists. "We must not rest
until these illegal clinics are wiped from the face of the earth!"
The crowd began to applaud with upraised hands, and the tiny
American flags waved like a red, white and blue benediction
before her. A moment later, she disappeared inside Air Force
Two, which was cleared for departure on Runway Three.

As Air Force Two lumbered toward takeoff for Washington,
D.C., Frances Reed Foster gasped in frustration at the Assistant
District Attorney who was once again refusing to provide her
with details of the raid on the Algiers abortion clinic, a raid
which killed her daughter. Frances knew only that the clinic
nurse, a woman named Nora O'Brien, had been arrested, and
that the nurse had been arraigned that morning, charged with
being an accessory to the murders of five unborn children. And
no, Frances could not see the arrested woman; Frances was not a
relative, and she was not of counsel either, the Assistant District
Attorney explained once again.

Two hours later, with the aid of her fat checkbook and the
writing of a personal check for $25,000, which the court clerk
then verified as to its authenticity, Frances Foster posted bail for
Nora O'Brien. The Assistant District Attorney could go to hell.

Frances Foster waited impatiently in the jail reception area for
Nora O'Brien to emerge from behind an electronically operated
steel mesh gate. Through the steel mesh, Frances glimpsed a tall
woman in a rumpled surgical smock standing at a counter. Although no one told her this, Frances knew the brown-haired
woman was Nora O'Brien.

A uniformed clerk behind the counter handed the woman something, and a moment later, the electronic gate swung open and Nora O'Brien emerged from behind it, holding her personal effects in a brown paper bag. Her face was mottled with exhaustion and she didn't recognize the woman who obviously was waiting for her.

"My name is Frances Foster. I'm Hillary Foster's mother. Hillary from the abortion clinic—"

"I remember Hillary."

"I posted your bail. I want to talk to you."

Across a wide and deep gulf, an abyss of time and fortune and circumstance, Nora O'Brien heard the cold measured voice and for a moment, she wanted to turn and go back through the steel mesh gate to the narrow bunk in the women's section of the New Orleans jail where she had spent most of the long night. But there wasn't any going back there. Well, OK, she thought. Hillary Foster's mother wrote the check; Hillary was my patient and her mother gets to talk to me. And so Nora O'Brien called on the old standby Registered Nurse part of Nora, who was needed just now to talk to somebody's mother about a patient who didn't make it. Except that Nora O'Brien would never again be a Registered Nurse in the United States. She looked into the cold gray eyes of the woman who had posted her bail. "It was your daughter's choice. We were taking good care of her until—"

"Until the police came," Frances said, finishing the sentence.

"Yes. Until then. We were doing the best we could," Nora said to Hillary's mother. Nora O'Brien felt the old standby Registered Nurse part of her begin to crack, as even stone will crack and fissure when under enough pressure. "They killed her, you know! These people." Nora swept one arm out, as it to encompass all that was around them in the hot and sticky New Orleans jail complex where she had spent the last fourteen hours of her life. They had been dark and miserable hours in spite of the peach-colored walls, which psychologists said would soothe and comfort the distraught and make peaceful the violent. Nora O'Brien had been isolated by the police since the Tactical Unit raid on their little underground clinic, hers and Mike Green's, except for brief and fruitless conversations with a young and anxious attorney, who would see her tomorrow, he said. Detectives from the Tactical Unit had questioned her for three hours, in the presence of the same young attorney, who continually nudged her from under the table when he was not chain-smoking, and she had not slept more than a few hours.

All night, Nora O'Brien had worried about Michael Green, about the blocky young doctor who, if anyone had asked her, she would have confessed to loving, in her way, in the only way she knew how to love him, which was as a colleague, an admirer of his small calloused fingers, a lover of the cowlick at the back of his head that created a whorl of dark brown hair which he attempted to slick back, unsuccessfully. "A very fine doctor was helping Hillary and—"

"Yes. Michael Green. He's dead, too," Frances said. "I—" Frances stopped. Nora's face stopped her; the horror and disbelief and grief that was boiling up in Nora's dark brown eyes, boiling up and overflowing. "I think we should get out of here," Frances said. She took Nora's arm and propelled her toward the door of the jail reception area.

Mike is dead. No. Nora O'Brien felt a terrible hot ball rising toward her throat. "My things—" she said.

"I have them."

Nora O'Brien felt Frances Foster shoving her toward the door. Mike is dead. The girl Hillary is dead. Nora stumbled. Frances caught her. Nora had not cried in a very long time. She was, after all, thirty-five now and big girls did not cry.

A few minutes later, they were in Frances Foster's rented car, and Frances was maneuvering it through the narrow streets of the

French Quarter, on their way to Hillary Foster's apartment. Nora O'Brien was slumped against the door on the passenger side, staring unseeing out the window, the passing buildings and side streets a blur, her old standby Registered Nurse self gone as surely as the little clinic she and Mike Green had operated was gone. She was wiping her eyes with a handkerchief that bore the sweet and strong traces of Joy perfume. It belonged to Frances Foster.

In Washington, D.C., on this hot and muggy afternoon, the late Hillary Foster's close friend Elizabeth McKinley was just arriving home from a business trip to San Francisco. Elizabeth traveled frequently in her job as an emergency management consultant, although she hated flying, airports, and out of town lunches with clients. As usual, she checked for messages first. She punched her message recorder reverse button and stood back to listen. The machine hummed. A three-digit dial moved in reverse. She watched the digit numbers shrink. Two hundred. One ninety-five. At one ninety, she punched Stop and turned the recorder onto Play.

"Lizzie? It's Hillary. Where are you? Don't be out of the city. I hate your fucking machine. Did you know that? Well, it's just after five down here in Mardi Gras town." Hillary's voice stopped. Elizabeth McKinley could hear the faint sounds of breathing. That was odd. Hillary was a very definite kind of person. She didn't have long pauses in her life. Elizabeth turned the volume up. Hillary's voice returned. She was talking faster now. "Did I tell you I hate this machine?" Another pause. "Look. I've got a problem Lizzie. I'm—" A sigh. "I'm just a little bit pregnant. Is that what they say? A little bit pregnant?" There was a pause on the recorder. Then Elizabeth heard a long breath. Drawn-out and long. "It's, ah, not the right time for me just now," Hillary's voice said.

Time for a cigarette, Elizabeth thought. Oh boy. Pregnant. How could she? Elizabeth looked at her fingers. They were trembling just slightly. Take a deep breath, Lizzie. Nothing to be afraid of. Everybody knows there are clinics operating. Well, shit.

Hillary's voice went on, piercing the still apartment. "I haven't told anyone. Lizzie?" Hillary's voice stopped. Elizabeth heard a sharp explosion of breath. "Will there be a little ghost, do you think? I can't think about it." Hillary's voice dropped to a whisper. Elizabeth leaned toward the recorder, straining to catch the words.

"—wrong time. I found out about a clinic operating in a place called Algiers. A doctor friend of mine I know from the Music Conservatory runs it. He's a terrific cello player. Really wonderful, and a nice man. I think I'll be real safe with him. He's an OB, Lizzie. Lizzie? Could you come down?" The voice stopped. "I don't have time to go out of the country. I'll be fine getting it done here. They told me to come on Thursday just after nine. God. Late at night in some dingy place. It's a nightmare. But—" She stopped. The recorder clicked past the silence. Elizabeth took a long drag on her cigarette. How could Hillary get caught like this? Damn!

"Don't tell my mother, Elizabeth. Do you hear me? God, I hate your machine! She doesn't need to know. Nobody needs to know but you and me. That's the way I want it. Thursday. Can you come? That's three days from now. Lizzie? Call me right away, will you? Tonight. I don't care how late it is." Her voice dropped. "Well. I'll wait for your call."

Elizabeth heard the click of the receiver. The recorder stopped. Thursday. The abortion would have been last night, then. Hillary is probably fine, she thought. Probably taking the day off to recover. Poor old Hillary. Well, I won't tell her mother; mothers need protecting from real life, she thought. She picked up the phone and punched in Hillary's number in New Orleans. The phone rang four times.

A familiar voice answered, but it was not Hillary; it was Frances Foster—God, she must have incredible maternal antennae, Elizabeth thought, concluding instantly that not only had Hillary's mother learned of the secret abortion; she had obviously flown down from New York to help and comfort Hillary. Well, good for her, Elizabeth thought. If anybody's mother would do that, it would be Frances Foster.

"Frances?"

"Yes. Who is this?"

"Lizzie McKinley. In Washington?" Elizabeth was comforted; Hillary was not alone after all.

"Of course. Hello, Lizzie."

"Ah, how is Hillary doing?"

There was a long silence at the other end of the telephone.

"Mrs. Foster?"

"Yes. I'm here." Another silence. Then: "Elizabeth, there has been a terrible accident," Frances Foster said. She cleared her throat, as if there were something stuck there. She was in the tiny living room of Hillary's apartment and answering the telephone had been an automatic gesture; the phone was at her elbow on a side table. Nora O'Brien was sitting across from her, on a loveseat, drinking a glass of wine. The air conditioner was going full blast and the apartment was beginning to cool off. "Really, I—" Frances stopped. I can't, she thought. Frances looked over at Nora O'Brien, who was fully alert now; Nora O'Brien had gathered herself together in some elemental way and now she rose from the loveseat and took the telephone receiver from Frances Foster's outstretched hand.

"Elizabeth, my name is Nora O'Brien and I guess you're a friend of Hillary's?"

"Yes. Her closest friend. What is going on down there!"

"Hillary is gone. She was pregnant and police raided the clinic where she was—"

"What the hell do you mean gone!"

"She's dead."

Elizabeth began to shiver. She clasped her arms together to stop the shaking. She was freezing. Freezing to death. I wasn't there, she thought. I wasn't there for her.

"Elizabeth?"

"Yesss."

"I was the clinic nurse. Hillary's nurse. They killed Hillary and they killed a very fine doctor who was trying to help her; Michael Green was a wonderful person." Nora O'Brien took a long deep breath, expelling it very slowly. Her hatred and rage would sustain her now; she knew that as surely as she believed in vengeance and she believed in it with every beat of her heart. "Hillary's mother just bailed me out of jail. Not for long, probably," Nora said. She drained the rest of the wine. "Are you OK?"

"Yesss," Elizabeth said.

"Have something stiff. And then you'd better get down here."

Chapter Four

Bougainvillea wound delicately around the iron balcony railing outside the dead Hillary Foster's window, twisting and turning in deep green, its dark shining leaves cool in the hot and muggy southern sun. Nora O'Brien, her reddened and half-closed eyes watering in the bright light coming through the window glass, saw that the bougainvillea had been trimmed recently, trimmed and watered; Nora's dead patient Hillary had been the gardener, the meticulous caretaker of the bougainvillea. The iron balcony faced St. Philip Street in the French Quarter, the fortified city of the Vieux Carré which had been planned and laid out by the French military engineer Adrien de Pauger in 1721. But the old fortified city had not shielded the dead Hillary; it had not shielded the dead Dr. Michael Green, M.D. and abortionist, either, and it would not shield Registered Nurse and accused felon Nora O'Brien.

Now Nora was here, in Hillary Foster's Vieux Carré flat, about to turn once again to Frances Foster, who wanted some answers, which Nora O'Brien did not have. Elizabeth McKinley, Hillary's friend, was on her way to New Orleans from Washington, D.C., and she, too, would want answers which were not there, not for Frances Foster or Elizabeth McKinley or Nora O'Brien herself. With all of her broken heart, Nora hoped that Hillary Foster and Michael Green, M.D., had gone swiftly, that the two of them had not lingered in the violent dark of the Algiers abortion clinic with the unclean hands of members of the New Orleans Police Tactical Unit on them, defiling their bodies; she hoped they had departed this life like Houdini escaped from his shackles in the underwater trunk, swimming swiftly and surely into the last great adventure. But with all of her yearning for this escape for the two of them, Nora O'Brien could not elude her sharp and agonizing memory of their last night in the abortion clinic in Algiers, for she remembered a long time passing before an ambulance came for them. And so she hoped for the blessing of therapeutic shock for Hillary Foster, who had surely hemorrhaged to death, and she hoped for the numbness of concussion and unconsciousness for Michael Green, who she believed had absorbed mortal blows delivered by at least one member of the New Orleans Police Tactical Unit. But all of this was conjecture, although her professional judgment bolstered it considerably.

Nora pulled down a creamy white window shade that hung over the window in Hillary Foster's apartment, blotting out the balcony, the bougainvillea, St. Philip Street, and the hot southern sun, but not the heat; even the air conditioning could not blot out the heat. In the dim light, and with the torpid afternoon just beginning, her first afternoon as an accused felon in the State of Louisiana, Nora O'Brien turned to face her dead patient's mother, Frances Reed Foster, who had posted Nora's bail, thus paying for this moment, and who wanted to know what had happened during her daughter's last hours on this earth. But Nora had not been in the kitchen converted to a surgery in the Algiers row house when police invaded it; she had been in the long hallway by the staircase, facing the wall, her arms up, her hands pressed against the wallpaper, fingers splayed out, while a member of the New Orleans Police Tactical Unit conducted a rough body search, and then she had been moved to the foyer for the long wait for the ambulance that did not come in time for Hillary

Foster or Michael Green. "The police killed them both," Nora said to Frances Foster. "The police. The Rights for the Unborn League. They were at the Superdome last night, celebrating the passage of the Amendment. Did you know that? Sanctimonious bastards."

Frances Foster sank back against the cushions of the loveseat. Well, she knew what Nora said was true, but she wanted more; surely her daughter's death was not just the result of this random violence against the clinics. She tried to picture the clinic in Algiers, across the Mississippi River, last night. Was it dark there? Dirty? Surely Hillary could have found a safe place. No. It was not safe; none of them are safe, Frances thought. She lifted her cold gray eyes to Nora O'Brien, searching Nora's drawn and pockmarked face, trying to see in her exhausted eyes something that would tell her more.

Frances sighed deeply. She remembered Hillary's face, her cold as marble body on the flat reinforced steel drawer in the subterranean morgue at the New Orleans police station. Looking up at Nora, with just the sound of the air conditioner humming in Hillary's apartment, just the sound of air moving through the whirring air conditioner fan between them, Frances asked for more. "Did she suffer?"

Nora O'Brien had seen faces like this before; she had been a public health nurse for thirteen years, after all, and she had spent the last six of them in the Sexual Assault Unit at Charity Hospital, witness to victims of brutality and suffering. As each year passed, the sexual assault cases, particularly the assaults against children, seemed to grow worse. Nora O'Brien had no explanation for this seeming rise in violence and could not deny that it was there. Nora moved to the sofa opposite Frances, sitting down heavily on the thick cushions. "Hillary was about ten weeks along; she was healthy and strong. Good vitals. No indication of problems. Mike Green was doing a simple suction abortion on Hillary when the police broke into our clinic," Nora said. "He would have been nearly finished. Something happened in surgery. I—." She remembered the sound of wood splintering from a heavy blow. And a scream; there was a scream from back there and then it stopped. Nora felt Frances' cold gray eyes boring into her. "I believe the police tried to stop the abortion; they were clumsy and they killed her. I believe she hemorrhaged; she bled to death while they waited for an ambulance to come across the river from New Orleans." Nora's voice softened. "She would have been in shock from the bleeding, Mrs. Foster; it would have been like a coma," Nora said.

Frances pressed her lips together, holding back her tidal wave of grief and rage. Hillary's face this morning, her expressionless face, so cold, with just her fine blonde hair still feeling like Hillary; was her face the still blank face of the unconscious? Did she know? Frances reached for this slender thread. "So Hillary wasn't in pain when she died?"

It was such a small comfort to give to Frances. "Probably not; not at the end," Nora said, speaking very softly into the hushed room, her voice just rising above the sound of the air conditioner. She reached for a bottle of wine that was on the side table and poured herself a glass of it.

Frances closed her gray eyes. So the police did kill Hillary; the police and the Rights for the Unborn League and First Lady Mary Holt Morgan killed Hillary, and Dr. Michael Green, who was with her in the clinic across the Mississippi River from New Orleans, in the black dark of a hot and humid southern night, and they would not be the last to die like this unless something was done to stop it. For the first time since her telephone rang last night and she answered the summons to New Orleans, Frances Foster felt her heart beat faster, not with fear and trembling this time, but with the fire of righteous anger welling white hot in her soul. "This must never happen again," she said. "We must stop it

from happening; we must stop these people. These murderers."
It was Hillary's choice and they had killed her for choosing. Oh,
the bastards.

Nora drank the wine she had poured herself, drinking the entire glassful, and then she slammed the glass on the side table; the
side table rocked, and a china lamp on the table rocked with it but
did not fall over. Nora O'Brien, in spite of her numbing exhaustion, in spite of the grief and loss and pain, felt a surge of renewed energy throb through her body; she felt a well of affection
begin to fill in her for Frances Foster, a well of understanding
beginning, and she felt the beginnings of hope.

Nora looked with direct brown eyes at Frances Foster, the
woman she had met only hours ago, the woman who had bailed
her out of the New Orleans jail, writing a check for $25,000 to
pay Nora's way out of there. "Back in the nineteen-forties and
fifties there was something called Jane's List," Nora said slowly.
"It was a series of telephone numbers; you called them one after
another and they led to a safe abortionist. We need a Jane's List
that will lead women to safe abortions," Nora said. But where
was safety; where was the safe place? "Sweden," she said. "We
would be safe in Sweden."

Out of the country, Frances thought. They were not safe in
their own country. At that moment, something was severed inside Frances Reed Foster; something that always had held her
like strong rope broke free. She realized they were ties, ties that
bound no longer. Frances Foster, Hillary's mother and sole survi-
vor now of the Reed Foster family, whose money could not buy
her daughter's life, now saw that her money might begin to buy a
Jane's List. Calculating swiftly, Frances figured that her entire
estate—everything, even the house at East Hampton—would
probably bring, if liquidated, around $10 million. Not enough;
they would need more money, she thought. Much more money. It
occurred to her that while she herself did not have enough

money, there were those who did. As Nora watched, waiting, Frances continued her mental calculations for some minutes. "About $100 million would get us well started," Frances said finally. She smiled gently at Nora, her wide mouth curving up in her first smile in many long hours. "We can get it, ah, from the First Lady and the League; they owe us and they should pay." She paused, allowing Nora to absorb this, but before Nora could reply, Frances continued: "We can kidnap the First Lady, Nora. That will get us the money. Here, have a little more wine, Nora. You look pale."

Across New Orleans, and far from the late Hillary Foster's Vieux Carré flat, a northbound flight to Washington, D.C., was about to leave the departure gate for Runway Four. First Lady Mary Holt Morgan had departed from New Orleans International Airport hours earlier, but Secret Service Agent Eugene Duffy was just now leaving. His was the "wheels up" assignment on this trip, and so he had remained on the tarmac as Air Force Two lifted off for Washington, D.C., checking the last of the security details, making sure there was no funny business during the last moments of departure. Duffy was flying home commercial, via USAir, and his flight had finally been called. It was a relief for Duffy to fly commercial for once, to be off-duty for once during his own takeoff and arrival. Eugene Duffy, who like all members of the Secret Service was on assignment from the federal Bureau of Alcohol, Tobacco and Firearms, had been a part of First Lady Mary Holt Morgan's personal staff for almost two years. He was a favorite. The First Lady liked to play pinochle with Eugene, who was a very good player and a good match for her. She played to kill and so did Eugene Duffy; their long running tally, accumulated mostly during her flights around the country on behalf of the Rights for the Unborn League, showed the First Lady ahead of him, but not by much.

Eugene Duffy had never expected to find himself playing cards with someone like Mary Holt Morgan; he was from the old mining town of Wallace, Idaho, carried to his present heights by a baseball scholarship to the University of Idaho and the friendship of his local congressman, Lyle Pellum, who liked baseball and helped the local boy get on with the Federal Bureau. Duffy was grateful to the congressman and to baseball. But Eugene Duffy had not been interested in a pinochle game on this particular southern afternoon, even with First Lady Mary Holt Morgan; he was instead morosely contemplating his next move with one Leslie Gibbons, who had announced over the weekend that she wanted to date other men. Her announcement had given rise to a murderous rage in Eugene Duffy's heart, but he was controlling it, and he was scheming to stop her; he was even considering an offer of marriage, although the thought filled him with dread, for he liked his freedom. In the hot and humid afternoon, Duffy heard the call to board the USAir flight. He shouldered his dark blue overnight bag and joined the line of passengers boarding USAir Flight 173 for Atlanta and Washington, D.C.

Eugene Duffy shuffled with the other passengers into the tourist section, going by the wide and thickly cushioned seats in First Class. All of the First Class seats were empty, all but one. In that seat, at the back of the First Class section and at a window, was Rights for the Unborn League Special Security Assistant Jack Riley, who flew First Class or nothing. Riley had never met Eugene Duffy, although he liked the Secret Service boys.

Jack Riley, who had led the raid on the Algiers abortion clinics, across the Mississippi River from New Orleans the previous night, had cancelled the flight he had planned that morning to Miami, for the League's Executive Director, Carlton Farnsworth, needed to meet right now about the clinic raid at Algiers. The raid had made the papers and the League didn't look too good on this one, Carlton Farnsworth had shouted that morning over the phone to Jack Riley; this was real bad P.R. for us, Jack, and we've simply got to do better on this kind of thing!

Well, Riley didn't like it either; he favored the quick and clean method in his work. The New Orleans Police Tactical Unit personnel, particularly the Tac-Unit sergeant, would not have been on Riley's short list for the crappy little raid in Algiers if he had been able to stop it. But once again, the League cooperated with the local boys and the local boys fucked up. Ah, the hell with it; the hell with New Orleans, Riley thought. He had been paid, and it was damn good money. Riley ordered a Bloody Mary and leaned back against the seat cushions. He opened his briefcase, twirling the combination lock with practiced ease. Papers stacked inside detailed investigative work concerning the financing of a network of underground abortion clinics. The clinics had begun operating shortly after final passage of the Twenty-Seventh Amendment to the Constitution; they seemed independent of one another, disorganized, and most were like the backyard outfit in Algiers. One doctor, maybe, one or two nurses. Small outfits. Mosquitoes. But the mosquitoes buzzed, didn't they, he thought. The papers in Riley's briefcase also included reports on violent incidents at some of the clinics, but none of the others had been as bad as this last one; somehow the Algiers clinic raid had gone to pieces on him.

Jack Riley pulled a slim manila envelope containing a confidential file on the death of Hillary Reed Foster from the briefcase. It was sketchy, pulled together in the last few hours. Riley spent the next thirty-five minutes going over the report, making small marks with a black felt pen at several points; points he thought mattered amid the rubbish thrown in there by the Tactical Unit, which was trying mightily to cover its wet and muddy tracks. One mark Riley made, a careful thin underline, was a mark under the name Elizabeth McKinley; her name had been found in the dead girl's papers. A second name underlined in the same fine black was that of Frances Foster, the girl's mother. Mrs. Foster lived in Long Island, and she had flown down that morning to identify the body. There was no information concerning the girl's father. Riley frowned. Frances Foster had bailed the nurse. Nora O'Brien, Registered Nurse, had walked out of the Women's Section of the New Orleans jail on the wings of a $25,000 check written by the Foster woman. A good check. Riley admired people who could write $25,000 checks, but he could not understand a check of that magnitude written for a stranger, especially when that same stranger was involved in your daughter's death. He needed time to think about this. The nurse could walk, he thought; she could jump bail no sweat and leave the Foster woman behind. And why wouldn't she? She was finished anyway; Nora O'Brien's days as a licensed nurse were over. Jack Riley dropped the Hillary Foster file into his lap and ordered another Bloody Mary. The name of Dr. Michael Green, M.D., abortionist, also was in the Hillary Foster file, but Jack Riley did not like to think about Dr. Green; he would let the New Orleans Police Tactical Unit sweat that one out.

By the time USAir Flight 173 banked east on final approach to National Airport, Riley had completed reviewing the Foster file, gone through most of the other files in his briefcase, and assembled a preliminary list of names.

He was just finishing yet another Bloody Mary as Flight 173 sank toward the Potomac River and closed on final approach to National Airport in Washington, D.C.

Fifteen minutes later, Jack Riley was in the old lobby at National, shouldering through the weekend crowds to a waiting limousine.

The low horizon of Washington approached as the limousine crossed the Potomac and sped north along the Rock Creek Parkway toward Georgetown. The limousine pulled off the parkway at the exit to the Naval Observatory.

Ten minutes later, Riley's driver pulled to a stop in front of a glass and steel structure that was national headquarters of the Rights For the Unborn League. The three-story building contained nearly 75,000 square feet of closely guarded floor space. An electromagnetic envelope of thin metal shielding was secreted between its heavily reinforced walls and the coat of reflective glass that surrounded the building exterior. The shielding prevented leaks of any electronic signals generated by the organization's communications system and provided security for an array of high-capacity computers.

Riley slammed the passenger door of the limousine and followed the driver through the hot and muggy Washington, D.C., sun to the building entrance. Wide glass doors opened automatically as they approached. A security guard in a gray uniform looked up from a black reception desk in the lobby and pressed a button on a console beside the desk. A computer screen blinked on. Riley's full name, John Brooks Riley, of Miami, Dade County, Florida, rolled up on the screen. In bright green lettering on the charcoal video screen, the short story of Riley's life thus far appeared. John Brooks Riley, born in Freeport, Texas, October 12, 1956; born in a white cinderblock house set back on a brown, weed-filled lawn two streets over from the Tex-Mex strip. John Brooks wanted more than the cinder block house. The University of Texas and then the Central Intelligence Agency made it good for John Brooks Riley, but he wanted it much better. For only money can buy beachfront condominiums and all that accompanies them in Miami, Florida; and so Jack Riley, after a fine career in the service of his country, became self-employed, available to high bidders. Soon, perhaps within five years, Jack Riley planned to retire, although he would be happy to call it quits much sooner than that and perhaps do a few hobby-type jobs now and then, just the interesting jobs.

In the lobby of the Rights for the Unborn League headquarters in Washington, D.C., the uniformed security guard who had been seated at the reception desk, reading the background report on John Brooks Riley that now glowed gently on his video screen, rose to his feet. "Go right in, Mr. Riley. The Director is expecting you." The guard pointed to a set of double doors to the left of the reception area.

Riley nodded, strode across the cavernous lobby, and pushed open the entrance doors to the offices of Carlton Farnsworth, Executive Director of the Rights for the Unborn League.

Carlton Farnsworth, dressed in a black pin-striped Savile Row suit, white combed cotton shirt and a red silk tie from the New York Jockey Club, was waiting inside, sipping a bourbon and branch.

Chapter Five

The good Kentucky bourbon and branchwater went down smooth, sliding cool and silky down Carlton Farnsworth's eager throat. It was late in the afternoon on Friday, late enough for a gentleman to have a cool drink in the privacy of his office. Carlton Farnsworth, Executive Director of the Rights for the Unborn League, leaned one fleshy hip against his polished mahogany partner's desk, the one he had brought over with him from the United States Department of Justice when he resigned as Attorney General of the United States to become the League's top officer, although not its President; the League Presidency belonged to First Lady Mary Holt Morgan. Carlton Farnsworth's resignation as Attorney General, which came at the earnest and heartfelt request for President Edward Morgan just thirteen months after Farnsworth finally had become Attorney General, was a sour note for Carlton Farnsworth, Harvard Law School, Class of 1966; the resignation was like sour candy under his tongue, sour candy he sucked secretly behind his smiling lips and his white, even teeth.

Carlton Farnsworth's teeth were set in a mouth that was small and slightly puckered, set in a face with remarkably even features; it was a face that served as a soft and perfect foil for Carlton Farnsworth's exceedingly bright blue eyes, which seemed to sparkle with warmth and joviality, especially when he smiled his perfect smile, which he did often, although his warm and beatific smile and his sparkling bright blue eyes masked utterly the inner workings of a ruthless and calculating mind. President Edward Morgan, no doubt at the urging of his wife Mary Holt Morgan, had asked Carlton Farnsworth to become Executive Director of the Rights for the Unborn League just as the coalition of Pro-Life groups from which the League had been formed launched its final assault on state legislatures across the United States, struggling for ratification of Article Twenty-Seven, the Human Life Amendment to the Constitution of the United States. Carlton Farnsworth, who had long nurtured a private dream of someday becoming President Farnsworth, Leader of the Free World, had been forced to take a benign and sparkling back seat to Mary Morgan as she campaigned across the country for the Human Life Amendment, treating him like a servant, like a smiling hired boy, she with her perfect golden hair and her glowing pink face. They fell all over her, all the little legislators, sucking up to her, brushing up against her, and all the while, he, Carlton Farnsworth, had pulled the hard strings and made the bargains and counted the damned votes, some one by one, until all the votes were in and the Human Life Amendment was a done deal.

Now the League was engaged in a concerted effort to crush the illegal abortion clinics, which had sprung up like unpleasant noxious weeds, blossoming in garages and back alleys and even in fine suburbs. The abortion clinics had begun operating after passage of the Human Life Amendment, and the Rights for the Unborn League was aiding state and local police, working with the Justice Department, lending all of the weight of its political strength and its organizational resources to the effort to stop the clinics. And now this incident outside of New Orleans Thursday night had gotten in the way. Farnsworth had received an oral report, of course, and the New Orleans Police Tactical Unit report had been faxed to his office. Jack Riley, his own man and the Special Security Assistant for the Rights for the Unborn League, had been on the scene down there in New Orleans, and it was obvious that old Jack had bungled his job. Well, the New Orleans Tactical Unit would take the heat anyway; the New Orleans boys could handle it. Still, Carlton Farnsworth disliked the slightest smudge of dirt on the pure white surface of the Rights for the Unborn League, for if he had not stepped joyfully into his position as its Executive Director, he was not unaware of the possibilities for himself therein, especially if the First Lady could somehow be shunted aside. He had therefore busied himself on this Friday morning and afternoon with a search for some wedge in the New Orleans incident through which he could drive the appropriate public relations position for the League in this situation. For this purpose, he had summoned Jack Riley, his special security agent, to Washington, D.C.

Leaning against his partner's desk, which was made wholly of the fine heartwood of Philippine Mahogany, Carlton Farnsworth smiled brightly and beautifically at Jack Riley, who had just entered his office. "So, Jack. Good flight?" Farnsworth smiled his widest smile. "This incident in New Orleans. I've been looking into it from here, and ah, I find out that the girl's mother bailed the abortionist's nurse out of jail?" Farnsworth acknowledged Jack Riley's affirmative nod and went on. "I thought that was unusual. After all, the nurse and the abortionist killed the woman's daughter, didn't they. Did you know the girl's mother has never been married?" Farnsworth's bright blue eyes sparkled. "It makes you wonder." Carlton Farnsworth raised his sandy eyebrows, lifting them like question marks over his bright blue eyes. "It looks like the girl's mother is trying to hide something, doesn't it." Farnsworth indicated with a wave of his free hand that Jack Riley could make himself comfortable on the deep ox-blood leather sofa opposite the desk, although Farnsworth himself remained in a half-standing, half-sitting position, leaning against his heartwood of mahogany desk. "I think we should look into this matter of the girl's mother. This Frances Foster woman," Farnsworth said.

Jack Riley poured himself a double shot of Farnsworth's Kentucky bourbon and eased his lean and hardened body onto the sofa. He could see the direction Farnsworth was heading; Jack Riley had spent much of his journey aboard USAir Flight 173 from New Orleans examining the circumstances surrounding the Algiers raid across the Mississippi from Old New Orleans. For Jack Riley, however, it was not the clean white image of the Rights for the Unborn League that caused this examination; it was his own reputation, his contract as the League Special Security Assistant, his personal standards for operations such as the raid on the Algiers clinic, standards which had been sorely violated by certain members of the New Orleans Police Tactical Unit. And now, from Carlton Farnsworth, Jack Riley detected yet another good reason for probing deeply into the Algiers matter; he saw an increased compensation package for himself in such an endeavor. Jack Riley took a long smooth drink of Carlton Farnsworth's Kentucky bourbon. "The Foster woman wrote a personal check for the bail on the nurse. She didn't blink on it. If the nurse walks, she's out a quarter of a million. The full freight on the bail bond," Riley said.

"She has old family money," Carlton Farnsworth said, smiling. "We, ah, ran her through our system this morning, just a quick and dirty look. It seems that there is quite a lot of money in the Foster family," he said. Farnsworth's mouth puckered and he took another measured sip of his glass of Kentucky bourbon and branchwater. "A fine old family. The girl should have known better than to get herself in, ah, trouble. Strange that she didn't," Farnsworth said, smiling his bright white smile, his blue eyes sparkling. He handed Riley a thin computer printout; the printout was a thumbnail sketch of information in Rights for the Unborn League computers on Frances Reed Foster, of East Hampton, New York. "We should look into this. Ah, just privately and confidentially, Jack. No need to formally involve the League," Farnsworth said.

Jack Riley took the printout and folded it in half, his tanned and slender fingers folding it the long way, creasing the printout in an exact straight crease. Riley had very smooth fingers and hands; they were almost completely unmarked, as if he had worn gloves all of his life, so that on whatever he touched, he would leave no trace. "This might be expensive," Riley said finally.

"It's not a problem. Whatever you need. Carte blanche for you Jack!" Carlton Farnsworth finished off his Kentucky bourbon and branchwater with a flourish. "Say, Jack. My wife and I are having a little gathering at the house tomorrow night. Why don't you come on out," Farnsworth said.

Jack Riley slid the folded printout on Frances Foster into the breast pocket of his jacket. Riley detested little gatherings, especially gatherings hosted by Carlton Farnsworth at his plantation house in suburban Virginia. "I don't—"

"Sure you do, Jack! I, ah, do believe you should come," Farnsworth said softly, his bright blue eyes sparkling once again.

What the hell. The drinks would be free. "Sure," Jack Riley said. So he would come to Carlton Farnsworth's gathering; so he would be one of Farnsworth's boys. It was, as Riley's grandfather would have said, long ago on the Texas Gulf coast, long before Jack left there and never went back, the price of the ticket.

Carlton Farnsworth, clapping Jack Riley on the back and smiling his bright smile, guided Riley to his outer office now that their personal business was taken care of, and now that Riley was prepared to take on this curious and suspicious situation involv-

ing the dead girl's mother, Frances Foster. Waiting anxiously for
Jack Riley was young and eager Brian, who was one of the Exec-
utive Director's new assistants. Farnsworth had assigned Brian
McClure to Riley for the balance of the day. Until six weeks ago,
young McClure had been a mere local youth coordinator for the
Binghamton, New York, chapter of the Rights for the Unborn
League; this volunteer position was undertaken while Brian Mc-
Clure was matriculating in Computer Sciences and Artificial In-
telligence at the State University of New York at Binghamton,
from which he was now graduated. Brian, who felt the hand of
Providence at his shoulder in his new position as Assistant to the
Executive Director of the Rights for the Unborn League, was
anxious to succeed at this new assignment.

In a very few minutes, Brian McClure found himself seated
next to Jack Riley in one of the small League offices down the
hall from Carlton Farnsworth's spacious suite. Young Brian just
had finished calling up current information on illegal abortion
clinic operations east of the Mississippi River.

Jack Riley, who was longing now for a Camel cigarette, noticed that the abortion clinic in Algiers, east of the Mississippi
River from New Orleans, was not on the list, but then the Algiers
clinic was no longer operating, Riley thought. The little backyard
outfit was gone. It was getting late; the hot July afternoon in
Washington, D.C., was already beginning to fade into the beginnings of a long and muggy night. Jack Riley was tired and young
and eager Brian McClure's hot breath on his shoulder reminded
Riley of the breath of an anxious woman, cloying and too sweet
and suffocating against him. He decided to give young Brian
something to do. "Brian, I want you to get me everything you
can find about this woman," he said, handing him the computer
printout on Frances Foster, which he had already read. "And I
want everything you can find about the classes of 1947, 1948 and
1949 at a place called the Crofton School in Connecticut," Jack

Riley said. From the brief file on Frances Foster, Riley had learned that Foster had attended the Connecticut girls' school. And so had First Lady Mary Holt Morgan back in the old days. Jack Riley smiled to himself. There was some kind of connection there; maybe there was an old school tie, the kind of tie that John Brooks Riley, formerly of Freeport, Texas, and now of Miami, Florida, would not have had.

Jack Riley left the anxious Brian McClure hunched over a computer screen at the Rights for the Unborn League as soon as McClure was safely started on his global search within the League computer system. McClure's fingers had been drumming ceaselessly on the keyboard, drumming like a drummer boy stepping smartly into battle, his fuzzy cheeks pink with excitement. What Riley needed now was a cool shower in his Washington, D.C., hotel room and a long cool drink.

Chapter Six

In New Orleans that Friday night, inside the Vieux Carré apartment of the dead Hillary Foster, her mother, Frances Reed Foster, and her nurse, accused felon Nora O'Brien, had been stretching tentative hands toward one another across the deep chasm of Hillary's death in the little backyard clinic in Algiers. And they had been discussing First Lady Mary Holt Morgan, President of the Rights for the Unborn League, and how to kidnap her and get away with it. For Frances Foster and Nora O'Brien had decided that the First Lady and her League should pay; they should pay for a safe abortion clinic in Sweden, and they should pay for airplane tickets and lodging and meals and incidental expenses for women who needed to leave the United States for safe, legal abortions in Stockholm, Sweden, and couldn't afford to do it. Frances and Nora knew this would not bring Hillary Foster and Dr. Michael Green, M.D., back from the dead. But in their grief, in the core of their broken hearts, the hot pure fire of rage burned brightly; this would sustain them in the weeks ahead. This would carry them on the complicated road to Stockholm; this and the $100 million Mary Morgan would pay them for her life. "She can get the money for us. She can get it from the President, and she can get it from the League," Frances said.

Several hours earlier, Frances Foster and Nora O'Brien had driven to Nora's apartment in the Kenner District, located in the greater New Orleans Metropolitan area, so that Nora could change her clothing; Nora still had been wearing the loose black slacks and light green surgical smock from the night before. When they arrived, they found that Nora's spacious apartment had been ransacked, quite legally, by members of the New Orleans Police Tactical Unit, who had been gathering evidence to use against Nora O'Brien at her trial. A copy of the search warrant had been placed carefully on Nora's kitchen table, and Nora's cat, a devoted gray and white mongrel named Max, was asleep on it, the sun from the kitchen window warming this well-kept and spoiled pelt. But Max awakened instantly when Frances and Nora arrived, for he had not been fed since Thursday afternoon, an entire day ago. Feeding him, Nora saw bits of blue serge clinging to his claws; she surmised that Max had defended, unsuccessfully, her spacious Kenner District apartment and she loved him for this. When Nora and Frances Foster returned to Hillary Foster's apartment, Max accompanied them, purring ferociously all the way across New Orleans, his claws working in and out, his cat eyes bright with anticipation.

Nora O'Brien and Frances Foster had been joined at Hillary's apartment in the early hours of this long hot Southern night by Elizabeth McKinley, Hillary Foster's closest friend, who did not get Hillary's message in time to come to New Orleans to help her, but who was here now. Elizabeth McKinley had flown from Washington, D.C., to New Orleans with the sound of Hillary's last message to her, the one Elizabeth found on her recorder, pounding loud in her heart:

"I found out about a clinic operating in a place called Algiers. A doctor friend of mine I know from the Music Conservatory runs it . . . Lizzie? Could you come down? . . ."

Now Elizabeth McKinley had been told what happened at the clinic, as nearly as Frances Foster and Nora O'Brien could piece it together. And something within Elizabeth was exploding; something was shattering inside like a terrible, grotesque Humpty Dumpty who took a great fall and couldn't be put back together again. And so when the shattering occurred, she rolled herself into a ball on the sofa, as if to protect herself from hitting the ground too hard, as if she herself were falling; from inside the ball, Elizabeth felt a strong hand on her back, patting and rubbing there. It was Nora O'Brien's hand on her, and then Nora's arms around Elizabeth, enveloping her, cushioning her fall. And she heard Frances rise up and leave the room, her footfalls soft on the soft carpet in Hillary's living room. Sometime later, perhaps it only was minutes later, Elizabeth heard Frances in the kitchen, doing the dishes that Hillary had left in the sink, doing them by hand, washing and wiping them and putting them away.

In the kitchen, after she had finished doing the dishes, Frances Foster gathered herself together once again. Without using a mirror, she recombed her white hair, refastening the barrettes that held her hair back at the temples; tomorrow morning, she would claim Hillary's body and take her home, but now it still was Friday, the day after the police had killed Hillary and Michael Green, M.D. Frances poured herself a glass of cold white wine, a Chablis, and joined Nora and Elizabeth McKinley in Hillary's living room. They looked expectantly toward her, as if for an answer to an unformed question, their faces turned toward Frances as they waited for her.

Frances wanted them to know more about Hillary, more than they knew now. Did they know she had a father once, an absent father that Hillary herself never knew? No. Something inside Frances wanted to tell them. "Hillary's father is dead," Frances said. "Maybe that's for the best. I don't think you knew anything about Hillary's father, did you Elizabeth?"

Frances was right and Elizabeth was sorry she was right. All the way to New Orleans, Elizabeth had been sorry; if only she had been home, if only she had able to talk to Hillary, maybe this would not have happened. At twenty-eight, Elizabeth McKinley had not known hardship or grief beyond the inevitable pain of adolescence and young adulthood; she had not known anger and rage beyond the anger of missed opportunity and perhaps some stray pieces of misspent youth. Hers had been, in spite of the early separation and divorce of her parents, a young life remarkably free of either turmoil or introspection, a young life lived on the fine free surface of things. Now this. The senseless murder of her dear old friend Hillary cut like the sharpest knife through her surface; it was a knife in her heart and now anger and rage and the pain of loss was pouring through the open cut. And Hillary's father is dead, too, she thought. "Hillary never mentioned her father," Elizabeth said, looking up at Frances.

"Hillary didn't know anything about her father. I think she thought she was the product of some kind of tragic love affair of mine," Frances said, sipping her glass of Chablis. "Would you like to hear about her father? Of course you would," Frances continued, not waiting for an answer. "I was in my mid-thirties, unmarried, maybe unmarriageable. Too independent. My mother used to tell me I had to watch out for that. But I wanted a child. So, I picked out an old friend to be the father; Harding Rogers was tall and handsome and willing and Hillary was born nine months later. She was blonde like Harding, fair like he was."

Nora O'Brien was listening, running her fingers over Max the cat's smooth gray and white ears, caressing them. "What happened to him?" Nora said. Her strength was returning; it was fueled by her desire for revenge and it had been ignited by Frances Foster and the idea that First Lady Mary Holt Morgan could be made to pay for what she had done. Nora O'Brien burned brightly in the gathering darkness of this New Orleans evening.

"He drank too much. I can't remember how many wives he had, or how many children," Frances said. "He drowned in a boating accident off the Maine coast. He was out with friends, and he was probably drunk out there, and then suddenly he disappeared. His body washed ashore a week later." Frances rose from the sofa and refilled her wine glass. "You know, I always suspected that Harding simply stepped off the deck of the yacht. Stepped into the black sea for one last adventure. Maybe Harding didn't want to become a dissipated old man; maybe Harding chose the long step into the water," Frances said. She could understand that now; she could understand choosing the long step into the water. Did her daughter Hillary know when she stepped into the darkness? Did she? Frances drank the rest of the wine in her glass and turned to Elizabeth, who had not been there earlier in the day and thus was unaware of their unfolding plans regarding the First Lady of the United States.

She turned to Elizabeth. "You realize the police killed Hillary," Frances said. "That, really, the Rights for the Unborn League killed her." She looked straight into Elizabeth McKinley's dark brown eyes. Frances had known Elizabeth since young Lizzie was a skinny eight-year-old coming over to the house to play with Hillary. Well, Lizzie is a big girl now, Frances thought.

Elizabeth McKinley felt Frances' gray eyes on her.

"Yes," she said.

"I believe Hillary had the right to choose an abortion. It was her choice," continued Frances. Frances motioned toward Nora O'Brien, who now was sitting upright on the sofa opposite Elizabeth McKinley. "Nora was Hillary's nurse at the clinic the police raided. Nora should not have been arrested. Dr. Michael Green should still be alive; Hillary should be here right now, recovering from a safe abortion." Frances stopped and took a long, deep breath. In her sixty-three years on this earth, in her darkest moments of those sixty-three years, and there had been some, she had never envisioned that her life would come to this; that she would become an outlaw in her own country, and that she would leave the United States and never return. In that moment, in her daughter Hillary's apartment, standing before Hillary's oldest friend Elizabeth, and with Nora O'Brien's fiery eyes on her, Frances Foster said a kind of mute goodbye to all that she had ever known, to all her familiar places, to all the sights and sounds and smells that had nurtured and comforted her and been her life up until now.

"This can't happen again," Frances said. "We won't let it. We have to cut off the head of this monster. We're going to kidnap the First Lady, Elizabeth. We're going to get $100 million in a kind of ransom for her, and we're going to establish a clinic overseas, probably in Sweden, with a referral network here for the clinic. A place women can call and come to and get help. The help will be free for those who can't afford it." Frances spoke very rapidly. Her voice hardened; it was a voice Frances Foster hardly recognized as her own. "This is going to take work and we need people to help. Nora is coming with me. We'd like you along. If you can't, we'll understand. All you have to do in that case is go back to Washington, D.C., and shut up." It was hard and brutal; there was no choice now. Elizabeth was with them or she was not, Frances thought.

Elizabeth McKinley, Hillary Foster's oldest friend, and the one who wasn't there when Hillary called her from New Orleans, felt herself rock back against the sofa as if from a physical blow. Mary, Mother of Jesus. The incantation from her Catholic girlhood came unbidden to her lips; her lips moved with it but no sound came. The was no sound at all in the room now; there was just a kind of thick stillness, thick and heavy and warm. What would Hillary do if it were me? The thought swam through the thick warm stillness to Elizabeth; what if I had died like that instead of Hillary? And the answer came, too, swimming toward her, direct and swift. Elizabeth McKinley had not been to confession in a very long time; she would never go to confession again. She raised her head and looked into Frances Foster's exhausted gray eyes. "How can you be sure we'll get the money?" she said. This was a different Elizabeth, different from the fine and accomplished young woman of a day ago, the one who had driven straight and true on a smooth highway uncomplicated by dark corners and dark alleys and swift and sudden turns and death itself.

Frances Foster smiled a thin tired smile. "I went to school with Mary Holt Morgan. She was plain Mary Holt then. Trust me, Elizabeth, the First Lady will pay," Frances said. And now Frances opened an aged door that had been closed for many years; a door whose rusting latch she herself had pulled open only a year ago. "You see, Mary Holt Morgan, our famous anti-choice leader, chose an abortion for herself when she was nineteen." Frances laughed; it was a short bitter laugh. "And now she stops anyone else from choosing. Oh how I loathe her! I despise her!" Frances stopped herself; when she spoke again, it was with that same hard voice, the one she didn't recognize, the one she would get used to now. "She was still in school and she kept the abortion a secret; it's a secret now, but I know about it because my father, Dr. Hugh Foster, was her abortionist."

It had been early last summer on Long Island, the beginning of a long sweet summer in East Hampton at the old Georgian house where Frances had lived most of her life; her parents had been given the big old house by her mother's family who had made their fortune in textiles. Frances had lived there alone since her parents' death more than twenty years ago. They had died just six months apart, her mother first, quickly, of a heart attack, and then Frances watched helplessly as her father, more slowly, began to disappear, shrinking into himself, as if he did not want to continue without his wife. Frances found her father one morning, still in his bed, his heart beating no longer.

Sidney Reed Foster and Dr. Hugh Foster, M.D., the obstetrician Sidney had married even though Dr. Foster did not come from the right kind of family, brought their only child Frances up in that house. Frances loved the old place; she had loved her parents, too, but it was her father Hugh Foster that she had adored with the steadfast adoration of a daughter for a father who took her by the hand into a larger world and promised her that world was hers for the taking and he would stand by her while she took it. And so Hugh Foster and his daughter, his beloved Frannie, joined in a kind of conspiracy together for much of her young life, a pact that permitted Frannie her adventures and protected her mother from acknowledging them.

Hugh Foster had grown up in Queens, New York, the son of a tailor who worked in mid-town Manhattan and took the subway home to the family's two-story house in Queens. Hugh Foster went to City University of New York and on to Columbia University School of Medicine, his parents' hearts bursting with pride at his every step. He met Sidney Reed when he was interning in obstetrics at Columbia-Presbyterian and she was working as a volunteer. He married her in spite of the textile fortune Reeds, and at every Reed family gathering, Hugh Foster drove this point home with his long, unkempt way hair that reached his shoulders, his insistence on backing every Liberal Party candidate in New York City politics, and his membership in the American Civil Liberties Union.

As a grown woman, Frances Foster once asked her father just why he had married Sidney Reed, who did not seem to share Hugh Foster's passions or his eccentricities, but who seemed instead to float calmly and serenely through a life of well-kept gardens and spotless linens.

"Why Frannie, your mother was the prettiest thing at Columbia-Presbyterian!" Hugh Foster said to his daughter. "And she's steady and strong as a rock. Stronger than I am, Frannie; you'll see that someday." And so she had.

Last summer, during the first bloom of summer, Frances had found her father's journals tucked away in the storage room above the old stable. Her mother had stored them there, each one carefully wrapped in white tissue paper; Sidney Foster had left the journals for Frances to find on some quiet afternoon. At first, reading them, Frances Foster had not understood what was there in the splotched ink handwriting. "Two this week. One last week." The notes were interspersed among jots and paragraphs that outlined, in brief, the busy Dr. Hugh Foster's medical practice. And then: "Told Helen C. if she carried to term, her baby would be acute spina bifida. Aborted fetus at seventeen weeks. That made three this week. One more tomorrow on Leslie M. Sidney sent one more to me for next week."

Abortions. Frances Foster, seated on an old piano stool in the storeroom above the stable, which had long ago been converted to a garage, had put down the journal, placing it gently on its opened wrapping of white tissue paper. He had performed abortions. In secret. Illegal abortions. So her dear disheveled father had raised his small sword for women when he could; he had aborted women when they asked him to, risking everything. She could picture him, anxiously patting his patients on the shoulder, consoling them, telling him it was their choice, their choice completely; they were safe with Hugh Foster. Sitting there on the piano stool, Frances saw that her mother, the serene, calm Sidney Reed Foster, had known all about the abortions, that she had probably known all along, that she had supported her husband in this. In the dusty storeroom, filled with the moldy smells of old

clothes and old papers and old memories, Frances had wished
fervently for an opportunity to talk to them both, to talk to Dr.
and Mrs. Hugh Foster once more now that she knew of this secret. But Hugh and Sidney Foster were gone, and Frances their
adored daughter had only the memory of them to keep her warm
there in the dusty storeroom.

Over a period of two weeks, Frances Foster read all of the
journals her mother had so carefully preserved. And in one of the
bound notebooks wrapped in tissue paper, Frances found the record of an abortion performed on Mary Holt Morgan. In the
fading hand-lettered writing of Dr. Hugh Foster, Frances learned
that Mary Holt the young student had come to him and he had
aborted her seventeen-week fetus; it was a second trimester fetus
which Dr. Hugh Foster removed from the body of a woman who
would go on to lead the Rights for the Unborn League, a woman
who would go on to call abortion murder. Folded carefully between the pages of the journal was a faded letter to Dr. Hugh
Foster from one George Holt, the father of Mary Holt Morgan.
The letter, jotted hurriedly on one page of blank white stationery,
thanked Hugh Foster for "taking care of Mary's little problem.
Rest assured, it will never happen again, Hugh!" George Holt
had written this in a big scrawling hand. The letter transported
Frances back to the Crofton School, the exclusive secondary
school in Connecticut where Frannie Foster and Mary Holt were
students together. She remembered Mary now, remembered the
scrawny blonde girl whose room was down the hall from hers on
the second floor of the senior girls' residence hall; she remembered that Mary Holt was perfect, perfectly dressed, perfect lipstick applied with a lipstick brush first. Frances Foster remembered that Mary Holt literally trembled with perfection, that her
manicured fingers shook when she handed in her papers, which
never had typographical errors, that her full lips were pressed

together in a perfect straight line when she arrived in Chemistry III, where she was Frannie Foster's lab partner.

In the storeroom above the old stable, sitting on the old piano stool, boxes of old papers and her father's journals scattered in haphazard piles and dusty stacks around her, Frances Foster remembered her schoolmate Mary, who had become First Lady of the United States. She remembered Mary's unconscious habit of pulling single strands of hair from the back of her neck, strands from just behind one ear. It was an odd and self-destructive, unconscious habit, this pulling of single strands of hair, one at a time, as if she were pulling them from the head of a doll, as if Mary Holt were committing tiny little suicides with each strand she pulled from the back of her own neck.

During those same weeks, while Frances Foster journeyed into the past in the storeroom above the old stable, First Lady Mary Holt Morgan, assisted by Rights for the Unborn League Executive Director Carlton Farnsworth, was leading the drive for final ratification of the Human Life Amendment to the Constitution of the United States, the Amendment which outlawed abortion. Frances Foster knew this as she read her father's papers, loving her father for his quiet struggle against hypocrisy, loving her mother for protecting him, for leaving his journals for Frances to discover when the time was right. Until the discovery of the journals, Frances Foster thought very little of First Lady Mary Holt Morgan, of her old schoolmate who became First Lady. Frances and the First Lady were worlds apart; there was nothing to think about. But then there were the lies, the hypocrisy, the false witness.

Frances Foster, in her late daughter Hillary's apartment in the Vieux Carré, the New Orleans French Quarter, now turned to Nora O'Brien and Elizabeth McKinley, who had been listening as she explained how she found her father's journals, how he was an abortionist, how he had aborted a seventeen-week-old fetus from the body of young Mary Holt.

"She'll get the ransom for us; she'll protect her little secret with all her little might," Frances said. It was late now, and Frances was very tired; she could wait no longer for Elizabeth McKinley, her daughter Hillary's best friend. "Well, Elizabeth?" Frances said, very softly, asking her now whether she was joining them or whether she was not.

Elizabeth McKinley's fine white skin was sticky with perspiration; she could feel the stickiness on her neck and she wished Hillary's air conditioning were better. Hillary should have come North for the abortion, she thought. I could have gotten her a safe abortion! But she didn't; she did the best she could right here, Elizabeth thought. Elizabeth wanted to play the last few days all over again, like the first time didn't count and she and Hillary could have another turn and play them right this time. Ah, but you don't get to play the turns again when you grow up. The first time counts; this time counts, nothing else, she thought. She looked up at Frances Foster, looking into the cool gray eyes, the tired eyes, of Hillary's mother. "I have to be with you for this," Elizabeth said, very softly, almost to herself, almost as if she were alone in Hillary's room. "Hillary's death has to mean something." And I have to mean something, too, Elizabeth thought, but she did not say the words.

On Saturday afternoon, late in the afternoon, almost at darkness, Frances Foster and Elizabeth McKinley boarded a plane for New York. The body of Hillary Foster, her body cold as marble, cold and still, was in the cargo hold of the aircraft; Hillary was going home.

Nora O'Brien stayed behind in New Orleans. But Nora and Max the cat were packing, very quietly, packing everything in Nora's Kenner District apartment in cardboard boxes. A preliminary hearing had been scheduled for accused felon Nora on the following Wednesday, at which she was to enter a plea to the charges against her stemming from the New Orleans Police Tactical Unit raid on the little backyard clinic in Algiers. Although Nora did not tell her young chain-smoking attorney this, she did not intend to be present for the preliminary hearing. By Sunday afternoon, Nora intended to be on her way to upstate New York, driving a rental car which Frances Foster had secured for her, driving to the famous village of Cooperstown, New York, home of the Baseball Hall of Fame. Nora intended to find a large summer rental in Cooperstown, a rental large enough to accommodate five or six women, who would be coming there soon, but they would not be on vacation, would they? No indeed, Nora thought.

In the midst of the packing, Nora reached over and smoothed the gray and white fur on Max's alert ears. "Don't worry, Max," she said. "You're coming with me."

Max the cat purred and switched his tail to and fro, to and fro.

Chapter Seven

Jack Riley squinted into the retreating sunlight; the sun was going down red tonight, red and hot and throbbing, like Jack Riley felt at the back of his neck tonight, stiff and throbbing and wanting to lie down in the cool grass beside a streambank, cool and alone. Instead he was crammed into a dinner jacket, his feet shoved into dress shoes, and he was driving up to the guarded gates of Rights for the Unborn League Executive Director Carlton Farnsworth's antebellum home in suburban Virginia.

Jack Riley didn't belong there; he belonged at home in Miami, home in the seventh floor condominium that looked out on the Atlantic. Riley ground out his Camel cigarette, lifted his foot off the accelerator, and eased the rental car to a stop in front of the heavily barred gate. Here we are, Jack, he thought. Now behave yourself. He lit a Camel and waited.

He was leaning back in his seat when a security guard tapped on the window. Jack Riley looked out at the guard and smiled. Private bulls. Of course. Well, it's not a problem for Jack, he thought. He pulled out his League security card and pressed it against the glass. The bull's face swam toward him in the gathering twilight. A powerful light blinked on. Blinding light. Riley raised a hand to his face; the light blinked off. He looked up to see the guard scuttling toward a stone guardhouse. A moment later, the gate swung open.

Static erupted on the car radio as Riley cleared the gateway; he leaned forward and turned the radio off. An alarm light blinked on the dashboard console. Riley smiled at the electronic interference. Leave it to Farnsworth and the League boys, he thought. The place is wired like League Headquarters, just like a government in exile would be wired. He sucked on the Camel. The engine of the rental car began to ping as the motor labored up the long, sloping drive.

Jack Riley, his neck still throbbing painfully, still hot and red, felt an almost physical revulsion come over him as the outlines of Carlton Farnsworth's antebellum mansion hove into view on the prow of the hill. The plantation house was all white, encircled by a fine white portico, and surrounded by row upon row of flower gardens rich with calla lillies and japonlica and datura, hothouse flowers placed there artificially and laboriously moved in winter back to greenhouses. The hot tropical flowers called back long sweet summers; but his summers had been consumed with gritty labor, sweaty hard labor to earn his way out of Freeport, Texas, far away from the old cinderblock house hard by the Tex-Mex strip. Money had already purchased for Jack Riley his own high cool piece of Miami, but never would it bring with it the remembered ease of antebellum summers and twilights on the portico watching the gathering darkness envelop the cutting gardens; he could find only discomfort among those who counted those summers as their birthright.

The mansion windows glowed like yellow lanterns; Jack saw figures passing to and fro in the yellow glow, passing like brilliant fireflies flitting through the lanternlights. He squinted at the figures in the windows. Through the glass you go Jack, he thought. Step through the mirror; step lively boy.

Five minutes later, Jack Riley found himself standing beneath a glittering chandelier in the main hall of the plantation house; music was playing, played by a string quartet, the players seated on folding chairs at the rear of the entry hall. Riley grabbed a glass of champagne from a tray, drank it down in one gulp, and took another glass; the champagne was just beginning to warm, just beginning to get that sickly warm taste champagne gets when it is poured too soon and served too late.

Around Jack Riley, and apart from him, the gathering of selected elite members of the Rights for the Unborn League, invited to the mansion by their host, Carlton Farnsworth, swirled in a pretty, vivid swirl through the public rooms on the first floor of the antebellum mansion. They were Episcopalians and Baptists and Catholics, and they were here, among their own kind, to celebrate once again the passage of the Human Life Amendment and to pledge themselves to an America rich in idealism again. They smiled beautiful smiles, with gestures graceful and long and true. Into this gathering came Jack Riley, their special security assistant, who was downing another glass of sticky champagne when he saw Carlton Farnsworth, his bright white smile beaming, his blue eyes sparkling like two stars. Farnsworth swept through the crowd toward Riley, nodding, smiling, touching hands and arms that were raised to greet him.

"Jack! Glad to see you could make it!" Carlton Farnsworth's champagne-reddened face bobbed toward Jack Riley. Clinging to Farnsworth's arm was a young blonde woman whose long, upswept hair was caught in a tortoise shell comb.

Jack Riley nodded and shook Carlton Farnsworth's extended hand; he was tempted to squeeze it, tempted to squeeze the fat out of those soft chubby fingers. With an effort, Riley restrained himself, but the thought of squeezing Farnsworth played on; Riley smiled a slight amused smile. Fucking Farnsworth is drunk, he thought. He glanced at the blonde. Well well.

"Lissy, meet Jack Riley," Farnsworth said, nudging the blonde. "Jack's on retainer for a special project with us."

Farnsworth laughed. "Better with us than against us, as they say. Isn't that right, Jack!"

"Sure." The champagne tasted stale. Riley wondered if there was any whiskey around. Nice little blonde piece he thought. He was beginning to enjoy himself; he was beginning to see an evening with possibilities.

"Now, Lissy, Jack here used to be with the United States Central Intelligence Agency, so be careful!" Farnsworth boomed. "Isn't that right, Jack!"

There should be whiskey somewhere, Riley thought. He took Lissy's outstretched white hand in his. My, my. "A long time ago," Jack Riley said to her. "Nice to meet you, Lissy."

"Actually, it's Lissandra," she said to him. "Lissandra Cochrane. Mother had very, um, romantic ideas." She turned to Farnsworth. "Carlton, would you mind terribly if I asked you to find just a small bit of brandy for me? I'm afraid champagne, um, doesn't agree with me." Riley felt her white fingers pressing against his palm. So it was Carlton to her. Well, well. Her hand was warm. A little damp.

"Lissy, honey, you can have anything your little heart desires," Farnsworth was saying. "How about you, Jack? A little more champagne?"

He felt her fingers trailing across his palm. Warm fingers. "A little whiskey would be appreciated," he said.

"No problem!" Farnsworth said. Riley watched Farnsworth's retreating back as he wobbled through the crowd.

Lissy turned to face Jack Riley; he felt the close heat of her. "He's an old friend of daddy's," Lissandra Cochrane said. She raised her blonde eyebrows up and opened her hazel eyes wider. Her blonde hair was a very light apricot color, and it gleamed beneath the chandelier in the main hallway of Carlton Farnsworth's antebellum mansion. She took Jack Riley's arm and squeezed it gently, her fingers just indenting the flesh of his forearm. "So, I'm stuck at this boring old party that's not even half over. Um, were you really a spy, Mr. Riley?"

"Jack. In a manner of speaking."

"How fascinating. Are you married?"

Why did they always ask him that? As if marriage made any difference, as if it mattered; it didn't matter. "No," Jack Riley said. He longed for a whiskey now. Whiskey and me, he thought. He felt her edge closer to him. "Do you work for the League, Lissy?" She was warm beside him, warm and soft.

"Oh no! I, um, have an art gallery in Alexandria," she said. "But you do, don't you! Daddy said you're looking for the renegade clinics. That's what he calls them. Evil renegades."

Jack Riley reached for another glass of the warm sticky champagne; he leaned against her as he reached, and he felt her pressing back. Her skin was so white, chalk white flushed with apricot; she smelled faintly of the gardens outside, smelled of the hothouse flowers forced into bloom alongside the graceful portico.

"Do you think the clinics are evil, too?" Her voice dropped to a whisper.

"I don't think about it. I'm just a hired hand, Lissandra."

"Oh." She straightened her back and dropped her shoulders slightly. The movement accentuated her rounded breasts and long graceful neck.

At that moment, Carlton Farnsworth reappeared. "Well! Are you two getting acquainted?" Farnsworth handed Riley a glass tumbler of whiskey and water and gave Lissy a tulip-shaped glass of something that looked like dark brandy. "Now, little girl, Mr. Riley here is an older, more sophisticated man. Your daddy might not approve," Farnsworth said. His reddened cheeks glowed and he grinned a glittering white grin.

Lissandra Cochrane tightened her grip on Jack Riley's arm. Riley felt her long fingers pressing harder, indenting into his forearm. "Now don't you worry, Mr. Farnsworth," Lissy said. I'm just going to show Mr. Riley around a bit. You go on now and see to your other guests and don't you worry a bit about Mr. Riley," she added.

Jack Riley drained the tumbler of whiskey and water. He was beginning to feel better; the tight hot burning at the back of his neck had disappeared. He knew it was the champagne, and the whiskey, and Miss Cochrane that had given him this relief, and he saw yet more comfort to come.

"God, how I hate that daddy crap," Lissy whispered to Jack Riley, breathing hothouse breath into his ear. "I haven't had a conversation with dear daddy in years. He's been too busy, um, saving the Christians. Are you a Christian?" She giggled and finished her brandy.

Jack Riley looked at the pretty, swirling crowd of elite members of the Rights for the Unborn League members. "I'm a hired hand," he said. He tapped Lissandra Cochrane's empty brandy glass with a smooth index finger. "Is there more where that came from?"

She closed up the remaining space between them; her shiny apricot hair brushed against his shoulder. "There certainly is, Mr. Riley. You just come with me. I know where everything is in this mausoleum," Lissandra Cochrane said. "Upstairs."

Jack Riley discarded his empty glass tumbler and followed Lissy up the winding center staircase. Following her, he saw that Miss Lissandra Cochrane did not wear undergarments. Not even pantyhose. She was wearing a black dress that was wrapped into a kind of knot between her breasts; the fabric clung to her body in soft folds. Jack Riley watched her as she skipped energetically up the staircase, skipping on long white legs, leading Riley away from the pretty swirling gathering at the foot of the stairs.

"Carlton would want you to see this," she called back to him as she swept along a wide upstairs hallway, watching him from over her shoulder. She waved an arm toward a row of gilt-framed oil paintings. "The Farnsworth collection. Awfully tacky, I think. Mr. Farnsworth loves it. He has no taste of course."

Jack Riley caught up with her; he was beginning to enjoy himself. A small smile played itself across his tanned face, reaching toward his dark brown eyes. "What's behind all the doors?" Riley said. He pointed to a series of heavy wood paneled doors that ran along each side of the hallway.

Lissandra Cochrane stopped and whirled around to him, pirouetting on her toes, raising her thin white arm above her head, smiling her blinding smile. "Bedrooms! Each with its own bath. Twelve bedrooms, twelve baths. Just in the main house." She sighed and dropped her arms to her sides. "Can you imagine? Oh, well. If you've got it, flaunt it! That's what I say." She stretched her arms out once again; she was all white and shining apricot, radiating toward Jack Riley.

Jack smiled back at her and moved toward one of the doors, opening it. The open door revealed a long spacious room, curtains drawn, lamps burning low. He could smell the beeswax on the softly glowing pine furniture. A hand knotted bedcovering was spread over a poster bed. He felt Lissandra Cochrane tiptoe up behind him; she peered over his shoulder into the dimly lit room, her soft breaths on his neck.

"This is Mr. Farnsworth's apartment," Lissandra said.

Riley smiled once again and loosened the tie on his dress shirt, snapping open the stays. "Where does Mrs. Farnsworth sleep?" he asked. He felt Lissy's fingers rubbing lightly across his shoulder blades.

"They have separate apartments," she whispered. "Mrs. Farnsworth has a lovely apartment at the other end of the house. Very private."

"Interesting."

"Yes." Her fingers moved to the back of Jack Riley's neck. "It's much too pristine in here, don't you think?" The fingers probed, rubbing in small circles. "Too much, um, tidiness or something. I really prefer things a bit more, um, casual, don't you?"

Jack Riley did want something casual, and he wanted a drink, too. Turning just slightly, he slipped away from Lissandra Cochrane and entered Carlton Farnsworth's private apartment, walking directly to a small cabinet in the corner; he recognized liquor cabinets when he saw them, even pine cabinets rubbed with beeswax. Expertly, he slipped a small bolt from the cabinet lock and opened the cabinet doors.

"This will be fine," he said, humming. Ah. He pulled an unopened bottle of Bushmills from the cabinet and tucked it under his arm and returned to Lissy, who was leaning against the doorjamb, watching him, her hazel eyes glowing, her apricot hair gleaming like a halo from the light in the hallway outside Carlton Farnsworth's private apartments.

She smiled a beautiful Southern smile and ran her pretty pink tongue over her soft full lips. "A man of unusual talent. Does that come from being a spy?" She took Riley's arm possessively. "You know, you're quite a handsome fellow, Mr. Riley. Quite dashing, actually."

Riley twisted the Bushmills cap off, tipped the bottle up, and drank deeply. The whiskey burned. He took a deep breath and turned back to her. "Call me Jack. How old are you, Lissy?"

Lissandra Cochrane tossed her pretty head back and looked up at Riley. "Twenty-three next week. I'm a Saggitarius." She giggled. "We, um, like adventure." She released his arm and skipped down the hallway to a door at the end of the corridor. "This one is more like it," she said, opening the heavy door.

Jack Riley, reaching her, looked inside. The bedroom was furnished in deep red. Red tapestry wallpaper covered the walls, and a gleaming dark wood bed was covered with a deep red quilt. He felt Lissy brush past him, black fabric on white skin.

Lissandra Cochrane pulled the red quilt back from the bed. Above her head, a wooden fan turned slowly, turning the heavy upstairs air. "Well, what do you think? Hmm?" She rubbed one hand along a thigh. "Do you know what the Christians say, Mr. Riley?"

Jack Riley didn't know what Christians said, and he didn't care. From the doorway, he looked long at Lissy, at her white skin glowing against the deep red of the quilt, at her gleaming hair, at her softly open mouth; she was the most beautiful thing in Carlton Farnsworth's antebellum mansion. "What do the Christians, say, Lissy," Jack Riley said.

She smiled a melting golden smile. "They say if you're going to sin, sin gloriously!"

Riley leaned against the doorway, watching her. He opened the Bushmills and drank another slug. "Ah, Lissy," he said finally. He closed the bedroom door, bolted it, and turned to her. The curtains were drawn, and in the dim light, with just the shadowed reflections of a small bedside lamp upon her, Lissy looked even younger than her almost twenty-three years. Her white skin glowed, and her apricot blonde hair tumbled to her shoulders when he removed the tortoise shell comb. She raised her arms, and smiling, mouth opening, gathered Riley into her arms.

He groaned as he rolled onto her, covering her slim body with his own. It had been a long time. Oh, Jesus.

Later, when they were lying together on the damp sheets, the tangled bedcoverings strewn on the floor along with their clothing, and when Jack Riley's fever of this night had left him like the outgoing tides had left him on the beach so long ago on the Texas Gulf Coast, he pulled himself away from Lissandra Cochrane, disengaging himself from her even as she snuggled against him, her damp apricot hair draped over his shoulder like a fan.

"Let's not go back," she said. "I don't feel like getting up and going back to a boring old party with boring old Mr. and Mrs. Farnsworth."

Riley reached for the Bushmills, disentangled himself from Lissy, and sat up on the side of the bed. "You wouldn't want Farnsworth to walk in here, sweetheart." The fever was gone; where was his tie? "Let's get dressed," Riley said. Her smell was on him, a not unpleasant smell, but it was time to go. Jack Riley did not think Carlton Farnsworth was all that much of a good old boy; he remembered that he had been summoned to the party by the Executive Director of the Rights for the Unborn League.

Jack Riley reached down and pulled Lissandra Cochrane to her feet. "I have to get back to Washington soon" he said. He turned away from her and reached for his shirt studs. Behind him, he heard Lissy sigh as she reached for her dress.

Riley was just closing the door to the bedroom and starting down the hall, Lissy at his side, when Carlton Farnsworth, who was holding a drink in his hand and panting slightly from exertion, appeared at the top of the staircase. Farnsworth was turning purposefully toward his bedroom when he saw them.

Carlton Farnsworth blinked his bright blue eyes at them. "Well! I see you've been taking a look around." He waved an arm toward the row of gilt-framed paintings. "Quite a collection, don't you think?" Farnsworth paused for a breath and lurched down the hall toward them. He put the champagne glass he was carrying on the floor. "Stuff tastes terrible. I came up to get a real drink; a gentleman should be able to have a real drink in the privacy of his room, don't you think?" Farnsworth said. He reached out and gripped Riley heavily on the arm. "So. What do you think of the place?"

Old Carlton is sloshed, Jack Riley thought. Drunk in his own bordello. "Nice place," Riley said.

"It's a replica of an old Louisiana plantation home. A true antebellum home. Exact replica," Farnsworth burbled. "Damned expensive, too. But what the hell. It's only money," he said gaily.

Riley heard Lissandra giggle softly beside him. Suddenly, he wished fervently that he was back at the hotel in downtown Washington, D.C. Or in Miami. Where there were no Carlton Farnsworths, no Rights for the Unborn League gatherings, even no Lissandra Cochranes. He began to move toward the staircase, but Farnsworth gripped Riley's arm once again and smiled a bright drunken smile.

"Say, have you seen my private rooms?" Farnsworth said. Before Jack Riley Riley could answer him, Farnsworth was propelling Riley and Lissandra down the hall and into his private apartment.

"This bed," Carlton Farnsworth said to them, as he drew them beside him into the dimly lit room that smelled of beeswax, "came from an old plantation house on the Mississippi, just outside of New Orleans." Farnsworth ran a soft white hand along the smooth pine headboard. "I had it refurbished," Farnsworth continued. "And under here," he said, gesturing to a drawer built into the underside of the bed, "is where they kept the bed linens and so forth." Farnsworth smoothed the creamy hand-knotted bedcovering, smoothing it fussily, as a fussy old man would smooth it, patting it gently all the while that he talked to them, almost as if he were alone in the dimly lit apartment, alone and far away in another world.

Carlton Farnsworth bent over and tugged at the drawer. "They stick a little," he said, panting and tugging. With a final wheezing effort, he pulled the pine drawer beneath the bed open; it was stacked with linens, packed tightly with them. Farnsworth began fumbling through the stack of linens, looking for something in the laundered and carefully pressed stack of fine white cotton sheets and pillow coverings. "It's in here somewhere," he mumbled. "Ah."

Farnsworth spread two oddly shaped white cloth garments on the hand-knotted bedcovering. Obviously old, the garments were starched and pressed, and they were stained in places with faint yellow stains. "Now, there are some real antiques!" Farnsworth said triumphantly, catching his breath. "Yessir, my daddy wore these back in the 1940s," Farnsworth said, beaming brightly at Jack Riley and Lissandra Cochrane.

Riley looked down at the starched and pressed white robe; a stain covered almost all of one side of the robe, and a much smaller and paler yellow stain discolored a portion of the hood on one side of the eye holes. Beside him, he heard Lissandra Cochrane suck in a breath.

"Oooh," she said. "I've never seen a Klan outfit before. Do you ever, um, wear it, Mr. Farnsworth? My, my."

Carlton Farnsworth laughed softly. "Me wear it?" "Well, only for a joke at parties." His bright blue eyes twinkled and he bobbed up and down slightly, as if he were bouncing up and down on his heels in excitement. "But only in the company of very close friends," Farnsworth said. He picked up the robe and hood, holding them delicately before him, hood in one hand, robe in the other, holding the garments as if they would shatter like something made of china, something precious and fine.

Holding the robe and hood in front of him, and looking serenely at Jack Riley and Lissandra Cochrane, who were standing very quietly in the dim room that smelled so sweetly of beeswax and deep polish, Carlton Farnsworth said: "Times have changed, as you both know. We have equality now in this country. And, I believe the South was the first to promote it, looking back. I think history will show that," he said soberly. "Integrated schools, for example. The South integrated first, you'll recall," Farnsworth said.

Riley had not spoken, for he did not know what to say and he always chose to say nothing instead of something. He noticed, however, that Carlton Farnsworth did not look very drunk right at the moment, although Riley had seen Farnsworth stumble at the top of the staircase and he was certain Farnsworth had come to his apartments to have a stiff drink all by himself.

Lissandra Cochrane moved beside Riley, shifting impatiently; she put one hand on Riley's shoulder, and then she reached out and tentatively patted the robe, patting it as if the fabric were something alive, something that could move suddenly if it were touched. "Were you ever at any, um, rallies, Mr. Farnsworth?" Lissy inquired.

Carlton Farnsworth's cheery face reddened and his soft small mouth, so small in his pink face, began to pucker as if he were sucking on something. Farnsworth put the robe back on the bed and placed the hood beside it. Bending over the garments, he smoothed a wrinkle on the robe. "As a very young child," Farnsworth said, smoothing the robe once again, running his hand over it, "I did accompany my daddy to one or two gatherings. By that time, they were largely ceremonial. My father was a member because he was a local businessman and it was expected." Farnsworth paused. "Many of the members were just farmers and businessmen, you know. People like us."

Riley watched Farnsworth fold the garments and put them back in the pine drawer. Not like me, he thought. But another voice inside whispered yes. Yes like you, Jack Riley, just like you.

"Well," Farnsworth said, turning back to them. "I'll be going downstairs now. The First Lady is due shortly, and I've got to get things ready for her." His little mouth puckered once again, puckering in distaste, which Farnsworth did not bother to conceal from Riley or Lissandra.

Mary Holt Morgan, First Lady of the United States and President of the Rights for the Unborn League was, in fact, on her way to Farnsworth's antebellum mansion at that very moment. She was inside her black bulletproof limousine, alone in the back seat, reapplying her lipstick, which had looked smudged the first time. A Secret Service agent was riding in the front seat beside the driver, scanning the road ahead, his eyes restlessly sweeping the highway, his fingers drumming impatiently on the short barrel of his compact machine gun, which was fully loaded. Mary Holt Morgan was in a poor mood this evening; her favorite agent, young Eugene Duffy, was off tonight. This irritated her because she had hoped to fill the hour between the White House and the Farnsworth home with a little game of pinochle with Eugene Duffy; the First Lady could not understand why young Eugene would prefer someone else's company to that of the First Lady of the United States, even on a fine Saturday night in June. Well, Eugene was young; there probably was a girl somewhere.

Rights for the Unborn League Special Security Assistant Jack Riley, who had managed to disentangle himself from Lissandra Cochrane long enough to escape the Farnsworth mansion, was back on the main road now, alone in his rental car, the dark Virginia night soft around him. There was not a breath of wind tonight, and the air was hot and heavy; Riley had removed his dinner jacket and his tie and his dress shirt was open to his chest. He switched the car radio on, lit a Camel cigarette, and settled in for the drive back to Washington. The radio station was playing a retrospective of Willie Nelson songs. Riley listened for awhile, but the music was drowned out by static that surged into the receiver; he cursed the cheap radio and switched it off.

Riley glanced at his watch. It was early. A few minutes before ten. He felt wide-awake, as if he could drive for hours. More whiskey, Jack. He reached under the seat for a bottle he kept there.

Just as he straightened, he saw the oncoming lights of a trio of cars round a curve in front of him. Suddenly, the lead car began a slow deliberate swerve into his lane. Riley felt a surge of adrenalin pound through his bloodstream. He looked quickly to the side. A narrow shoulder. Perhaps four feet wide. Then a ditch. He leaned on the horn, but the oncoming lights did not swerve away; they came on, drifting further into his lane. Now they were closing, bright yellow and white lights, closing in on Jack Riley, crowding him, shoving him out of the way, trying to kill him.

They were here. The bright arcs blinded him; in the blindness he jerked the wheel of the little rental car, pulling it onto the shoulder. A front wheel ground onto the shoulder. The car heaved and shot toward the ditch, wheels grinding along the shoulder, spitting gravel, skidding, throwing the car toward the ditch in an out-of-control slide, carrying Riley into the black darkness. With a last desperate heave, he forced the wheel into the skid, turning into it, trying to stop the powerless slide into the darkness; he felt his stomach muscles contract as the car pitched toward the ditch. The rental car tilted. Riley cramped the wheel. The bright white and yellow lights swept over the rental car and were gone.

The rental car wobbled on two wheels, hesitated, then bounced back onto the shoulder. Riley pumped on the brakes and the rental car skidded to a stop. A trio of red taillights, far behind him now, swept around a long curve, sweeping across the horizon like bright red jewels in the dark night; the red lights rose up on the horizon, rising on a swell, and then they were gone.

Jack Riley leaned back in the driver's seat and reached for his whiskey; the bottle was half-empty, rolling back and forth next to the accelerator. He pulled the bottle onto the seat beside him. The whiskey tasted hot and bitter on his throat as he swallowed, swallow after swallow. He shuddered as a tremor swept his body.

Riley knew the trio of cars had been a motorcade. The First Lady's limo in the center? Well, sure, he thought. Why not. She was on her way to the party at Carlton Farnsworth's antebellum mansion, the Rights for the Unborn League party with selected members of the League present to greet her. He remembered Farnsworth in his dim private apartment upstairs in the mansion, the pinched expression on Farnsworth's face when he said the First Lady's name. Farnsworth is her boy, Riley thought; he is her chubby errand boy. And in the rental car, in the darkness at the side of the road, Jack Riley smiled a terrible thin smile.

He pulled back onto the main road. Have another drink, Jack, he thought. It's still early. He drove on into the dark Virginia night, driving toward Washington, D.C.

First Lady Mary Holt Morgan, secure in her limousine, had not noticed any passing cars on the way to Carlton Farnsworth's home and the Rights for the Unborn League party; she rarely looked out the dark tinted windows of the limousine when she traveled, for she did not have time. Mary Holt Morgan, if she was not playing pinochle with Secret Service Agent Eugene Duffy, or with a substitute for Duffy, tried to spend those moments on something useful, something that mattered, like reviewing new candidates for the League Board of Directors. She did not want Carlton Farnsworth, long-time friend and political ally of her husband, President Edward Morgan, to get himself out of her reach; she did not entirely trust Carlton Farnsworth, but then Mary Holt Morgan did not entirely trust anyone. She was nobody's dummy.

Chapter Eight

On Sunday evening, at the end of a murderously hot and sticky summer day in Washington, D.C., young and eager Brian Mc-Clure, Carlton Farnsworth's shiny new Assistant at the Rights for the Unborn League, brought his just-printed League files on Frances Foster to League Special Security Assistant Jack Riley, who was in his air-conditioned hotel room waiting for them. Mc-Clure also was to deliver information on the Crofton School in Connecticut, which Frances Foster had attended in the old days, along with First Lady Mary Holt Morgan.

Earlier in the day, Riley had found the apartment Elizabeth McKinley lived in; she was not at home, and no, the building manager did not know where she was, and it was none of the building manager's business anyway.

Riley, who was smoking a Camel cigarette and drinking a glass tumbler of Bushmills whiskey only slightly diluted by hotel ice and water, now turned to bright and shiny Brian McClure: "Are these the complete files, Brian?" he asked.

McClure positively vibrated with eagerness. "On Frances Foster," he said. "I conducted a global search of the system and you have every item on her." McClure frowned and knitted his brows together in an unconscious parody of mature, thoughtful concern. "Our cupboard was pretty much bare on the Crofton School," Brian noted. "So, I called there, and they promised to mail the records as soon as they're duplicated. So, given the mails, I'd say the material might be here by around the end of the week."

Riley closed his eyes. The end of the week. He would have to call up there himself in the morning. He wanted the Crofton School material; Frances Reed Foster and Mary Holt Morgan had gone to school together and the material was important to him.

"Is there something wrong, Mr. Riley?" Brian McClure asked, his blue eyes fastened on Riley. McClure had lost control of his mature knitted eyebrow expression; it had collapsed with the first sign of disapproval, which Brian assumed from Jack Riley's tired expression.

"No," Riley said. He ran one hand across his forehead. He needed to get young Brian out of his hair; he wanted some time to think. "You've done a great job, Brian. Fast work."

McClure brightened once again. He still was smiling when Riley closed the door to his hotel room, sending Brian home for the evening.

In his hotel room, Jack Riley unfolded all of the computer printouts—the complete Frances Foster file and the thin printout that Carlton Farnsworth already had given him. He pulled a torn-out page from a newsmagazine from his pocket and dropped it onto the polished wood beside the printouts. The page pictured Morgan cutting the ribbon for a home for unwed mothers in Bayonne, New Jersey. The accompanying article said Morgan first became a pro-life activist during her student days at the Crofton School in Connecticut.

Riley paced in a circle around the table, circling the printouts and the page from the newsmagazine. Maybe it didn't matter that they went to school together; still, it was an intriguing element to this potentially lucrative puzzle. He circled the polished table like a sculptor would perhaps circle an unfinished statue, peering

at the material from all angles, drinking it in as he sipped reflectively on his glass tumbler of Bushmills and water and melting
ice. The First Lady smiled up at him from the newsmagazine as
he circled around her. Riley had to admit to himself that it was
the First Lady who drew him; it was she who fascinated him, she
who had driven him off the road last night, she who had been
standing straight and tall and righteous before the Rights for the
Unborn League crowd gathered at the New Orleans Superdome
while he, Jack Riley, was bent over in the darkness outside the
little backyard clinic across the Mississippi River in Algiers,
storming the gates of Hell for Mary Holt Morgan.

Finishing his Bushmills and water, he gathered the printouts
together into a neat pile. He slipped the newsmagazine page in
between the folds of the printouts. He was restless. Unsettled. He
dropped the printouts into his briefcase, locking it carefully, and
went downstairs to the hotel lobby. Pushing past the lines of hotel
guests who were checking out on this Sunday night in Washington, D.C., Riley headed outside and down the street toward the
blinking lights and soft music of a small piano bar.

On Monday morning, his head thick and pounding with a
hangover, Jack Riley returned to Rights for the Unborn League
Headquarters and to young Brian McClure, who continued to be
assigned to Riley.

Riley closed his eyes. Aspirin chased with a Bloody Mary had
not been enough to relieve his pounding headache. He opened his
eyes and looked over at Brian McClure, who was seated next to
him at a computer console in the library at League headquarters.
This morning, Riley wanted answers to his questions about
Frances Foster and the First Lady and the Crofton School. "How
far from here is the Crofton School?" Riley asked Brian, who
had been waiting for instructions, his young slender hands poised
expectantly over the computer keyboard.

"In miles?"

Jack Riley sighed and closed his eyes once again. "Yes. In miles. Just approximately," he said softly.

McClure patted the computer keyboard delicately, tapping the keys but not pressing them into commands. "Let's see. The school is not too far from Westport, so that would make it about 240 or 250 miles. Maybe as much as 260," McClure added, knitting his brow maturely. "I can get you an exact figure if you wish."

Riley detested the thought of a long hot drive over the expressways from Washington, D.C., to Westport and the Crofton School. Well, he could take the air shuttle up there, he thought. The shuttle from National Airport to La Guardia and a rental car to the Crofton School. He picked up a pencil and tapped it on the edge of the console table. He had never been to a place like the Crofton School; places like Crofton were a universe away from where Jack Riley grew up, going to school with all the Mexicans in Freeport, Texas. Riley smiled to himself. Well, he could sure speak Spanish as well as any Mexican.

"Mr. Riley?" Brian had taken his fingers off the computer console and dropped them into his lap.

Riley was beginning to dislike young and bright Brian McClure. Maybe it wasn't the kid's fault, Riley thought. But the kid was so anxious; McClure's anxious eagerness grated on Riley.

"Sorry, Brian. I was just thinking about something. Say, would you mind getting me some coffee? Get me a regular with sugar, will you? Isn't there a cafeteria in this place?"

McClure rose eagerly from his seat in front of the computer console. "Sure, Mr. Riley. No problem. The League has a pretty good cafeteria here, as a matter of fact. They serve just about everything."

After Brian McClure left, Riley eased himself into the empty seat in front of the computer console and tapped into the system file on known illegal abortion clinics. The file had just been updated. Humming to himself, and tapping the keyboard with his long smooth unblemished fingers, he began to scan the Southeast region. Now the backyard clinic in New Orleans was listed; there was a CLOSED notation beside it. Riley took some comfort in the CLOSED notation; it was as if the notation had wiped clean the messy business in Algiers, as if some organized conclusion had been reached there. He scrolled down, past Georgia and North and South Carolina to Florida. Well, well. There were two entries for South Florida, both in Miami. One of the entries gave a location that was not far from his own high cool condominium in Miami Beach. Riley smiled to himself, smiling his thin terrible smile. Miami Beach was his neighborhood; what went on there might not be the League's business. The League should stay out of there, he thought, remembering the New Orleans Police Tactical Unit. He, Jack Riley, would just take care of that untidy little problem right now. Very gently, Riley pressed the Delete key. The Miami Beach listing sucked itself through the computer cursor and disappeared.

He closed up the computer file on illegal abortion clinics and picked up a telephone next to the console. In a moment, a League telephone operator answered.

"Would you get me the Crofton School in Connecticut, please? I think it's near Westport. The student dean's office if you can," he added.

"One moment," the voice said. It was a young woman's voice, a chirping kind of voice. Riley cradled the telephone receiver against his shoulder and reached into his jacket for a Camel cigarette. What the hell, he thought, smiling once again. The smoke was hot in his throat. He leaned back in the console chair, and stared up two television cameras positioned at angles near the ceiling. Tiny red lights beamed from each camera. Riley pursed his lips and blew a smoke ring at the cameras. "Take that," he said to the cameras.

The telephone receiver came to life.

"Your call is coming through now, sir." The chirping operator's voice was brisk.

From the Crofton School near Westport, Connecticut, came a low-pitched New England voice. "This is Dean Adele Pearson, Mr., ah, Riley?" she said.

Jack Riley straightened in his chair beside the computer console at Rights for the Unborn League headquarters. "I believe my associate, Brian McClure, spoke with you earlier about some student records."

From Connecticut, Riley heard the sound of papers being moved. "I remember Mr. McClure. He asked us to send him a certified copy of our student rosters back to the end of World War II," Dean Pearson said.

Her voice was remote; Dean Adele Pearson sounded much further away from Jack Riley than the simple distance from Washington, D.C., to Connecticut. "That's right," Riley said. She sounds like somebody's piano teacher, he thought. Now you will practice the scales, please; rap rap on the piano stand with her baton. From the beginning; rap rap. He could see her standing there. Someone like her. Did she look like a piano teacher? Jack Riley's headache pounded.

"Well, then. Is there some problem, Mr. Riley?" Dean Adele Pearson said to him, her voice carrying low and calm across the vast distance between her office at the Crofton School and the Rights for the Unborn League library, where Jack Riley sat beside the computer console.

He blew another smoke ring into the eyes of the Rights for the Unborn League cameras above him. "Look, Miss, ah, Pearson, could you and I go over some of this on the phone? Just the student enrollment material," he said.

"I'm afraid we do not give out information concerning our alumnae over the telephone, Mr. Riley." Dean Pearson cut the edges of each syllable off with her neat little baton.

Riley sucked on his Camel cigarette. "Sure. But this is a special case. So, if you don't mind," he said.

From Connecticut, the sound of papers being moved came once again, as if papers were being neatly stacked right next to the telephone receiver. "The Crofton School has to be careful," Adele Pearson said from Connecticut. "You'll recall that we agreed to certified mail in your case. But that is as far as we go, Mr. Riley. On the advice of the school's attorney. You do understand."

Jack Riley stubbed out his Camel cigarette in a paper clip box beside the computer console; he picked up the cigarette butt and began to tear it apart, bit by bit. The telephone receiver was silent. She was waiting. I could send Brian up there, he thought. No. Keep Brian out of this. This one was his personal project. "When are you open up there, Miss Pearson?" He tossed the shredded bits of cigarette butt into a wastebacket next to the console.

"Nine to four-thirty. Weekdays," she said. "May we expect you then, Mr. Riley?"

Riley threw the contents of the paper clip box into a wastebasket. "Yes," he said finally. "Tomorrow, if that's convenient." Teacher, teacher. He imagined her with a baton.

"Tomorrow will be fine."

Brian McClure arrived back in the Rights for the Unborn League Library soon after Jack Riley had completed his unsatisfactory conversation with Dean Adele Pearson. On a small plastic tray, McClure brought Riley a cup of coffee, an unopened container of orange juice, and a bran muffin. "Here you are," McClure said. "And I thought you might like a muffin. They make excellent bran muffins in the bakery downstairs," he added, smiling brightly at Riley.

"This place has a bakery?" Jack Riley had not taken the time to survey personnel facilities inside the Rights for the Unborn League headquarters.

"Oh, yes. Complete cooking facilities. And storage for food supplies," McClure replied.

"Food supplies?"

Riley watched McClure shift uncomfortably, rocking back and forth on his heels. "It's, ah, part of the preparations for unusual operations," McClure said. "If something should happen, some kind of incident, then the League would be able to continue operating."

Well, well. Jack Riley pulled his crumpled package of Camel cigarettes from his shirt pocket. "What kind of incident, Brian?"

McClure's blue eyes widened. "Well, any kind," he said. "A disaster, for example. California dropping off in an earthquake. You know what I mean."

Riley retrieved a Camel from the crumpled package. "Sure," Riley said.

"Uh, Mr. Riley?"

Riley looked back at McClure. Brian had put the tray on the console table and now he was standing behind it, waiting. "What is it, Brian?"

"You're not allowed to smoke in here."

Jack Riley smiled a thin smile at Brian McClure, and he kept smiling as McClure's eyes, which had been fastened on Riley, dropped to the deep royal blue carpeting and his baby soft eyelashes brushed his fine cheekbones. Riley put his package of Camel cigarettes back in his shirt pocket. He decided that a drive to Connecticut in his air-conditioned rental car would not be all that bad; it would be a relief. He decided to skip the air shuttle and instead take a long quiet drive tomorrow to the Crofton School. There was plenty of time for a drive like that tomorrow; he would make the time.

It was just past noon on the following day when Riley drove his rental car through the entrance gates of the Crofton School; the high wrought iron gates reminded him of the entrance to Carlton Farnsworth's antebellum home in Virginia. But this was not somebody's dream of the Old South reincarnated outside Washington, D.C.; this was an incarnation of snotty Yankee country, wasn't it. A new, unopened bottle of Bushmills whiskey was under the front seat on the driver's side of Riley's rental and as he approached the entrance to the Crofton School, he wanted very much to pull over and open it and let the whiskey warm him and sustain him and nourish him before he passed through the entrance gates. He forced himself to ignore the urge for the whiskey; he would satisfy himself after his meeting with Crofton School Dean of Students Adele Pearson.

The red brick buildings of the Crofton School were set in a perfect U-shape facing a broad expanse of green lawn bisected with brick walkways. In the distance beyond them, Riley could see a gymnasium and athletic fields. The lawns had been clipped and mowed within the last twenty-four hours; he could smell the unmistakable odor of freshly cut lawn. The sprinkler system was on, and waves of water spray spiraled from a dozen sprinkler heads set on the broad green lawns. Riley sidestepped the spiraling spray as he strode up the red brick walkway that led to the building in the center of the campus. Walking up to it, climbing the set of red brick steps that led to the main entrance, Jack Riley noted a small bronze plaque above the double doors. "The Crofton Academy for Young Ladies, founded 1837." Well, well, he thought. Watch your step, Jack.

Well-oiled hinges moved soundlessly when he pushed the main door open. A small, hand-lettered sign directed visitors to an office down the hall.

Riley's heels clicked on the polished wood floor. It gleamed with arcs of polish. The hallway smelled of wax and linseed oil. A door stood ajar at the end of the hall; Dean's Office was stenciled in black letters on the frosted glass doorfront.

He saw a woman in her middle forties seated at a desk inside the simple office, her head bent over a stack of envelopes. There she is, he thought. Teacher, teacher. "Miss Pearson?" She looked up at the sound of his voice.

"Yes," she said. She smiled a pleasant, impersonal smile and waited for the stranger to introduce himself.

Her voice was surprisingly soft, not like the voice he remembered from his telephone conversation at the headquarters of the Rights for the Unborn League. "I'm Jack Riley. From the Rights For the Unborn League," he said.

Dean Adele Pearson's polite expression froze on her face and she drew her shoulders back as if something taut and strong were pulling her shoulder blades together from behind. She moved the stack of envelopes to one side and stood up. "Do you have some identification, Mr. Riley?"

Now Jack Riley recognized her voice; now it was the same one he had heard on the telephone yesterday at Rights for the Unborn League headquarters in Washington, D.C. Now she was the piano teacher once again, just as she had been on the telephone before, rap rapping on the piano stand with her baton. But she had no baton; Dean Adele Pearson was holding a fountain pen, which she had been using to personally address the stack of envelopes on her desk. Riley reached into his jacket pocket and pulled out his plastic-embossed League identification card. The card included his fingerprints as well as his picture. He smiled and handed the identification card to Adele Pearson.

She examined the card for a long time, as if she were memorizing every detail of it. Everything. She turned the card over in her hands and then she handed it back to Jack Riley, handing it back to him as if it were an unclean thing, an untouchable object. "Your identification seems to be in order, Mr. Riley," Dean Adele Pearson said. "You understand that our students and our alumnae have certain Constitutional rights. And that they have a right of privacy," she said, drawing herself up, holding Jack Riley in her direct unflinching gaze.

To Jack Riley, her crisp piano teacher voice seemed even sharper now, undiluted by long distance telephone lines. "Sure," he said. She intimidated him with her piano teacher voice and her bony shoulders and her tight thin mouth. The hell with her. "I'm interested in your class rosters from 1947, '48, and '49," Jack Riley told her. He would ignore this bitch and get on with it.

"Class rosters from that era would be in the school archives, Mr. Riley," she said. "They are not kept in this facility."

Well, she would have to get the fucking records, Riley thought. He noticed a wooden bookcase with glass doors against the wall opposite her desk. Two lower shelves were filled with school annuals. The upper shelves contained trophies, ribbons and several engraved plaques. One trophy was for a first place in women's crew at the National Junior Women's Finals. "Were annuals published then? School annuals?"

"Yes. Crofton students have always published an annual."

"With class rosters?"

"Sometimes. But they're not always accurate."

Adele Pearson came toward Riley, gliding around her desk to him. She was a slender woman of medium height. Her black hair was streaked with gray. It was cropped short and combed into a smooth and glossy style that accented her high white forehead. She walked around him to the bookcase and then turned to face the Special Security Assistant for the Rights for the Unborn

League. "Mr. Riley, the Crofton School is concerned about your inquiries. First our rosters. Now our annuals?"

More than anything at that moment, Jack Riley wanted a drink; his dry throat was dusty and he was tired of Dean Adele Pearson. "I think my associate, Brian McClure, explained that this is a security matter, Miss Pearson," he said. The bitch should shut up and cooperate. "I can get a court order. It would make the newspapers. Maybe even television." He smiled gently and cocked his head at her.

Adele Pearson drew herself up to her full height of five feet five and one half inches. To have that man's hands and his sickening fingers on Crofton School materials, examining them, investigating them, delving into the personal lives of her students, was almost more than she could stand. The Rights for the Unborn League was an organization she detested with a pure hot loathing that made her tremble with fury. For Dean Adele Pearson, who had been born in Dover-Foxcroft, Maine, to Jessica and Theodore Pearson of the old Maine Pearsons, had like all the Pearsons before her carried out her duty all of her life and those duties had included the provision of aid and comfort to Crofton students who needed abortions and didn't know where to get them.

The passage of the Human Life Amendment had not stopped Adele Pearson from providing this assistance; it was her duty and she would carry it out. Her students were first and the Rights for the Unborn League could go to Hell. And so on this early afternoon in 1998, standing only a few feet from Jack Riley, the Special Security Assistant for the Rights for the Unborn League, Dean Adele Pearson was terrified that the loathsome security agent had somehow discovered that she helped her students. For she was only human and she was afraid. Her fear, which she was controlling with an effort, and which had been pounding in her heart since the first call from the Rights for the Unborn League on the previous Friday, manifested itself in her sharpening voice, in the way she drew herself up, holding herself rigidly, as if to ward off a blow, and in the two pinpoints of reddened flesh at her cheekbones. She would have to let him see the school annuals; she could see that from the way he stood there, smiling that smirky smile at her. Dean Adele Pearson wanted to ask Jack Riley why he cared about the classes of 1947, 1948 and 1949; she wanted to ask him why the League cared about the students from those years; those students were old now, in their sixties. How could they matter to the League? She closed her eyes once, giving herself a tiny moment of blessed privacy.

"As I said, it's a security matter, Miss Pearson," Riley said, prodding her, smiling gently, waiting for her to reply.

Adele Pearson stared at the loathsome creature from the Rights for the Unborn League once more. "I see," she said to him. She turned and inserted a brass key into the bookcase lock, and for the first time since this incident began, since League representative Brian McClure called her on Friday, her composure began to wobble dangerously. Her hands trembled violently as she turned the brass key in the lock and opened the glass doors to the bookcase. "There! Go ahead and look, Mr. Riley!" She stood up quickly and brushed past him to the doorway. "Some of the annuals are old and fragile. Please be careful with them." She turned and was gone.

Riley looked at the empty doorway. He could hear her retreating footsteps echo down the hall. He turned back from the doorway and scanned the rows of annuals. There. 1947. 1949. The space between 1947 and 1949 was empty. Riley shrugged and pulled out the '47 and '49 annuals.

Standing beside Adele Pearson's desk, he began to leaf through 1947. Crofton had 537 students that year. There was no mention of a Frances Foster. Or a Mary Holt.

Riley picked up 1949. The pages were glossy even now, nearly fifty years later. There were black and white photographs of a science class, with groups of students standing solemnly beside Bunsen burners and test tubes. The print was small under the pictures. Riley squinted at the lists of names.

Squinting, reading the fine small print carefully, Jack Riley found them. The two of them. Frances Foster and Mary Holt, lab partners in chemistry, the caption said. Lab partners. Schoolmates.

Jack Riley turned the pages. There was Mary Holt, astride a horse. The caption said Mary Holt, an accomplished equestrienne, planned to tour England and Ireland after graduation. He closed the annual and began rubbing his fingers over the raised Crofton School lettering on the annual cover. Well, Jack Riley didn't tour anywhere after his graduation; he worked like a dog on the shrimp boats so he could get the Hell out of Freeport, Texas.

At that moment, Dean Pearson reappeared. She was carrying a manila envelope, which she handed to him stiffly. "These are copies of the class rosters for the years 1947, 1948 and 1949. If there is nothing more, I have many other things to do today," she said. She had recovered her composure. Now she wanted to finish with Jack Riley and the Rights for the Unborn League; she wanted to hear the door close behind him. If the League was investigating her, then so be it.

Riley put the school annuals on her desk beside the stack of envelopes she had been addressing when he arrived. There wasn't much in the annuals, but he had made the connection between Frances Foster and First Lady Mary Holt Morgan. He would see where the road went next. "That's all for now," he said to Dean Pearson, who continued to stand stiffly before him, waiting for an answer.

"Goodbye, Mr. Riley," she said.

Driving back to Washington, D.C., taking his time, nipping now and then on his new bottle of Bushmills whiskey, Riley decided to take a few days off from the investigation and go home to Miami. There had been nothing in the newspapers that day on the incident at the little backyard clinic in Algiers, across the Mississippi River from New Orleans; maybe the incident of last Thursday night was going to fade away. Maybe people would forget about it, at least for awhile. Of course he did not want them to forget entirely, for then his special, private services to Carlton Farnsworth, his very expensive additional services, might not be necessary.

In Westport, Connecticut, that evening, Adele Pearson seated herself at her kitchen table in the small Half Cape house where she had lived alone for fifteen years and began reading the Crofton School annuals for the years 1947, 1948 and 1949. Jack Riley and the Rights for the Unborn League were looking for something in the annuals, and in the rosters, which also were spread out on her kitchen table, and she was determined to find out what it was. The young faces of long ago that smiled out at her from the pages of the annuals were Crofton School alumnae. And in a way that she could not define, especially since the women from 1947, 1948 and 1949 were much older than Adele Pearson herself, they still were her students and she would protect them if she could.

Chapter Nine

Dean Adele Pearson closed the 1948 Crofton School annual and picked up 1949. She was tired now; her eyelids drooped, heavy with fatigue. She had read over every line of every page of the annuals for 1947 and 1948, but the shiny pages, graying with age and smudged black ink, had not revealed a reason for Jack Riley and the Rights for the Unborn League to thrust their loathesome hands into Crofton School business. Resolutely, Adele Pearson opened the 1949 annual; there must be something there. She tilted her head back and closed her eyes. Was it possible that their search in the old files was a ruse? Maybe they were really investigating Adele Pearson and not the classes of 1947, 1948 and 1949. Her strong straight shoulders dropped and her hands rose to her face and covered her mouth, as if to cover a moan that would escape if she did not trap it inside her body and stifle it there.

She had helped just one student first, just young Jennifer Long, who cried and said her parents would kill her if they found out; they would make her come home and they would lock her in her room, Jennifer had said, her tear-stained face red and splotched and pleading. Couldn't Dean Pearson help her! Didn't Dean Pearson know somebody? Somebody who could help her get rid of it!

How could Dean Adele Pearson refuse? She couldn't. And four days later, while the late evening television news was being broadcast into the quiet living rooms of Westport, Adele Pearson had driven Jennifer Long to the rear entrance of a small clinic in Westport, a family practice clinic, where Jennifer was unburdened of a thirteen-week fetus by a Nurse Practitioner. Driving back to the Crofton School two hours later, with Jennifer huddled under a blanket in the back seat, Adele Pearson had been terrified that a local police patrol car would pull them over, that she somehow would make a mistake as she negotiated her way over the dark streets of Westport and a Westport policeman would pull her over and see Jennifer in the back seat and instantly surmise that an illegal abortion had just taken place and Adele Pearson was responsible for it. She had pictured her arrest and the scandal and the snuffing out of her career. She would lose her position as Dean; they would have to get rid of her, of course, and she would go to prison. Her life, her carefully planned and decent, accomplished life, would shatter before her very eyes.

Adele Pearson had literally trembled with relief when she drove through the gates of the Crofton Schools grounds that night. She had tucked Jennifer safely away in her room on the second floor of the student dormitory, and she herself had slept on her sofa in the sitting room across the hall from her office. She slept often in the sitting room; the cozy sitting room, with its worn chintz window coverings and its battered but scrupulously clean Chippendale furnishings, was almost like a second home to Adele Pearson.

Months later, a second student came to her. Once again, there was a terrifying midnight journey to the family practice clinic in Westport. Once again, there was overwhelming relief as they passed through the Crofton School gates to safety.

The journeys that came after that, the half-dozen or so journeys to the family practice clinic with her students, had taken their toll on Adele Pearson, torn as she was between her allegiance to the Crofton School and all that it stood for, and her loyalty and loving concern for each Crofton student. How could she not help them? How could she stand by and watch any of their lives be ripped apart by an unwanted pregnancy? Well, she could not stand by. And so she took care of them, trembling with fear, shaking with it as she drove over the dark streets of Westport, Connecticut, praying for safety once again, praying for an end to another terrifying night. Adele Pearson longed to be brave on those nights; she yearned for a courageous heart, for a reckless heedless warrior's soul. She hated herself for being so filled with terror that she could hardly keep her gloved hands firmly on the steering wheel of her car.

Hunching over her kitchen table, she began to read the 1949 Crofton School annual. Maybe the Rights for the Unborn League really was looking for something from that far back, from half a century ago; maybe they really didn't know about Adele Pearson and the late night drives into Westport. She began to turn the pages of the 1949 annual, turning them slowly, one by one. There was the LaCrosse team. Then the Latin Club. Two pages of poetry by the Class of 1949, old fingerprints smearing the last few lines of a sonnet into a blurred gray smudge. There was the Senior chorus, their stiff smiling faces looking out at Adele from the page.

Adele Pearson squinted at the tiny lettering underneath the photograph of the Senior Chorus, peering at the names written there. Sandra McBride. Emily Littlejohn. Sarah Pointer. Mary Holt.

Adele Pearson sat up. Of course. Mary Holt Morgan, First Lady of the United States. President of the Rights for the Unborn League. Adele had not forgotten that Mary Holt was a Crofton School graduate, but wasn't the First Lady younger than this? This Mary Holt, the one in the picture with her dark blonde hair in short severe waves, the one with her mouth set in a straight line, would be sixty-three. Well, The First Lady could have lied about her age. Women did, Adele thought. Looking at the picture of the Senior Chorus, Adele Pearson felt relief wash over her. A lump grew in her throat, and seated at her kitchen table, the school annual for 1949 open before her, she began to weep. She wept silently, letting the tears fall, letting them run down her cheeks. So they weren't looking for her after all; the League didn't know about the abortions. Jack Riley, the League Security Assistant, had come to Crofton School because of the First Lady. If the Rights for the Unborn League was having some kind of security problem that involved the First Lady, it wasn't Adele's business. Even if Mary Holt Morgan had been a Crofton girl. Adele didn't care about the First Lady. Except to be ashamed of her and her Rights for the Unborn League and her Human Life Amendment.

Adele Pearson wiped her tears away with a tissue and closed the Crofton School annual for 1949. She would go through the entire annual tomorrow, when she wasn't so tired; she wanted to make certain there was nothing else in there that might interest the Rights for the Unborn League.

Almost directly east of Westport, across the sluggish summer waters of Long Island Sound to the eastern shore, Frances Foster lay dry-eyed and wide awake in her bed. The old Georgian house in East Hampton was eerily silent; there were not even the usual night sounds of the house settling to break the silence. Elizabeth McKinley was asleep in the guest room down the hall, held fast in the dreamless sleep of exhaustion.

They had buried Hillary Foster that afternoon, just the two of them, slipping her into a silent grave beside her grandparents in the old cemetery outside of East Hampton. Frances stared up at the dark ceiling in her bedroom, remembering the warm afternoon, the sunlight playing on the ancient maple trees and neat hedgerows that circled the little graveyard, the thudding sounds of earth striking Hillary's casket as the workmen began to cover her over for all time.

Downstairs, the clock above the mantlepiece began to chime; it was midnight. Frances threw back her bedcoverings and rose from her bed. She was warm; she left her wrapper in her bedroom and padded downstairs wearing just her long thin cotton nightgown and her old corduroy slippers. Purposefully, Frances made her way along the narrow back hall behind the kitchen, striding in the darkness, knowing from deep memory every inch of the house she had lived in nearly all of her life. She opened a door at the end of the hall and flicked on a lightswitch; light from a single overhead bulb illuminated the steep staircase leading to the basement. Gripping the handrail with one hand and lifting the hem of her cotton nightgown with the other, Frances stepped quietly down the stairs. She was a ghostly figure as she floated down the staircase, her cotton gown rippling behind her, her white hair loose from its barrettes, the last chimes of the mantlepiece clock echoing behind her through the still house.

Frances stopped at a closed door at the bottom of the staircase, took a small key from the wall beside the door, thrust it into the lock, and gently pushed the door open, slowly, as if there were something heavy behind the door, something that pushed back. But nothing was pushing back at Frances Foster; nothing but memories. For this was Hillary Foster's old playroom, her old secret room where people had to knock and say the password before they came in.

The plastered walls of the playroom were painted a fading yellow. White curtains festooned with dancing bears covered a casement window at the rear of the low-ceiled room. There was a child's desk in one corner, faded yellow paint gone to dust. A dappled rocking horse, mane nearly gone, red saddle worn almost to the bare wood, reposed peacefully just inside the door, as if it still was waiting for its rider to return. Frances reached out to the rocking horse, running her fingers through the tattered mane. "Good horse," Frances whispered. "Good boy." Frances leaned against the door, pressing one shoulder against the wood molding, pressing it against her body through the thin cotton gown. For a moment, Frances heard all the lost sounds around her, the lost echo of high pitched voices, the laughter ringing clear and sweet, the footsteps running toward her. Frances breathed deeply, a long slow ragged breath, her mouth twisted with grief and longing and pain and loss. "Dear God," Frances said. "Dear God, if there is one."

She turned and left the playroom, climbing the staircase to the kitchen. She sat down heavily in one of the chairs pulled up to the scarred old pine table in the kitchen, sitting in the dark. The enormity of what she was planning to do struck her now, striking like a heavy blow. She had been walking fiercely step by step through the days since Hillary's death, her rage sustaining her, driving her on, driving her like fire drives animals from a forest, hurtling them forward to escape. Kidnap the First Lady. How would they ever get away with it? She was heavily guarded; she was probably never alone. Even if they could get her, would they get the money? Would they get away afterwards? Frances Foster clasped her hands together and stared into the darkness as if she were searching for something in the dim shadowy light of the kitchen, searching for something hidden there, something dangerous that could strike out at her. They could all be killed, she thought. Young Elizabeth McKinley. Nora O'Brien. And herself. She could die too. She drew in a long breath, filling her lungs like a swimmer would fill them before diving into the water; she realized that she didn't care if it killed her.

Frances rose from the table and turned on the overhead light. She took a lined yellow pad down from a shelf and put on a pot of tea. Then, settling herself back at the table, she began to make a list. They would need a bank account in Switzerland, another account in Stockholm, and a line of credit for both accounts. They would need several vehicles, perhaps a van and a station wagon. She would need to gather everyone together. Their meeting at Cooperstown, New York would be ten days from now, the Saturday after next; Frances hoped Nora O'Brien could find a quiet place for the meeting. She put down the yellow pad and picked up her mug of tea. The kidnapping itself; how would they kidnap First Lady Mary Holt Morgan, President of the Rights for the Unborn League?

Somewhere, Frances Foster thought, there would be a small space of time when Mary Holt Morgan would open herself to them, when the First Lady would be the little lone chicken in the chickenyard, clucking selfishly at her little pile of corn.

Frances Foster sat bolt upright in her kitchen chair. Of course. The First Lady's hair. Frances remembered Mary Holt at the Crofton School; she remembered Mary and her hair, her constant perfecting of it, her torturing of her dull blonde hair into precise waves. She remembered the habit Mary Holt had of pulling strands of her hair from the back of her neck, plucking the hairs out one by one. Mary Holt Morgan had never broken the nasty little habit; Frances remembered seeing the First Lady on television not long ago, reaching unconsciously for the back of her neck. Frances Foster began to speculate dreamily. Now the First Lady's hair was golden and shining; now her hair was a perfect golden halo framing her pretty pink face. Frances smiled and sipped her tea. There might be a bald spot back there from the hair pulling; the First Lady might be bald at the back, right at the hairline. Oh, she wouldn't want anyone to know about that, Frances thought. Not even the White House staff; everyone knows they don't keep their mouths shut. No, she would have to go outside the White House to keep her beautiful hair golden and

shiny, to bleach and tone it and artfully conceal the bald spot.
And the First Lady would be alone for her little cosmetics ses-
sions, for coloring and styling her hair and for polishing her pink
little face, which glowed with the unmistakable flush of frequent
chemical face peelings. That was when Mary Holt Morgan
would be the little chicken in her chickenyard, grooming her
feathers with her little beak, hoarding her secret pile of corn,
cluck cluck clucking selfishly to herself, Frances thought, finishing her cup of tea in the still kitchen.

Reaching over to a pine sideboard by the window, Frances
picked up her new copy of *First Lady: The Mary Holt Morgan
Story*. Surely the unauthorized biography would include something about Mary's beautiful golden hair; surely her biographer
would not leave out such an important detail, Frances thought.

The biographer had left almost nothing out; the First Lady's
carefully styled hair was the result of nimble and creative work
by Roberto Quintero, the famed hairdresser and complexion renewal expert who worked out of a small, exclusive salon in
Georgetown. There was no mention of a bald spot. Maybe Roberto knew when to keep his mouth shut, Frances thought. She
put the Mary Holt Morgan Story down on the table beside her
yellow legal pad. Elizabeth McKinley would have to find out
more; Elizabeth would have to visit Roberto Quintero's Salon in
Georgetown. Frances was grateful for Elizabeth McKinley, who
was fast asleep upstairs, but who would be leaving in the morning for Washington, D.C., where she had lived and worked for
more than five years. For all of her fervent desire to succeed,
Frances did not think they would prevail without the help of her
daughter Hillary's oldest friend. Elizabeth was an emergency
planner; her entire professional career had been built around
planning for crises and managing rescues of people and property.
Frances had decided that kidnapping the First Lady was a kind of
rescue, and that creating a safe place for women to go for abor-

tions was its own kind of emergency, a crisis which Frances Foster and Elizabeth McKinley and Nora O'Brien and others would rise to meet.

It was nearly 2:00 A.M. when Frances Foster turned out the kitchen light and went up to bed, to sleep this time, fitfully, throwing her arms out, tossing like a small boat on a heavy sea.

In the morning, Frances Foster sent Elizabeth McKinley back to Washington, D.C.; Elizabeth had a lot to do in the nation's capital over the next ten days. After Elizabeth left, driving Frances' old station wagon, and carrying Frances' copy of *First Lady: The Mary Holt Morgan Story*, Frances placed a call to her attorney, Matthew Adair, in New York City.

After a few short preliminaries, Frances got right down to business with Matthew Adair, who had been her personal attorney for more than thirty years. She told Matthew that she wished to liquidate her entire estate, everything, all of it, and she wanted the funds, after taxes, to be placed in a personal account in Zurich, Switzerland.

Adair objected strenously to this move. It was a bad time to liquidate and even if it weren't, he would never advise liquidating an estate of this size. Didn't she know how much was involved there? He was dreadfully sorry about young Hillary; of course he had read about it in the papers. It was a great tragedy for her; the loss of her child was insupportable, his heart went out to her. Did she plan on having a service? Oh, the service was yesterday. He hadn't known. The service was private. Well, he could understand that. But now it sounded like Frances was leaving the country. Surely, with all her ties here—.

"What ties, Matthew?" Frances said, finally interrupting Matthew Adair's long pleading monologue. "There are no ties left."

"You have friends. You have me, for God's sake!" Matthew Adair said, for he loved Frances. He had loved her for many years; especially after the death of his wife Lucinda four years

ago. It should have been the most natural thing in the world for
Frances to come to him after Lucinda was gone. But she didn't;
she really seemed to prefer that solitary life of hers out there in
East Hampton. Now this. Adair was deeply alarmed. "Frances,
give yourself a little time to get over this. You're being much too
hasty," he said.

Frances listened calmly. "I'm not going to get over it, Matthew. Not ever. Now do as I say," she urged.

Matthew Adair sighed inwardly; he knew her too well to argue
anymore. "All right, Frances," Matthew said. "I hope you don't
regret this later."

"I won't regret it, Matthew," Frances told him.

She was drawing a line through the note on her yellow pad that
had Matthew Adair's name on it when the telephone beside her
began to ring. She didn't recognize the woman's voice, and when
the woman identified herself, announcing that she was Dean
Adele Pearson from the Crofton School, Frances' old alma mater, Frances grew impatient. She contributed regularly to the
Crofton Alumni Fund and she didn't appreciate this telephone
solicitation.

Dean Adele Pearson had never spoken directly to Frances Foster; she had never met her in person. Frances Foster was a name
on her contributing alumni list, and Adele's previous communications with Frances had been handwritten thank you notes for
Frances' contributions to the Alumni Fund. This morning, Adele
Pearson had read the 1949 annual. When she came to the photo
of lab partners Mary Holt and Frances Foster, an alarm had
sounded. Frances Foster. There had been something in the newspaper about her just a few days ago. Then Adele remembered;
Frances Foster was the mother of the girl who died in the raid on
an illegal abortion clinic in Louisiana last week. The article had
hinted that the Rights for the Unborn League had been involved
somehow. Adele Pearson had shuddered at the news of the raid.

What if the police raided the family practice clinic in Westport one night while she was there? What if they raided the clinic and arrested her? It was another danger, another risk to add to all the other risks she was taking. Now the Rights for the Unborn League was at Crofton School; Rights League agent Jack Riley had surely seen the photograph of Frances Foster and Mary Holt. And Riley had told her he was investigating a security problem.

It had taken Adele Pearson a full hour to pick up the telephone and call Frances Foster, a full hour in which she sternly told herself that she had a duty to her students, even to her older alumnae; the Crofton School's protection and concern extended even to the grave. Mrs. Foster had sounded impatient when she called, saying briskly that she already had made her Alumnae Fund contribution this year. "Oh no, it's not about that!" Adele Pearson said. She swallowed hard and continued. "Mrs. Foster, someone from the Rights for the Unborn League was here yesterday, asking for information about the years when you were at Crofton. I don't know if you knew this, but your classmate Mary Holt is First Lady Morgan now?"

In her kitchen in East Hampton, Frances Foster drew herself up in her chair. Were they investigating her? Was it possible? Anything was possible. "I know about the First Lady. She's President of the Rights for the Unborn League, too," Frances said. "Did the security person ask about me directly, Dean Pearson? Did he use my name?" Maybe this is a terrible coincidence, she thought.

"He didn't mention any names, Mrs. Foster. But I—." Adele Pearson paused. "I read about your daughter Hillary's death. I am so very sorry about your loss. I wondered if there might be some connection," she said, her voice trailing off uncertainly.

Frances pushed aside her wishful thinking for a coincidence. So they want to know all about Hillary and me, she thought.

They're going to blame us for what happened in New Orleans; they're going to make it our fault. "The bastards," she said.

"Yes," Dean Adele Pearson said. "If there is anything I can do, Mrs. Foster."

Frances wrote the name Adele Pearson on her yellow legal pad. "I appreciate that, Dean Pearson. There may be a time soon when I do ask for your help," she said.

Hanging up the telephone, Frances Foster drew a line under Adele Pearson's name. She had heard the fear in Adele Pearson's voice; it had taken some courage for the Crofton School Dean to call her this morning. The Rights for the Unborn League was a terrifying presence even from a distance. Frances put on another pot of tea. Nora O'Brien would be calling soon and Frances wanted to tell her about Dean Adele Pearson; they would have to be even more careful now.

It was just past two that afternoon when Elizabeth McKinley pulled into the parking lot of a Howard Johnson's off the Washington-Baltimore Expressway near Font Hill, Maryland. Frances Foster's old standard-sized station wagon was not air-conditioned and Elizabeth was hot and sticky and tired from the drive from East Hamptom. She slipped into a bright orange booth, ordered a diet cola and a chef's salad and opened Frances' copy of *First Lady: The Mary Holt Morgan Story,* the latest unauthorized biography of the President of the Rights for the Unborn League. The paperback book was thick with grainy photographs of Mary Holt Morgan, and it included an exhaustive index, which Elizabeth turned to immediately, looking up 'H' for Hairdresser. "See Quintero, Roberto," it said. She turned to Quintero. Under "Quintero, Roberto," were three page-number annotations, one for a photograph and two for narrative references. On the second reference, on page 127, Elizabeth McKinley found what she was looking for. The First Lady's close friend Roberto did her hair himself, often coming to the White House; on occasion, the First Lady went to Roberto at his exclusive salon on "K" Street in Georgetown.

Wild horses would not drag from the lips of Roberto Quintero the details of the First Lady's visits to his salon; he had created her enduring and elegant hairstyle as a kind of statement, a beautiful signature for her sophisticated look and that was all he would reveal. Roberto Quintero was certainly not going to share her secrets with some grubby little biographer looking for sensation!

Elizabeth stabbed at her salad; the lettuce was wilted and she was not hungry anyway. Frances Foster was right; the First Lady might be vulnerable at Roberto Quintero's. It was worth a shot. Elizabeth decided to call the Quintero Salon now; she was worried about getting an appointment before the meeting in Cooperstown. They had to know when the First Lady traveled out of the White House to the hair salon on "K" Street. She didn't want to think about what they might have to do if the hair salon scheme would not work. She had no idea how else they could get close enough to Mary Holt Morgan; it might take months and months. It would mean trying to take her during a public appearance; it would mean increasing the risk, increasing the already large chance for failure. Elizabeth knew that successful emergency management meant encircling the disaster; it meant control and containment and not a circus. No bright lights, no capacity crowd.

She did not want to wait months and months; she did not want to wait even a single month. She wanted it to be tomorrow. Elizabeth rose and walked to a telephone booth at the back of the Howard Johnson's restaurant. The telephone buzzed interminably before a smooth contralto voice from Roberto Quintero's Salon on "K" Street answered. No, Mister Roberto was not taking on new clients just now, the contralto voice purred, but one of his assistants could squeeze her in Thursday next; that would be absolutely the earliest that they could work her in. Young Jonathan was Mr. Roberto's newest assistant, but he was really quite good, quite creative. Would that be satisfactory? All right, then. Thursday next it was.

Returning to her salad and diet cola, Elizabeth McKinley spent the next forty-five minutes skimming through *First Lady: The Mary Holt Morgan Story*. Most of her salad was still on her plate when she left the restaurant and turned back onto the expressway for Washington, D.C.

Driving home, maneuvering Frances Foster's old dark blue station wagon through the clogged traffic into the District of Columbia, Elizabeth McKinley pictured the First Lady in Roberto Quintero's Salon. She pictured Mary Holt Morgan with her pretty little head laid back against the shampoo sink, her hair plastered flat against her skull, her pretty neck arched back, her white throat open. A person could slit that throat in one easy stroke while the First Lady was having her shampoo, Elizabeth thought. One quick hard stroke and it would be over for the First Lady; she would bleed to death, choking and gurgling on her blood, gasping and drowning in it. She wondered if the First Lady would know what was happening; if her eyes would bulge in terror, if she would grab her throat and try to press it back together.

Chapter Ten

In a third floor courtroom of the New Orleans Parish Court-house, with the noontime heat hanging heavily in the still air, Judge Averill Higginbotham III, his neck red and sticky from heat and impatience, motioned young Robert E. Lee Johnson to the bench. There were far too many Robert E. Lee Somethings coming before Judge Higginbotham these days. He wished these young mothers would let that name go. This Robert E. Lee, the Johnson boy, was stick tall and thin and his sleeves stuck out a bit too much from his shirt cuffs for Averill Higginbotham's taste; well that was the way with the court-appointed boys, he thought. Higginbotham waggled a stubby manicured finger at young Robert E. Lee Johnson. "Where is your client, Mr. Johnson!" the judge hissed.

Robert E. Lee Johnson, court-appointed attorney to accused felon Nora O'Brien, whose preliminary hearing was to have been two hours ago, blinked his eyes rapidly at Judge Higginbotham, desperately searching for a reply. He could not find Miss O'Brien; Johnson did not have five cents of an idea where she was. "I believe she has been unavoidably delayed, your honor," he said. "I, uh, believe she is ill, sir."

Judge Averill Higginbotham III had heard that one so very many times before that he could hardly contain himself as he loomed over the sharp-shouldered figure of Nora O'Brien's court-appointed attorney. "When will she be disposed to come before us do you think, counselor?" he said softly, grimacing in distaste at Robert E. Lee Johnson.

The attorney uttered a little prayer to the God of poor young lawyers. "I believe she will be in, uh, renewed health next week, your honor," he said. Robert E. Lee Johnson vowed to bring the bitch in next Wednesday if he had to drag her in by the hair. He smiled hopefully at the judge.

Higginbotham paused and squinted at young Johnson through cynical blue eyes. He wondered if young Johnson's client had perhaps defied his court and skipped town, skipping out on a $25,000 cash bond. Well, Judge Averill Higginbotham III was looking forward to presiding over this particular case, in which the Registered Nurse, Nora O'Brien, was accused of being an accessory to the murder of these helpless babies in that filthy illegal abortion clinic over in Algiers. Higginbotham felt it was about time for him to move up to the Louisiana Supreme Court this year. This nasty case, over which he would preside with firm impartiality and glacial calm, would surely be closely followed in the Louisiana media, perhaps even in the national press. It came at a good time for Averill Higginbotham III. "Very well. The hearing is postponed to Wednesday next," he said. Higginbotham leaned even closer to Robert E. Lee Johnson. "And she'd better be here!"

Leaving the New Orleans Parish Courthouse, Johnson drove directly to Nora O'Brien's apartment in the Kenner District. His client did not answer her door, which didn't surprise him. The Monday, Tuesday and Wednesday editions of the New Orleans newspaper were on her doorstep. The curtains were drawn on her windows, but one curtain did not quite reach the bottom of the window and Johnson peered through this opening, through the slit between the window ledge and the top of the curtain, his tall thin body hunched over the window. It was dark in there and he couldn't see very well; the dim room looked like her bedroom. A pigsty, Johnson thought. The room was a mess; the bed seemed to be piled high with the lumpy shapes of blankets or clothes and the closet doors were open.

Robert E. Lee Johnson's back began to hurt; he straightened up and walked to Nora's front door. Maybe the door would open if he wriggled it hard enough; it was a tacky little door with a cheap lock. But the door would not open under his insistent prodding and shoving. He was afraid to actually break in, to batter the door down. What he had been able to see, however, led him to conclude that his client Nora O'Brien may have gone somewhere far away from New Orleans and Judge Higginbotham's courtroom.

Johnson sat down on the steps in front of Nora's apartment building, sitting in the hot and muggy afternoon sun, smoking another of his cigarettes. He would have to find her. He had never had a case like this one assigned to him before, one that would mean publicity, maybe even his picture in the newspaper holding her hand as he asked the court for mercy for this misguided and contrite woman. Robert E. Lee Johnson squashed out his cigarette on the apartment step; he would hire private cops, by God, he would do it all to get that woman back into the courtroom beside him.

Far to the north of New Orleans, in the cool reaches of upstate New York, accused felon Nora O'Brien, who did not plan to see Robert E. Lee Johnson ever again, or appear in the courtroom of Judge Averill Higginbotham III ever again, was just pulling into the outskirts of historic Cooperstown, home of the Baseball Hall of Fame.

Nora patted the smooth gray and white fur of her cat Max, who had traveled with her all the way from New Orleans, traveling in the bucket seat beside her, working his claws into the upholstery to protest the constant movement of the car, which he loathed with all of his cat loathing. "Not much longer, Max," Nora said soothingly. They had turned north on Highway 28 outside of Oneonta, New York, earlier that morning; Nora was glad to be off the Interstate and onto the quieter New York State Highway. They had been traveling north since Sunday afternoon, traveling away from New Orleans Police Department investigators and New Orleans courtrooms, and away from Charity Hospital, where Nora O'Brien would never practice her profession again.

Nora's deepest regret, if there were any regrets right now, was that she had not been able to claim the body of Michael Green, M.D., and take him away from the morgue in New Orleans to some place where he could rest in peace. She did not even know if anyone else had claimed Michael Green's body, or if anyone would. Surely someone would, she thought; surely someone from his family had already come for Michael Green. In her conversations with Frances Foster, it was Michael's face that Nora kept remembering, looming up in her consciousness like a ghost that would not rest; she knew that Michael Green would want her to kidnap the First Lady and begin the safe clinic in Sweden. Nora O'Brien knew that as surely as she knew that they might fail. Hers was the heart of a realist. She knew that there was only the barest chance that they would succeed, that anyone could see that they were naïve fools to believe that they could get away with kidnapping Mary Holt Morgan, get $100 million out of her, and get safely out of the country.

Inwardly, Nora compared their scheme to going ahead with chemotherapy on a late stage cancer. Sometimes people hung on for months; many times they were gone just as fast. But then there were a few who made it; there were the few who lived and nobody really knew why those very few survived and all the rest did not. She had always suspected that there was something in the personality, some key ingredient, that joined the survivors. Nora patted Max the cat once more. So they would be among the survivors, she and Frances and Elizabeth McKinley and whoever else Frances brought in to this thing. They would cut out the cancer and they would survive it. And if they didn't? We'll be like Scarlett O'Hara, Nora thought. We'll think about that tomorrow. She smiled to herself, a wide smile that slashed across her wide Irish face and gave it warmth. It was a beautiful smile, although Nora did not know that; she did not think there was anything beautiful about her face. Her face, with its expanse of flesh over prominent bones, the pockmarks of adolescent acne blurred with maturity, was the face of a woman of the rocky fields of old Ireland; it was a strong face.

Nora slowed the compact car she was driving and turned off the highway, driving toward the town center of Cooperstown; she supposed the road would pass by the field where Abner Doubleday invented baseball. Driving slowly now, Nora began looking for it. The road was surprisingly thick with slow-moving traffic, and the occupants of every car seemed to be wearing baseball caps. Nora herself had played a distinguished game of softball once upon a time, pitching for her junior girls team. Her size had given her the advantage of strength, and her pitches were big and strong and fast.

But Nora was not in Cooperstown, the tiny community redolent of baseball, to relive her glory days as a softball pitcher; she was here to set up the upstate New York meeting for Francis Foster and Elizabeth McKinley and whoever else Frances decided to bring in to this. She and Frances had decided that the village of Cooperstown, hidden deep in the green and hilly Leatherstocking region of upstate New York, and packed with tourists in summer, would serve them well as their temporary headquarters. After all, who could question a gathering of old friends and baseball fans on a sunny summer weekend in Cooperstown.

Nora did not see Abner Doubleday's ballfield, but she did see a Motel Six sign blinking on and off ahead. She turned in the motel driveway and pulled into an empty space near the entrance. At mid-week, the motel had a vacancy. She registered herself as Frances Foster, of East Hampton, New York, and booked a room through Friday. Then Nora hauled her overnight bag and Max the cat to a room on the second floor and collapsed on the bed. Nora was tired, and while she did not care to admit it, she was a little afraid. Her preliminary hearing had been scheduled for this morning; she wondered if there already was a warrant out for her arrest. If it hadn't happened already, it would happen soon.

She had never been a fugitive before. Was this what it felt like? Would her picture be circulated to police departments? Would they call her family in Chicago? Nora O'Brien had not called home since her arrest last Thursday night; she could not have withstood the shock and horror in their voices when they discovered what she had done. It had been a long time since Nora had been home. She wrote sometimes, and sent cards at appropriate times, but she could not bring herself to go home to Chicago once more, to see their hurt questioning faces and watch them pressing once again for some explanation of why dear Nora was so unlike their other four children, who were all married and right here in Chicago.

Nora decided not to think about it. She propped herself up on the bedpillows and dialed Frances Foster's house in East Hampton. Frances answered the telephone almost immediately. "It's Nora," she said. "I'm in Cooperstown."

Frances Foster was glad to hear that. She had been shaken by Adele Pearson's call this morning; it had never occurred to her that the Rights for the Unborn League would begin investigating her. It was dangerous for them and Frances wanted to move faster because of this. She told Nora about Dean Adele Pearson's call. "I don't think they know anything. I don't think they have any idea of it, but this makes everything harder," she confided. "Have you found a place for the meeting?"

"I just got here," Nora said. "A half hour ago." So the League was after Frances and the New Orleans police were after her.

Frances decided that even in Cooperstown at the height of the tourist season, they could not risk renting motel rooms. A summer house rental would be better. "Look, Nora, I think we should rent a house instead of motel rooms. Take a house for the rest of this month and for August," Frances advised her.

Nora leaned back against the pillows. "OK," she said. She looked up at the ceiling. "My preliminary hearing was this morning in New Orleans. There may be a warrant out for me. They may even be circulating my picture."

There was a silence at the other end of the telephone as Frances Foster absorbed this. She made a note to herself to ask Matthew Adair to check on that; attorney-client privilege was a wonderful thing. "They won't find you, Nora," she urged. "Use my name for everything, even to buy gasoline." Frances had given Nora O'Brien a sheaf of credit cards before she left New Orleans; the cards would be useful now. Nora O'Brien sounded tired; she sounded discouraged to Frances. "Nora?"

"Yes. I'm here," Nora said quietly. With one hand, she began to rub Max the cat's gray and white belly.

Nora O'Brien did not lose her child, Frances thought. She didn't lose her only child like I did. "I want you to know that you don't have to go through with this," Frances said.

In Cooperstown, in her motel room, Nora O'Brien continued to stare up at the ceiling. She wanted to go through with it; she wanted them to pay. It was what she lived for now. "I know that. I'm not fading away, Frances. It's just that—" She took a deep breath. "I don't know if anyone came for Mike Green. Hillary's doctor? I don't know if anyone came to take care of Mike," Nora told her. "I don't like to think of him lying on a slab in the morgue down there all alone."

Frances Foster realized that she had not thought much about Michael Green, M.D., in the last few days; she had been too busy burying Hillary and beginning their plans for the kidnapping of First Lady Mary Holt Morgan. And she realized that Nora O'Brien was grieving, that she too grieved for all that was lost and would never be again. She wondered suddenly if Nora had called her mother, if Nora's mother would understand. "I'll find out about Mike Green for you, Nora," Frances said. It would be another item to add to the list of things Matthew Adair would be doing.

Nora O'Brien felt better after that. Hanging up the telephone and laying back on her bed in the Motel Six room, with the curtains drawn and the color television droning, Nora began to leaf through the telephone book, looking for a rental agent. If she could just be sure that Mike Green's body was out of the morgue and that someone had taken him from there to give him a decent burial, she would be all right. Would they buy him a stone? Would there be a marker for Mike Green? She resolved to buy him one if nobody else did. She found a rental agent and made an appointment for the following morning. She was looking for a spacious summer rental, she told the agent, yes, a balance of the summer through Labor Day. Something large. She was expecting family and friends. It would be a kind of family reunion. Yes, near Lake Otsego would be nice. She understood that the lake was lovely this time of year and something in a quiet area near Otsego would be lovely. Would there be any pets? Oh no, Nora O'Brien told the humming rental agent. No pets.

That evening, Nora walked to a delicatessen near her Motel Six room and returned with a commodious bag of deli food, which she shared with Max the cat, who picked the shrimp out of his salad. "It's all right, Max," she said, running her free hand over his fur. "Everything is all right." Max the cat purred contentedly beside her, his pink tongue lapping up the last of his chicken and cream cheese plate.

On Thursday morning, Nora O'Brien met with a delighted rental agent in Cooperstown, New York, and used Frances Foster's American Express gold card to make a substantial deposit for the summer rental of what the rental agent breathlessly described as an exquisite Italianate Victorian estate on one acre in the prime Cooperstown Village historic district, a rare find. Elizabeth McKinley, meanwhile, was in Georgetown, an area of prime real estate in the District of Columbia. She was in a tiny restaurant on "K" Street, across the narrow avenue from Roberto Quintero's nationally famous salon, where First Lady Mary Holt Morgan, esteemed President of the Rights for the Unborn League, was known to have her hair done and her complexion pinked.

By waiting, and tipping her waiter very generously, Elizabeth had been able to secure a window seat, and from this vantage point, she was able to observe the comings and goings at Roberto Quintero's salon. Her fettucini was almost untouched on her plate, and now the waiter was hovering solicitously, wondering if the pasta perhaps did not please her delicate palate? Like an obedient child, Elizabeth forced herself to eat the pasta; she was not hungry, but she did not want the waiter buzzing around her like an irritating mosquito.

There was a passenger load zone in front of Roberto Quintero's, but it was never empty. Limousines pulled in and out at brief intervals, and on occasion, limousines were double-parked in front of the salon. The front door to the salon was heavy and wooden, thickly painted with black semi-gloss enamel, and a brass knocker with the name Roberto Quintero etched in small letters on a brass plate was the only sign that indeed this was his famous establishment. The windows on each side of the black salon door were faced with black shutters; the wooden building itself was about fifteen feet wide and like many structures in Georgetown, it listed slightly to one side. Elizabeth McKinley concluded that an alleyway at the rear of the building would provide their best hope for bringing a van close enough to the salon to get the First Lady out the back door and into their escape vehicle, which would have to resemble a commercial delivery van. A delivery van would not be out of place in the alley behind "K" Street.

She sipped a glass of white wine and stared thoughtfully out the window. The First Lady's limousine would almost certainly be at the front door, in the passenger load zone, but surely the Secret Service would have someone at the back door, perhaps in a car back there. The thought discouraged her. They must be crazy to think they could get away with this. The Secret Service could block the tiny alleyway and "K" Street itself; they could prevent anyone from getting close to Roberto Quintero's while Mary Holt Morgan was in there. And why wouldn't they? Maybe trying to kidnap her while she was having her hair done wasn't the best way. Maybe there was some other way, Elizabeth thought.

She stared out the window once again, staring intently at the narrow building that was the home of Roberto Quintero's salon. The tall narrow building, its thin clapboards painted a dark mustard color, was one of a row of similar wooden buildings on "K" Street. Each window on all three stories was faced with the black shutters, and there were window boxes on each; the window boxes were a brilliant riot of red and green, thick with blooming begonias. The false front above the third story had a window in the shape of a diamond in it. False front, Elizabeth thought suddenly. Was the roof flat? Was there a staircase up to the roof? A fire stair? Sitting in the restaurant and looking across "K" Street at Roberto Quintero's Salon, Elizabeth felt her heart begin to pound. And she was thankful for every fire service seminar and workshop she had ever attended while completing her master's degree in Emergency Management. Three-story commercial buildings, even narrow converted buildings like this one, had fire stairs to the roof.

Elizabeth McKinley left the restaurant on "K" Street so abruptly that the waiter barely had time to reach her with her check. She paid him in cash, once again tipping very generously as she hurried out the door. Watching her retreating figure, the waiter didn't care if she was hurried; she was a good tipper and she could do a fifty-yard dash through the damned restaurant for all he cared.

She crossed to the other side of "K" Street, darting through the heavy slow-moving traffic to the front door of Quintero's Salon. She stopped there for a moment, and then walked on, going next door to The Chocolatier, a sweets shop. The Chocolatier was in another wood frame building with clapboard siding; the building was perhaps twelve feet wide, but it was a full three stories tall. A tiny bell tinkled as Elizabeth went inside the cool air-conditioned shop, where a row of glass cases filled with expensive chocolates, pralines, marzipans, and jellied confections ran along one wall, running all the way to a steep narrow staircase in the rear. Walking to the back of the shop, examining the white chocolate confections in the last case next to the stairwell, and looking carefully up the staircase, Elizabeth could see that the staircase went all the way to the third floor. A clerk dressed in a chocolate brown blouse and trousers and a crisp white apron was watching her, smiling, waiting. Elizabeth pointed to the white chocolate almond bark. "A quarter of a pound please," she said.

The clerk scurried to fill her order, giving Elizabeth more time to look around. When the clerk handed her the order of almond

bark, Elizabeth paid her, in cash. Elizabeth McKinley smiled at
her pleasantly. "Where do the stairs go?" she asked.

"Oh, our kitchen is upstairs," the clerk answered. "Candy
making takes a lot of room. We store supplies on the third floor,
and then we vent the cooking heat through to the roof."

"Really. Do you have a roof garden?"

"Oh, no. Just a fire stair and a fire door. Fire code, you
know," the clerk said wisely.

Elizabeth felt little tingling thrill go through her body. "Ah,"
Elizabeth said, smiling once again at the clerk. Leaving the Chocolatier, with the little bell tinkling behind her as she closed the
door, Elizabeth walked to the corner of "K" Street, and turned
down the side street to the alleyway behind "K." The alley was
very narrow, perhaps eighteen feet wide, and it was swept clean
of litter and debris. Commercial garbage containers were placed
at strategic points, and No Parking signs were nailed to the walls
at approximately ten foot intervals all the way along the alley.
The Secret Service will pay no attention whatsoever to those No
Parking signs, Elizabeth thought. And neither will we. Walking
briskly, she walked the entire length of the empty alley to the next
side street. There were no cars parked in the alleyway, although a
delivery truck lumbered cautiously through just as Elizabeth
reached the other end. She turned to watch the truck. It stopped
in front of a blue painted door near the end of the alley and the
driver got out, opened the rear doors of the truck, unloaded a
carton by hand and muscled it through the door. The driver was
back in his van and gone in a very few minutes. So delivery
trucks stop in the alleyway, Elizabeth thought. Commercial
trucks can park back there for short periods and nobody bothers
them.

Driving back to her apartment, Elizabeth McKinley began to
feel some hope. With luck, and good planning, they might succeed. By the time she pulled into her parking space and shut off

the engine of her car, Elizabeth was humming a little tune to herself. She was thinking about First Lady Mary Holt Morgan, the President of the Rights for the Unborn League, thinking of the First Lady thrown over Nora O'Brien's shoulder like a sack of potatoes on the roof of Roberto Quintero's Salon, and she was thinking of Mary Holt Morgan's inert body stuffed into a nice clean carton from The Chocolatier, going out to a delivery truck on a clean little hand cart. Oh, there was a lot to do. Elizabeth was beginning to feel a little thrill of excitement pulsate through her body as she thought of all the things they had to do. She was beginning to feel reckless with it, as if she were galloping a horse over uneven ground, tempting fate, living dangerously. She wondered how much she was capable of, how much she might be tempted to do. Was this how soldiers felt when they oiled their guns, when they got ready? She had never felt this way before, not in her whole life; she liked the feeling.

On Friday, Elizabeth McKinley returned to "K" Street. She wore her $750 suit from I. Magnin in San Francisco and her hair was neatly parted in the middle and drawn into a plain page boy behind her ears. She had applied makeup, very sparingly. She looked elegant and expensive, like a young congresswoman, or an accomplished attorney or lobbyist. Well turned out. Equal to anyone at Roberto Quintero's Salon. This time, she did not stop at the black entrance door; she went inside, walking quietly over the soft gray carpet to the reception desk, where a contralto-voiced woman waited to greet her.

"I believe I have an appointment for next Thursday," Elizabeth said to the woman. "Elizabeth McKinley with Jonathan, Mr. Quintero's new assistant?" She waited as the woman flipped through her appointment book to next Thursday.

"Yes, I see we have you down here. Is there, ah, some problem, Miss McKinley?" The contralto voice purred approvingly at Elizabeth.

Elizabeth felt a hot reckless feeling pulsate through her body. She smiled and stepped up on a small mental stage, just like an actress would glide into the lights. "Well. I'm afraid I'm just a bit nervous about this. Kind of like going to the dentist. I was in the neighborhood and I thought—" She smiled helplessly and touched her hair with both fingers, touching it at the side of her temples, where her thick brown hair was pulled back behind her ears.

"I'm sure everything will be fine, Miss McKinley," the contralto voice assured soothingly. "Not to worry, dear."

Elizabeth smiled again. "Of course." She licked her lips. "If I could just see the salon," she said. "Familiarize myself with it. Silly, isn't it?"

The woman stood up and came around the desk to Elizabeth. She was tiny, perhaps five feet tall, and she was dressed entirely in black. Her hair, which was coal black, was pulled back into a shiny old-fashioned chignon at the nape of her neck. She reminded Elizabeth of her old ballet teacher. She took Elizabeth's arm. "I understand. My dear, I'm Annabelle, the salon coordinator, and I can assure you that you are just entirely safe with us." Her contralto voice dropped lower as she patted Elizabeth's arm. "We'll just take a little tour, you and I, and then you'll feel so much better about this," she said, leading Elizabeth into the salon.

The inside of Roberto Quintero's Salon was a quiet buzz of activity. The floor was divided into cubicles, with a shampoo area in the back. No one looked up as Elizabeth McKinley and Annabelle walked through the salon; the perfumed air was heavy with the smell of disinfectant and peroxide. Wooden fans suspended from the high ceiling turned slowly, moving the still air. Elizabeth felt Annabelle patting her gently on the arm as she walked beside her, a tiny black bird amid the shiny chrome and soft carpeting.

"Our hair is our glory, isn't it," Annabelle whispered. "We're very mindful of that here at Roberto's. You won't see our clients going about with those stark terrifying new cuts," Annabelle said.

Leaning over Annabelle, speaking softly, Elizabeth confided: "I understand even the First Lady comes to Roberto these days." She smiled at Annabelle, smiling innocently at her, smiling encouragement.

"That's right," Annabelle whispered.

"The White House staff tells me she is very pleased with Roberto's work," Elizabeth said, encouraging Annabelle once more.

"Oh, do you know Mrs. Morgan personally?" Annabelle looked up at Elizabeth with new respect as the two of them continued their promenade to the rear of the salon, turning back at a white painted staircase and moving slowly toward the front, like an odd little couple out for a stroll.

"I'm with the Administration," Elizabeth said smoothly.

"How nice for you!"

They were passing the cubicles again; there was not much time left. Elizabeth decided to press her advantage while she had it. "Is the First Lady due in soon?"

They went on past the last cubicle. "Not for another three weeks now," Annabelle said. "She's due in on the 14th for her touch-up. That's confidential of course," Annabelle whispered.

"Of course." Elizabeth smiled another gentle smile, and she thanked dear Annabelle as she left Roberto Quintero's Salon that afternoon. Elizabeth still was smiling, and she was humming to herself once again, when she returned to her apartment, where she sat down with pen and paper and drew a rough outline of the interior of Robert Quintero's Salon and the interior of The Chocolatier next door. Next week, when she went in for her appointment with young Jonathan, Roberto's newest assistant, she would find out more about what was upstairs in Roberto Quintero's Salon.

As Elizabeth McKinley worked on her outlines of the interiors of the shops on "K" Street in Georgetown, Frances Foster was laboring over certain paperwork in her kitchen at East Hampton, New York. Her attorney, Matthew Adair, was continuing, under protest, the liquidation of her estate, and he also was in touch with the Parish of New Orleans, inquiring about the disposition of the body of Michael Green, M.D. Frances had refused to answer him when he asked why she wanted to know, but he was getting suspicious. Poor Matthew.

It was nearly eight that evening when Frances Foster's telephone rang. The caller identified himself as Robert E. Lee Johnson, the court-appointed counsel for Nora O'Brien in New Orleans. Speaking rapidly, Robert E. Lee Johnson informed Mrs. Foster that Miss O'Brien had not shown up for her preliminary hearing today and he was very much afraid that Miss O'Brien had, ah, left the area. Regrettably this put the entire $25,000 in bail that Mrs. Foster had generously provided for Miss O'Brien's release at risk, he told her gravely. He didn't know whether Mrs. Foster was aware of this awful possibility?

Why no, she wasn't. Frances wrote Robert E. Lee Johnson's name down and took his telephone number, just in case she should learn something and need to get in touch with him.

"You understand bail will be forfeited if Miss O'Brien does not show up next Wednesday for the rescheduled hearing?" Johnson told her, shouting into the telephone, as if she might otherwise not hear him calling all the way from New Orleans.

Frances held the receiver away from her ear. "I don't know what I can do for you, Mr. Johnson. I have no idea where she is, as I told you," she said.

Robert E. Lee Johnson was not sure he believed her. After all, he couldn't understand why this Foster woman would bail the nurse in the first place. Hadn't her daughter died in the police raid? It didn't make sense to him, considering that Nora O'Brien had without doubt played a part in that girl's death. "I'm going to put a few people I know on this, Mrs. Foster. For my client's own good," he said.

Frances said she understood and she would certainly call Mr. Johnson should his client turn up. She appreciated his concern for her bail funds.

After Frances extricated herself from the conversation with Johnson, she sat for a long time at the kitchen table, not writing anything down, but simply sitting, sipping her tea, looking out the window at the broad expanse of green lawn rolling away from the old Georgian house where she had grown up. It was getting so complicated. Robert E. Lee Johnson didn't concern her; he sounded young and anxious and inexperienced. But who were these people he was sending to look for Nora? Who were they? She hoped that they at least were not part of the Rights for the Unborn League; surely she could hope that they were just local investigators of some kind. People like Nora's young court-appointed attorney perhaps.

Chapter Eleven

On Sunday morning, a purposeful Frances Foster boarded a commuter flight at the tiny East Hampton airport and flew to JFK in New York City. With only minutes to spare, she strode from the commuter airlines terminal at Kennedy down the wide polished corridors to the Piedmont Airways gates, where she boarded a flight to Dulles Airport outside of Washington. Her harried personal attorney, Matthew Adair, had reported to her earlier on this bright and beautiful Sunday morning that Stephen Green, younger brother of the late Michael Green, M.D., had claimed his brother's body on Saturday afternoon in New Orleans and removed it to Harrisburg, Pennsylvania, for burial. So Michael Green, M.D., would be laid to rest in a small private cemetery outside of Harrisburg, beside a younger sister who had died in infancy, and he would carry to his silent grave the truth of the events that night in the little backyard abortion clinic in Algiers. Rest, Dr. Michael Green, Frances Foster thought as she settled into her First Class seat on Piedmont Airways Flight 365 to Washington and Atlanta. A reticent Matthew Adair had also reported to Frances that a preliminary hearing regarding the disposition of a felony case brought by the Parish of New Orleans against one Nora O'Brien, Registered Nurse, had been continued until this coming Wednesday. He had spoken to Miss O'Brien's attorney, Robert E. Lee Johnson, as a matter of fact, and Johnson had been pleased to hear from him. Mr. Johnson was extremely concerned about his client; he had been unable to locate her and he was resorting to extraordinary means to find her, including the hiring of private detectives. And by the way, Matthew certainly hoped Frances understood federal statutes regarding unlawful flight to avoid prosecution and the harboring of a fugitive? Matthew Adair was growing very suspicious indeed; he did not altogether trust this new Frances Foster, so unlike the old Frances he used to know. "I warn you, Frances," he told her urgently over the telephone that morning, "if you skate toward the thin edge on this matter of the nurse, there could be serious trouble."

Sipping her tea in the early morning light as she sat at her kitchen table, her long cotton wrapper drawn around her, her feet snug and warm in her old corduroy slippers, Frances had made another note on one of her long yellow legal pads. She decided to ignore her counsel's obvious alarm. "Tell me, Matthew," she said, "if Miss O'Brien were to leave the country, would the authorities try to extradite her?"

Over the telephone from his home across Long Island Sound in Darien, Connecticut, Matthew could be heard shuffling some papers in his study, from where he was calling Frances. "Probably not. The Human Life Amendment and the whole mess surrounding it have not made us any friends abroad," he admitted, sounding snappish and tired. "I hope that's a parenthetical question, Frances," Matthew added. He wondered if perhaps Frances needed to be on some type of medication just now, something that would get her through these initial stages of grief over Hillary's death, something that would quiet her down and prevent her from doing anything rash. If it was not too late already. Matthew Adair was afraid to ask Frances just how much she did know about the apparent disappearance of Nora O'Brien. Splitting hairs, he decided that since there was no actual warrant out on O'Brien, he could broach it. "Frances, do you have any idea

where Miss O'Brien might be just now?" Matthew asked her
gently, lowering his voice as if he were questioning a reluctant
grandmother in the witness box.

Poor Matthew, Frances thought. "No," she said, sipping more
of her tea. It was not a lie; Frances really did not know exactly
where Nora O'Brien was right at this moment, as she was speaking to Matthew over the telephone. She didn't know exactly
where Nora was. When she had talked with Nora an hour earlier,
Nora had been getting ready to check out of her room at the
Motel Six; today was the beginning of her tenancy in the Victorian house in Cooperstown's Historic District.

Hanging up the telephone after her conversation with Matthew, Frances had continued thoughtfully sipping her tea. She
remembered her telephone conversation with Robert E. Lee
Johnson. So the people Nora's court-appointed attorney had
hired to help find Nora were private detectives. Frances tried to
recall what Nora had told her about her departure from New
Orleans, whether there was anything in Nora's leavetaking that
would be helpful to private detectives. Only if they began looking for credit card purchases in the name of Frances Foster, she
decided. She made another note on her yellow legal pad, finished
her tea and went upstairs to dress.

Frances dressed casually for her flight to New York City and
Washington, and except for a roomy canvas tote bag, she did not
take any luggage, for she expected to return to the house in East
Hampton very late on this same Sunday evening. During the
short flight from Kennedy Airport to Dulles, Frances Foster
went over the thick sheaf of notes she had been accumulating.
She was past the point of questioning what they were doing now,
very long past it. Now she was resolute. She wanted to succeed;
anything less would be an expensive, empty gesture and Frances
Foster did not like empty gestures. By the time the flight touched
down at Dulles, Frances had reviewed all of her notes and she

was ready for a long scenic drive into the foothills of the Appalachian Mountains with Elizabeth McKinley, who was meeting her at the airport.

Elizabeth McKinley was waiting for Frances outside the baggage claim area for Piedmont Airways; she was driving Frances' old blue station wagon, and she had a thermos of coffee beside her in the front seat.

The two women did not go into the District of Columbia from Dulles Airport; they turned south instead, driving past the green fields of the Manassas National Battlefield, site of the First and Second Battles of Bull Run, which were won by troops of the Confederacy in the War Between the States in the hot and bloody summers of 1861 and 1862. They turned east below the old battlefield, driving toward the Appalachian Mountains, and at the junction of Highway 29 and Interstate 66, Frances pulled a map of Virginia from her bag and activated a stopwatch. It was a new one, which Frances had purchased from a sporting goods store in East Hampton on Friday. The stopwatch calculated seconds, minutes and hours, and it bore a tiny computer within its steel heart that also could calculate mileage and distances. Today, the stopwatch and its tiny built-in computer would give them information on how long it would take them to travel the approximately 120 miles between the District of Columbia and a location just beyond the small community of Middletown, Virginia, where a secluded old farm was available for lease in the Appalachian foothills.

On the way past Manassas, Elizabeth McKinley told Frances about her visit to "K" Street in Georgetown. Frances had been right; the First Lady's hairdresser took care of her in the family quarters at the White House, but on occasion, Mary Holt Morgan traveled to Roberto Quintero's Salon in Georgetown for a special appointment. Such an occasion was about to occur, and according to the very kind and helpful salon coordinator, Annabelle, this occasion would be on August 14 next. A little over two weeks from now. That was not much time, and they might want to use the First Lady's August 14 appointment for a rehearsal, a kind of mock drill, Elizabeth suggested. She wanted to get this done as much as Frances did, and she was impatient with any delays, but a trial run might be a safer way; it might save them later. "It would give us a chance to work out any glitches," Elizabeth said to Frances.

Frances considered the idea of a rehearsal. But then she thought of Nora O'Brien, Accused Felon, and her court-appointed attorney and his private detectives, and she thought of the call she had received Saturday morning from Adele Pearson, Dean of the Crofton School, her old alma mater. She remembered that voice trembling on the phone as Adele Pearson told her about the visit of the Special Security Agent for the Rights for the Unborn League. Well, I'm afraid too, Frances thought. "We don't have time, Elizabeth," she said. "These people will never stop." She told Elizabeth McKinley about the incident at the Crofton School with the Rights for the Unborn League and about Nora and her court-appointed attorney and his private detectives. "We don't have time," Frances repeated.

Elizabeth's heart sank. It would be so much more dangerous this way. So much more could go wrong. The salon would be nearly impregnable after the First Lady arrived on August 14th; the Secret Service would almost certainly block the front and rear exits and they might block the entire alleyway behind "K" Street. The hell with them, she thought. "So we'll do it right the first time," Elizabeth said. She began mentally revising her plan. "We'll have to be inside the salon building before she gets there," Elizabeth said. She poured herself some of the coffee from her thermos. It was Gold Rush blend, deep and dark and rich and strong.

Elizabeth needed the strong coffee; she had been awake most of the night before, trying to work out a detailed plan to kidnap the First Lady from Roberto Quintero's Salon. Already, she had decided that First Lady Mary Holt Morgan would be vulnerable at that moment, more vulnerable that on almost any other occasion outside the White House. The Quintero Salon was familiar territory to the Secret Service; there probably would be no one in the salon except Quintero, Mary Holt Morgan and one or two Secret Service agents. And Elizabeth McKinley had decided they could count on fewer agents than usual within immediate sight of Mary Holt Morgan, and on the slight relaxation of vigilance that would come with being on safe and familiar territory. This was their edge; this was the very small opening.

Elizabeth handed Frances her rough schematic drawings of Roberto Quintero's and The Chocolatier next door on "K" street in Georgetown, and she explained that each three story building included a staircase to the roof, which was sealed off by a fire door, and that the two buildings, like many buildings in Old Georgetown, were butted against one another with perhaps a foot of air space between them. "We can take her out by the fire door in the salon building, transfer to the other roof, and come down through the chocolate shop," Elizabeth explained. She smiled to herself as she drove along, drinking deeply of the dark Gold Rush blend coffee, maneuvering the old blue station wagon through the Sunday afternoon traffic. In her few hours of restless sleep the night before, Elizabeth had dreamed about First Lady Mary Holt Morgan for the first time. In the dream, the First Lady was angry with Elizabeth; she was standing over Elizabeth pointing her finger at her, and the First Lady's wide full red mouth was twisted with rage. Elizabeth remembered her heart pounding in the dream, pounding in a fierce thrill of excitement. She took another swallow of her coffee and pulled herself back to the present. Beside her, Frances was poring over the drawings.

"We can use a delivery truck and roll her out of the chocolate shop in a small crate," Elizabeth said to Frances. They could nail the crate shut, just like a coffin would be nailed shut, Elizabeth thought, her strong rich coffee warm and soothing in her throat, warm all the way down.

Frances Foster looked out the window at the rolling Virginia countryside. "How long would we have before they discovered she was gone?" Frances said. This part of the planning, the portion involving the abduction itself and the escape from the District of Columbia, belonged to Elizabeth; it was she who knew the District, and it was she who was the emergency planner, who would know what the authorities were likely to do.

"Two or three minutes," Elizabeth replied. She was worried about the shortness of time; she knew that if they killed Roberto Quintero and the Secret Service agents inside the salon with the First Lady, killed them very quietly, with silencers perhaps, that the two or three minutes would expand considerably. But Elizabeth did not suggest this because she knew Frances would rule it out; she didn't want any killings. Privately, Elizabeth thought they would be very lucky to get away at all. Thinking about these things, she felt a rush of adrenalin rocket through her body. It's just the excitement, she thought. It was just the idea of so much danger that made her feel that way. Up to now, she had been thinking only of getting Mary Holt Morgan out of Roberto Quintero's Salon and into The Chocolatier and out the door in a roomy chocolate crate. She had given little thought to what lay beyond "K" Street in Georgetown. But they would need a plan for that, too, she thought. They needed a plan that would get them safely outside the District of Columbia. "We may have trouble getting out of the District into Virginia," she said thoughtfully. "The police might have enough time to set up roadblocks on the bridges."

Roadblocks. Frances put down the schematic drawings of Robert Quintero's Salon and The Chocolatier. She hadn't considered roadblocks. They must cross the Potomac River to reach Virginia; the river became a barrier to Frances, a barrier to cross. It was too bad they couldn't just swim across the Potomac, she thought. Not swim. Float across. "What about using a boat? I still have the *Reliance*," Frances said. The *Reliance* was the Reed Foster family's wooden-hulled cruiser. It had been built in the mid-Fifties in Norway and the Norwegian Spruce that lined her hull was as sound as the day she was launched. Frances had kept the *Reliance* long after her parents died, long after her last cruise on Long Island Sound with her father. The *Reliance* was an object of sentiment for her, almost a member of the family. Suddenly she wanted to use the *Reliance*. It was not just to save them from roadblocks; it was because of Dr. Hugh Foster, because of her father, the abortionist. Frances still could remember him at the wheel, singing to himself in the wheelhouse, whistling and singing and pointing out all the seabirds to little Frannie. In a way, using the *Reliance* would keep things in the family, she thought. "Yes. Let's use the *Reliance*," Frances said firmly.

They were on Interstate 66 now, approaching the northernmost foothills of the Blue Ridge Mountains. Beyond them, the Appalachian Mountains stretched across eastern Virginia. Elizabeth, driving into an afternoon sun, thought about Frances Foster and the *Reliance*. Possibly using a boat would work; it was mid-summer and the Potomac River was clotted with yachts and cruisers. The *Reliance* could slip among them like a silver fish, slipping swift and away with its cargo, away to Virginia. "We could bring the *Reliance* into the Tidal Basin," Elizabeth said. "It would mean going across the District from Georgetown to get to the Basin," she said, "but I think we could do it." She poured herself another cup of Gold Rush blend coffee.

Frances smiled to herself. She was thinking of her father, of Hugh Foster at the wheel of the Reliance, his yachting cap askew, the long white scarf he always wore when aboard the Reliance flying in the wind. He would have helped us, she thought. He would have piloted the Reliance for us.

They were approaching the highway exit for the town of Front Royal now. In another thirty minutes or so, they would be at the cutoff for Middletown.

On Saturday, in one of many telephone calls she made from her kitchen in East Hampton, Frances Foster had engaged in a warm conversation with one Thomas B. Tuttle, owner and operator of Tuttle Real Estate in Middletown. Yes, he certainly did know of a small secluded farm that could be leased for recreational purposes, he told Frances. There would be a substantial deposit, of course, and it was an 'as is' rental, if she understood what he meant there!

The old Fletcher Place, as Middletown Realtor Thomas B. Tuttle had described it to Frances, giving her exact directions to the old place, was about ten miles beyond Middletown. Very private it was, Thomas B. Tuttle told Missus Foster. A dandy spot in the country, right in the foothills of the Appalachians. Indeed yes. And a real bargain. He could get a real fine deal for her on this one, Thomas B. Tuttle had told Frances over the telephone, between sucks on his stogie.

As Elizabeth McKinley, accompanied by Frances Foster, drove the old blue station wagon away from the Potomac River and the District of Columbia and deep into the limestone foothills of the Appalachians, Jack Riley, Rights for the Unborn League Special Security Assistant, was returning to the nation's capital from Miami, where he had spent the last four days of a vacation. On Monday morning, Riley was to see Carlton Farnsworth, who wanted a progress report on Jack's little project; he wanted to know what Jack Riley had unearthed thus far on this matter of Frances Foster and that young daughter of hers who was murdered by the Abortionist in the clinic in Algiers, across the Mississippi River from New Orleans. The League was in business to help these young mothers, after all; why, its whole reason for being was to stand by these mothers and their babies, to protect them from criminal exploitation and even death at the hands of those murderers. Yes indeed, Carlton Farnsworth wanted a progress report on the whole matter; he wanted to get to the bottom of it, by God.

Riley checked into Washington's Roosevelt Hotel on Sunday afternoon. It was murderously hot in D.C. on this mid-summer Sunday, and Riley was tempted to stay in his hotel room with the air conditioner on full blast and the shades drawn on the windows. He was sorely tempted to do this, and to open his fresh bottle of Bushmill's Irish Whiskey and lay down on his cool bed and drink Bushmill's over ice until he fell asleep. Riley was tired of the Rights for the Unborn League; he was sick to death of Carlton Farnsworth and his sparkling blue eyes and his bright white smile popping out from behind his puckered little lips. Riley opened the Bushmill's and poured himself a little shot. The money, Jack Riley thought. Think of the money, Jack. He downed the little shot of Bushmill's, and pulling on his wrinkled cotton jacket, he left his room at the Roosevelt Hotel. He was on his way to an apartment in the District of Columbia that was the home of Elizabeth McKinley. He wanted to talk to her about the late Hillary Foster and Hillary's mother, Frances Foster. Elizabeth McKinley's name and address had been found among Hillary Foster's personal effects, and the same Elizabeth McKinley had accompanied Mrs. Foster when she claimed her daughter's body in New Orleans.

Her apartment was about two miles from the Roosevelt Hotel, in a three story apartment building near the downtown area. It was a relatively new building, and every window on the first floor was barred with ornate black wrought iron bars. Standing at the apartment entrance, Riley picked up an intercom telephone and dialed the apartment number listed for E. McKinley. Her apartment was on the third floor and she did not answer the intercom.

So Elizabeth McKinley was not at home on a hot and muggy Sunday afternoon in Washington, D.C. What had Jack Riley expected? He smiled to himself and dialed the number listed for the building manager. The man who answered at the building manager's apartment had a heavily accented, guttural voice.

"Who is?" the man shouted.

Riley did not like talking over intercoms. He wanted the building manager down there in the lobby, facing him. "Security for the Rights for the Unborn League," he said into the receiver, speaking slowly and carefully.

There was a burst of static on the intercom line. "Who is?"

Jack Riley grimaced. Well shit. He didn't want to waste any more time on the fucking intercom. "POLICE!" he shouted.

The intercom filled with static once again. Then the line went dead. A moment later, the building manager appeared at the entrance door. The manager was a short stubby man, dark and swarthy. A day's growth of beard shadowed his face, and he stared unflinchingly up at Jack Riley, his black eyes narrow and appraising as he stood in the doorway, blocking it with his heavy bulk. "Identification," he said to Riley, working slowly and emphatically over the word.

Riley pulled his Rights for the Unborn League identification card from his pocket. Wordlessly, he handed the building manager the card. The card included his photograph and fingerprints; Special Security Assistant was written in bold black type under his name and the card was personally signed by Carlton

Farnsworth, Executive Director of the Rights for the Unborn League and former Attorney General of the United States.

The building manager turned Riley's identification card over and over in his thick hands, squinting at the words on the card and at Jack Riley's picture and at his fingerprints on the card. Then he looked up at Riley, looking long and hard at him through snapping black eyes, and finally thrust the card roughly back into Riley's outstretched hand. The manager stood staring at him now, blocking the doorway, appraising Riley, his black eyes traveling up and down Riley's lean body, examining him. When he finally spoke, it was to spit out a single word. "NO!" he said. He turned away, slamming the apartment building door in Jack Riley's surprised face.

It took a moment for Riley to realize that the building manager was gone, that he was not going to let Jack Riley into his building, or even talk to Jack Riley about what he wanted there. Well, well, Riley thought. The little Mex bastard. Riley didn't like to have doors slammed in his face; he didn't like it one little bit. He would take care of that little Mex bastard later.

A few minutes later, Riley was on his way to Rights for the Unborn League headquarters near the Naval Observatory. He decided that he wanted to conduct a little computer search for Elizabeth McKinley; he wanted to see what the League computers might have on her. He would have done the same thing on the little Mex bastard, but the building manager had not given him time to get his name.

Arriving at League headquarters, Riley ordered a cold turkey sandwich sent up from the League kitchen and set to work at a computer console in the League library. The offices were open and humming with activity on this Sunday afternoon; the League did not rest on Sundays or on any other day.

The new stopwatch Frances Foster was holding clicked past 127 minutes as they passed Middletown. They were deep into the foothills of the Appalachians now, driving toward the limestone heart of the mountain range.

Now they turned onto a dirt road. The chassis of the old blue station wagon rattled as Elizabeth McKinley forced the heavy car over dusty ruts and potholes. A barbed wire fence ran along one side of the road; the fence posts leaned, overwhelmed by red maple and birch hard against the old wire and old fence, pressing into the narrowing road. From the dirt track, she turned onto a rutted lane that ran between two low hills into a narrow valley. Elizabeth ground the transmission into second gear. Then first gear. The wagon track turned, then burst into a clearing.

A saltbox house covered with weathered shingles sat in the center of the clearing, high on a gentle knoll. A leaning barn, the remnants of a chicken coop, and a long low woodshed sheltered the house on the north side. There was a yellow pickup truck parked beside the house, and Thomas B. Tuttle, proprietor of Tuttle Realty, Middletown, Virginia, was standing beside his yellow pickup, his pearl gray fedora clapped jauntily on his head, his chest thrown out, a wide welcoming smile on his gaunt face revealing his chipped and nicotine-stained teeth.

Tuttle was looking forward to meeting Missus Foster. She sounded like a quality woman to him, and now that was a real solid vehicle she and the other lady were driving there. Watching as the blue station wagon with its two occupants rumbled to a stop beside him, Tuttle experienced the little thrill of the chase he always got when he honed in on a potential customer. He hoped Missus Foster wouldn't draw back when she saw the old Fletcher Place; the last renters had been hard on the old farm. Well, the price was right; she couldn't complain about that! He went right over to her, to the passenger side of the blue station wagon, and helped her out like a gentleman would. "Missus Foster?" he

said, looming over her like a tall ungainly crane wearing a
fedora.

Frances Foster smiled gently at him. "Yes. You must be Mr.
Tuttle," she said. "My, it's warm out, isn't it," she said, backing
away a step. Frances looked over at Thomas B. Tuttle's yellow
pickup truck. There was a Rights for the Unborn League bumper
sticker on the rear bumper.

Tuttle saw her looking at the bumper sticker. He didn't miss
much, old Tom Tuttle. He smiled in delight. "I am the Middletown coordinator for the League," he announced proudly, drawing his tall skinny frame up. "Virginia ratified, as you may
know, three years ago. We were a very early ratifier of the Human Life Amendment," he droned on ponderously. "Of course
my county, this here is Frederick County, has been an abortion-
free zone for eight full years. We saw to that locally," Thomas B.
Tuttle said, drawing himself up still further.

Frances Foster took another step back and looked away from
the yellow pickup and it's bumper sticker. So here was a gentleman who decided on behalf of the women of his Frederick
County when they would bear children; here was a man who
knew what was *right* for them. She looked up at Thomas B. Tuttle's sincere smiling face and she reminded herself sternly that
there were much bigger fish waiting for the frying pan and she
should let this one go by. For as much as she wanted, at that
moment, to grab Mr. Thomas B. Tuttle by his skinny neck and
wring it until he was dead, she wanted still more to have First
Lady Mary Holt Morgan at this Frederick County farmhouse just
over two weeks from now. Mary Holt Morgan was the head of
this monster. Thomas B. Tuttle was a curling fingernail, a piece
of dirt under its claw. Behind her, Frances heard a car door slam
and she realized Elizabeth was out of the station wagon, standing
beside it. She waved an arm toward Elizabeth. "This is an old
family friend, Miss Smith," Frances said warmly to Tuttle. She

motioned toward the farmhouse, which was about fifty yards from where the pickup truck and Frances' station wagon were parked. "If we could see the house?" she said, smiling once again at Tuttle.

He tapped the brim of his gray fedora with long nicotine-stained fingers and nodded toward Elizabeth. "How do," he said to her. She didn't look too important to Thomas B. Tuttle. Kind of a hanger-on, it looked like. He started toward the farmhouse and motioned Missus Foster and the Smith girl to come along with him. "You certainly can see the old place," he said brightly. "It's quite a place. A real antique, you might say!"

The old saltbox house was dark and damp inside, and the kitchen floor slanted slightly. A living room ran across the front of the house, joining a small bedroom; the kitchen, an old pantry, and a bathroom took up the back, and a narrow staircase led upstairs to four small bedrooms. Built on a knoll, the saltbox commanded views on all four sides; it would be a difficult house to approach without being seen by occupants inside, Frances decided. The outbuildings would shelter several vehicles. The house did not have electricity, but there was rudimentary plumbing. It was a sound structure, and the old farm was secluded. It would work for their purposes, Frances thought, and they didn't have time to be choosy anyway.

Thomas B. Tuttle was overjoyed when Frances Foster signed the paperwork and wrote a little old check for the deposit and two months rent right there in the house, right after she toured the place. Missus Foster was a quality woman, no doubt about it. He offered to take them both to lunch right there in Middletown that afternoon, but Missus Foster begged to excuse herself because she had to get back to New York, she said. Well, Thomas B. Tuttle could make it another time, then. He would just go on now, and let them kind of take possession of the Fletcher place right now, but if they needed any little thing, why they were to call him right up and he would be right out here to help. Yes, indeed.

Frances and Elizabeth spent more than an hour in the old saltbox farmhouse after Tuttle's departure. There were many things to do in the house, many details to take care of there. The saltbox and the entire Fletcher Place would be their temporary refuge a little over two weeks from now and they did not want to make any mistakes that would compromise their blossoming plans. Before they left the place, they completed a list of supplies and incidentals that they would need. Among the items on the list were several three-quarter inch plywood sheets cut to size, cut to fit the interior molding of several windows in a second floor bedroom. The plywood sheets would go over the windows of the smallest bedroom, the one at the back of the house, where the saltbox ceiling slanted down almost to the floor. That was to be First Lady Mary Holt Morgan's room for the short time she would be with them, and they did not want Mary Morgan to get any ideas about crawling out of any second floor windows; they wanted her tidily tucked away in her dark little room, tucked away under lock and key by her little self. Poring over the list, Frances and Elizabeth added several other items before they closed up the saltbox house and began the drive back to the District of Columbia.

It was after 8:00 P.M. when Elizabeth McKinley dropped Frances Foster off at Dulles International Airport for her flight back to New York. Driving back from the old Fletcher Place outside of Middletown, Virginia, in the old blue station wagon, a kind of exhaustion had overcome them both, and they spoke very little on the trip back. Neither of them had slept a full night since Hillary Foster's death, and the strain was beginning to tell on them both. And they were another step closer to a point beyond which there could be no return for either one of them.

Chapter Twelve

It was a pitch black upstate New York night; there was no wind, no sound except the sound of automobile wheels running on pavement, and the sound of a station wagon engine as it labored up a long hill. Frances Foster's old blue station wagon shuddered as it struck a pothole near the top of the rise, and the motor began to ping, the engine starved of propulsion. Elizabeth McKinley, who had been driving since early afternoon, driving from Washington, north through Maryland and Pennsylvania to upstate New York, shoved the station wagon into third gear as she reached the crest of the hill and turned west along a darkened road that cut through a tunnel of oak trees grown wide, branches reaching out, almost touching overhead. Elizabeth was tired; her eyes were red and raw and dry, gritty with exhaustion. She was nearing the outskirts of Cooperstown, New York, now, the little village of 2,300 that was the home of the Baseball Hall of Fame, and not incidentally the location of a summer rental by one Frances Foster of East Hampton. It was Frances Foster's second summer rental of the season; the first was a farmhouse outside of Middletown, Virginia, in the still and remote foothills of the Appalachian Mountains. Both rentals were for what was left of the entire summer season, all the way through Labor Day in early September.

A map and directions to this upstate New York summer rental, a Victorian house in the Cooperstown Historic District, were on the front seat beside Elizabeth. It was Friday night, actually early Saturday morning, since midnight had passed more than an hour ago, and less than two weeks remained before Thursday, August 14, the day First Lady Mary Holt Morgan was to have her special private appointment with Roberto Quintero at his salon.

Elizabeth McKinley was borne to upstate New York on this black night on the wings of her remaining stores of energy, and on a certain excitement that surged in her veins, beating like a constant drum. On the previous day, her excitement had pounded in a fearful cadence as she entered Roberto Quintero's Salon on "K" Street in Georgetown to have her hair cut by young Jonathan, Mr. Quintero's newest assistant. Leading her into the recesses of Roberto Quintero's Salon, and reassuring her all the while, was Annabelle, the salon coordinator, who as usual was wearing all black. Tiny Annabelle had been particularly anxious to guide her new customer Miss McKinley through the shoals of Roberto's Salon, for Miss McKinley had paid an extraordinary personal visit to the salon during the previous week to make certain she was in very capable hands, and Miss McKinley also was with the Administration of President Edward Morgan, whose accomplished wife, Mary, was one of Roberto Quintero's most valued customers. Elizabeth McKinley was indeed entitled to the very best treatment at Roberto Quintero's Salon, and Annabelle was quite determined that she would get it. Annabelle had therefore introduced her to young Jonathan herself, cautioning him, much as a rich maiden aunt would caution a young nephew, to do his very best for Miss McKinley.

Elizabeth McKinley had found herself in a cubicle with Jonathan, in one of a row of cubicles that ran along one side of the interior of Roberto Quintero's Salon. Facing her, and smiling gently, was young Jonathan, who was about twenty-five years old and of slight, wiry build; his was a nice helpful smile, nothing to be afraid of, it said. But it was Jonathan's eyes that startled Elizabeth. They were an extremely light blue, an almost transparent blue, as if lights were on behind them, and set in Jonathan's slender, aquiline face, and punctuated by his light eyelashes and eyebrows and his light blond hair, his light eyes seemed to glitter across a long distance at Elizabeth, glittering transparently like clear water in bright sun. Elizabeth had been unable to gaze directly into Jonathan's eyes. Sitting down in the salon chair, she instead looked at herself in the mirror in front of the two of them, and then when she shifted her eyes to Jonathan's reflection, she looked not really at him but at a point in the air next to his left shoulder. As she and Jonathan began discussing Elizabeth's hair, she was able to move her gaze back to herself, focusing now on her thick dark hair. They decided to simply trim it an inch or two, and she declined Jonathan's suggestion that he cut her some soft bangs that would sweep across her forehead.

"They would be very pretty, just brushing your eyebrows," he said, indicating the direction with his thin black comb. "They would go just so. Like little feathers," he said, smiling gently once again, his spotlight eyes upon her face in the mirror.

"Maybe next time," Elizabeth said. She smiled back at him in the mirror, looking at that same spot that was near his left shoulder. "Maybe I could wait and come back in two weeks," she said to his reflection. "On August 14," she said.

First Lady Mary Holt Morgan would be in Roberto Quintero's Salon on August 14, seeing Roberto himself. Elizabeth smiled toward the spot in the mirror once more. Jonathan was fluffing her thick brown hair at the sides now, making her hair float on his fine slender fingers. She saw him close his eyes as if in thought. It was a relief when he closed his eyes, as if a strong light had been shaded from her face.

"August 14 would not work," Jonathan said softly. "Perhaps the day before or the day after the 14th. The salon will be closed on the 14th itself," he said, his slender fingers just brushing the sides of her neck. "We will give your hair a bit more fullness here, a bit more lift," he said.

Elizabeth lifted her chin. Around her, outside the cubicle, she could hear the soft murmur of voices, the occasional hiss of a water spritzer and the whine of hair dryers. "Closed on the 14th? Really. Are you remodeling?" she said. She pictured the First Lady in Roberto's salon chair, in the chair Elizabeth herself was sitting in right now; the First Lady would have her head back, and her pretty white neck would be open to them, inviting them, and she would be telling Roberto Quintero just what she wanted done today. But Roberto would not get his little job done because he was going to be interrupted. It would be a terrible interruption, too, Elizabeth thought. Maybe Roberto would never again groom and coif First Lady Mary Holt Morgan; maybe she would never return from her little interruption.

Jonathan lifted Elizabeth's hair still higher, to just below her ears. "No, we are closed on August 14 for a special customer," he told her, sighing slightly, as if the closure were for a funeral, perhaps to dress and coif and carefully make up a body.

Elizabeth laughed. She decided it was time to prompt him a little bit, time to ease him out of his secretive little corner. "I know the First Lady is coming on the 14th, but I didn't think you'd close the salon for the whole day for her," she said. She saw Jonathan's eyebrows lift questioningly. "I'm with the Administration," she added confidently. She smiled at Jonathan. "I don't work for her directly, thank God." She had seen the quick look of disdain pass over Jonathan's features at the mention of the First Lady; she had seen his face droop when he spoke of the salon closure on August 14.

Now Jonathan's face relaxed. So Elizabeth McKinley worked at the White House. Well! She could be a very valuable customer for him; this was a stroke of luck, he thought. And he heard the disdain in her voice; he had heard her just about come right out and say what a real little prima donna that Mrs. Morgan was. As if they didn't know that already here at Roberto's. "We have to close for the whole day whenever she comes," Jonathan said. "Her schedule can change, so we never know the exact time. You'd think she could be more considerate! I guess First Ladies don't have to be considerate like other people. Well, she's one of Roberto's important clients, so there you are!" he said, the spotlights of his eyes wide and bright and indignant. He bent over her slightly then, peering at her hair from the underside of her shoulders.

Elizabeth McKinley took a breath. So young Jonathan didn't like First Lady Mary Holt Morgan; so nobody at Roberto Quintero's liked the bitch. How nice. Elizabeth smiled into the mirror and lowered her voice to a whisper. "She can be a little bit hard to work with. Mrs. Morgan has very definite ideas about how she wants things. Very strong ideas," Elizabeth confided.

Roberto straightened and stood directly behind her, his hands holding her hair evenly on each side of her face, floating there like rafts holding the turned under masses of dark brown hair. "You can say that again. Everyone but Roberto has to leave, the whole staff, and only Roberto can touch her. Even for her shampoo! And you know she only comes here for her coloring touch-ups and her face peels," Jonathan said resentfully. "Roberto has to do everything for her, just like a servant. She's so exacting and secretive, too. It's wearing on Roberto, and he loses money on her anyway," Jonathan added, pulling his scissors from his breast pocket.

Elizabeth nodded sympathetically. "It's the same way at the White House," she said. She looked around the cubicle. "I'll bet she even complains about the chairs here," she whispered, smiling.

"Oh, she wouldn't sit down here! She goes upstairs, to Roberto's private salon room on the second floor," Jonathan said. He began to snip bits of Elizabeth's hair, snipping minute stray hairs.

"Really. I'd like to see the private salon room," Elizabeth McKinley pressed. Inwardly, she soared. The First Lady would be on the second floor; it was a stroke of luck for them. Moving her up one flight of stairs and then up the fire stairs to the roof would be half the trouble of moving the First Lady up a full two flights before they could even reach the fire stairs.

"No problem," Jonathan admitted. "You can go up and look around after we're finished. You can go anywhere you like up there." He stood back from her now, squinting at her through his spotlight eyes. She had nice hair. Thick with body. It was another stroke of good luck. "What do you do at the White House?" he said.

Elizabeth McKinley looked serenely at Jonathan's reflection in the mirror in front of her, looking once again at the spot above his left shoulder. "I'm an emergency management specialist. Part of a management group," she said, smiling at the spot.

"Ah. So in case of a nuclear war, you'll be in the bomb shelter with the President?"

"Something like that," Elizabeth lied. Jonathan will never know the difference, she thought. He'll never know what happened; he won't even be here. At a gesture from Jonathan, she had stood obediently then and followed him as he led her to another cubicle for her shampoo.

Now it was a day and a night later, and she was far from Roberto Quintero's Salon, driving into Cooperstown, New York, in her nice new haircut and with her newly revised and detailed schematic drawings of the first, second and third floor interiors of the salon and the interiors of The Chocolatier, next door on "K" Street in Georgetown. It was on the car seat beside her, right next to the map and directions to the Cooperstown house that Frances Foster had sent to her earlier this week.

Elizabeth peered into the darkness, slowing the station wagon as she passed the town line for Cooperstown. She was coming to a stoplight ahead, its red light blinking on and off, on and off. Elizabeth slowly braked to a stop and lifted up the map, holding it near the windshield, where the glow of a streetlight on the corner illuminated the finely drawn directions to the house in Cooperstown. Yes, she was to turn left here, onto a street that was lined with houses set far back on large lots, their porches shadowed by maple and oak in the thick green leaf of summer. She shoved the station wagon into second gear, slowing as she passed a stockade fence stretching for a hundred yards along the roadside. Its high narrow pickets threw black shadows beside the arcing headlights. Frances had told her to watch for an ornate black gate; it would be right after a stockade fence and Elizabeth should be careful or she would miss it. The stockade fence passed by; then her headlights arced onto a large black wrought iron gate. There was a small light burning on one side of it, like a yellow ship's lantern would burn far out to sea. There it is, she thought. She pulled the station wagon to a stop in front of the gate. The motor idled, a low rumble beneath her. Steam rose from the hood. Beyond the iron gate, Elizabeth could see the dim outlines of a Victorian house; light was escaping from the downstairs windows, seeping out from beneath closed window shades. The upper floors of the house were dark.

Elizabeth McKinley blinked the station wagon headlights three times, switched them off, and killed the motor. It was pitch black outside and the Victorian house behind the iron gate seemed far away. Elizabeth could hear the sounds of a warm summer wind slipping through a nearby tangle of oaks. The station wagon motor ticked softly as it cooled. She pulled the collar of her cotton jacket closer around her throat. Sitting in the darkness, her head resting against the upholstery, she tried once more to organize the long mental list she had made for herself. On the seat beside her was a folder with her schematic drawings and a list of supplies they would need. She had tried to anticipate everything, but she knew this could not be done; they could only try to cover any mistakes as best they could. But there would not be room for any mistakes on August 14, not if they were to succeed; she knew this, too.

Elizabeth peered into the darkness once more. Had they seen her? Did they know she was here? In the distance, somewhere in the darkness, she heard the high-pitched scream of a small animal. Then silence. Elizabeth shivered; it was almost a shudder, almost as if something had run over the back of her body. What was the saying? Something walking over your grave; a ghost walking over your grave. Elizabeth ran both hands across her temples; she was sweating, sweating in hot beads of perspiration that were beginning to run down her face and the back of her neck.

The station wagon trembled as the passenger door jerked open. A flashlight swept over Elizabeth's face, roved around the inside, fastened on three crates in the back seat, and came back to Elizabeth McKinley. The light was blinding in her eyes. She raised her hands up, shielding them from the harsh glare. Abruptly, the light went out.

"Elizabeth, it's me, Nora," the woman holding the flashlight said urgently. Nora O'Brien leaned into the seat on the passenger side. "Start the motor. Use your parking lights. I'll get the gate."

The passenger door slammed shut as Elizabeth turned the key in the ignition. The motor whined, sputtered once, then caught.

She switched the parking lights on; in their faint yellow beam, she could see Nora ahead of her, pushing the gate open. Elizabeth eased up on the clutch and the station wagon jerked into life, rolling through the graveled entrance onto an asphalt drive.

The gate clanged shut behind her and a few seconds later, the passenger door yanked open once again. Nora slid into the passenger seat beside Elizabeth and slammed the door. "It's a circular drive," Nora said. "There's a garage in back. Drive around to it."

Elizabeth's eyes began to water from the strain of peering into the darkness. She wondered who was at the Victorian house besides Nora, who would be there tonight and tomorrow as they gathered over the schematic drawings of Roberto Quintero's Salon "K" Street.

She turned the station wagon toward the rear of the house, driving toward a long, low garage. There were three garage doors, and one was pulled open, although there was no light on inside. Elizabeth eased inside, the parking lights pooled light on the concrete floor of the garage. Behind her, she heard the garage door closing, shutting out even the shadowed night light from outside the garage. She switched off the engine. Nora O'Brien was out of the station wagon even before the motor sputtered into silence.

The garage was suddenly flooded with light from an overhead fixture. Elizabeth McKinley saw Frances Foster now, standing at a narrow back door, her hand just leaving the lightswitch. Elizabeth reached behind the driver's seat and pulled out a small overnight bag. She was tired; her legs ached and her neck hurt from the long drive. But a long night was ahead; Frances and Nora would have many questions to ask her, and she wanted to answer them all.

Frances strode toward Elizabeth; she was wearing a long striped caftan, and her white hair was smooth and shining, held back at her temples by her barrettes. She looked fresh, as if she had just arisen from a long and satisfying nap. But Frances had not been napping and it was nearly two o'clock in the morning in upstate New York. It was not sleep but the prospect of success that had invigorated her; it was the almost literal smell of victory that had removed any trace of weariness from her body and from her very soul. She wanted to hear everything Elizabeth had to report now; she didn't want to wait until morning to hear it. "Hello, Elizabeth. How was the drive?" Frances asked. She opened the back door of the staion wagon and picked up one of the boxes. Beside her, Nora picked up the second and Elizabeth picked up the third, smaller one which she balanced beside her overnight bag.

The small box felt heavy to Elizabeth; her forearms burned with it. "The drive was OK," she confessed. She put the box down and reached inside the car for her folder of schematic drawings; she was pleased with them, and she was pleased with her planning so far. The tired feeling began to leave her as she followed Frances and Nora through the small rear door of the garage and into the house.

Frances led them past the kitchen into the old parlor of the carefully preserved Victorian house in Cooperstown's Historic District. An enormous sword fern in a creamy china pot stood before the marble fireplace, and the parlor furnishings were heavy and overstuffed and uncomfortable. The parlor had a still, museum-like quality to it, as if life inside this house had stopped a very long time ago and now visitors came to sit stiffly and gape but not to touch. There were shades behind the lace curtains in the parlor windows, and the shades were drawn behind the closed curtains.

Two women who had been sitting on a deep red tufted velvet sofa rose as Frances Foster, Nora O'Brien and Elizabeth McKinley walked in, carrying the boxes, which were stacked beside an upright spinet piano in the corner of the parlor room. Frances, who might have been introducing bridge players to one another, then raised an arm in the general direction of the two women who still were standing, waiting. "Let me introduce everyone," she announced, smiling. "Adele Pearson and Nancy Todd," Frances said, gesturing to the women who were standing by the sofa. "This is my daughter's friend Elizabeth McKinley. And you've all met Nora already." To all four, she said: "One more woman will join us in Washington later, but she couldn't be here tonight." Frances Foster spread her hands out, gathering them all in, beckoning them to be seated, just as if she were hosting a social hour on a sunny afternoon in East Hampton, instead of in Cooperstown, New York, at two o'clock in the morning.

Crofton School Dean Adele Pearson, who was wearing a sensible skirt and blouse and her pearls, sank back down against the uncomfortable sofa. Well, she was here and there probably wasn't any turning back now, was there? She could hardly believe that the visit by Jack Riley of the Rights for the Unborn League to the Crofton School in Connecticut had come to this, and so very rapidly, too. After she had discovered the photograph of Frances Foster and First Lady Mary Holt Morgan in the 1949 Crofton School annual, and after she had made her timid call to Frances Foster in East Hamptom, New York, events began to overtake Adele Pearson and now here she was. She would have wished otherwise; she longed, really, to be home in her little house in Westport, safely asleep in her bed and far away from this dangerous business here in Cooperstown. But Adele Pearson had offered her assistance to Frances Foster when Adele first called Frances and this was an offer she would not take back, not when it was made to a Crofton alumna.

It had been a few days ago, Wednesday, to be exact, when her telephone rang at the Crofton School with the call from Frances Foster that changed everything. And on Thursday, Frances Foster was in her office with the door shut and almost before she realized it, Adele Pearson was telling Frances about her late night journeys to Westport with her Crofton School students, and the abortions, and the terrible dread fear of getting caught. And here was Frances Foster, telling Adele Pearson about her daughter Hillary and the illegal abortion clinic in Algiers, across the Mississippi River from New Orleans, and the raid by the Rights for the Unborn League, and her murder and the murder of Dr. Michael Green, M.D. Oh, the horror of it. The injustice. And so when Frances Foster had carefully unwrapped her plan to kidnap First Lady Mary Holt Morgan, bit by bit, like an enormous, elaborately wrapped package, Adele Pearson had nodded with perfect understanding, with sympathy and agreeing with Frances and swearing to keep her mouth closed about it at the same time. It was only logical that Dean Adele Pearson be offering to help Frances Foster once again, offering herself up to Frances and the others and offering to risk all those terrible dangerous risks.

Frances had been so soothing and so sure and so understanding of Adele's fear. It would be too much for Adele to take part in the actual kidnapping, Frances understood that, but Frances needed someone she could trust utterly with the important task of making sure their funds were properly accounted for in Switzerland. Had Adele been to Switzerland? No. It was a lovely country and their banks were discreet. Adele would be fine in Zurich, Switzerland; no one ever need know that she had done anything more than take a simple vacation in Switzerland with its walking tours of Alpine villages and its fabulous shopping.

And Adele Pearson found herself agreeing with Frances, agreeing that, yes, Adele could go to Switzerland, and open the bank accounts in Zurich, and wait there to make sure the deposits arrived. Yes, she could do that, especially since the Crofton School year did not begin until a week after Labor Day and she could be sure of being safely home in Westport by then, with no one ever knowing of this courageous and important role she had played in establishing their new free abortion clinic in Sweden.

Adele Pearson had arrived in Cooperstown on Friday afternoon, coming by train to Albany, and then by rental car from Albany to Cooperstown. Her rental, a Plymouth Reliant, was parked in the three-car garage now, safely out of sight of prying eyes, and her bags were upstairs, in one of the guest rooms. Adele Pearson had already been to her travel agent and in less than two weeks now, on August 11, she would be leaving for her little vacation in Switzerland.

Now as she sank back against the hard Victorian sofa in the parlor of the house in Cooperstown, she murmured appropriate greetings to Elizabeth McKinley, who had just arrived from Washington, and who looked very tired and drawn, as if she had not slept in quite some time. Adele Pearson regretted that Elizabeth McKinley and Nora O'Brien were not Crofton School girls; Adele would have felt much better if they had been Crofton alumnae. But that was beside the point, wasn't it. After all, First Lady Mary Holt Morgan was a Crofton School alumna too, although Dean Adele Pearson wished with all her heart that this were not the case.

Nancy Todd, who had been in Cooperstown since early Friday morning, was not a Crofton School girl, either. She was from Queens, New York, from the late Dr. Hugh Foster's old neighborhood. She had known Frances Foster since childhood, when the two of them had teamed up against Fatty Murphy and his friends to beat the crap out of them at pick-up basketball. She and Frances had prevailed against Fatty until Fatty turned thirteen and all of a sudden towered over them and began to make up for all the defeats that had occurred whenever Frannie and her father and mother visited Nancy Todd's parents in Queens. All through the years, through Nancy's brief and disasterous first marriage and then her divorce and her marriage to Frank Todd, she and

Frances had remained dear friends, seeing one another often, sharing the pains and pleasures of their maturity.

And then Hillary Foster was murdered in Louisiana, and Frances had called Nancy last week and asked can you help, and Nancy Todd had jumped right in. "I don't care what happens afterward, Frances!" Nancy Todd had shouted over the phone after Frances cautioned her about the danger. "Those creeps have to pay for this. The fucking bastards!" And when Frances had asked her about her family, about her daughter Christine, who was thirty-two now, the moment came when Nancy lost some of her fabulous fiery bluster. "She's one of them. She's a member of the Rights for the Unborn League, Frances. An organizer for them in Queens. I don't know where I went wrong," she said, her voice very nearly breaking over the telephone to Frances. "She's so self-righteous, Frances. I don't know where it came from. So cruel. She doesn't know what it was like for us," Nancy Todd had said.

Nancy Todd and Frances, in this telephone conversation, did not discuss what had happened six months after Christine's birth, in February of 1967, when a second pregnancy so soon had terrified Nancy Todd and she had decided not to carry it to term. Nancy remembered climbing a staircase, a long flight of wooden stairs at the back of a brick building in Queens in late February of 1967, on a bitter cold afternoon, and going inside a small little room at the top of the staircase, and seeing an old man who said he was a doctor and putting her feet in makeshift stirrups on his examining table and hearing him breathing asthmatically, breathing harsh labored breaths as he performed a dilation and curettage on Nancy Todd with his ice cold instruments. Always after the abortion, Nancy could not hear the sound of labored breathing without remembering once again the sharp asthmatic breaths of the old man at the top of the staircase.

Now she was here, in the parlor of this ridiculous old Victorian house in Cooperstown, plunging into deep water with her whole stocky body. And Nancy Todd felt alive, vivid and alive and strong and purposeful; she had not felt this way in a very long time, certainly not since the death of her beloved husband Frank of a smoking-induced heart attack five years ago. Nancy Todd looked long at young Elizabeth McKinley, who was sitting in a wing chair next to the fireplace, the giant sword fern on the hearth at her feet. She's so young, Nancy thought, as she nodded and smiled hello; she is so damned young. She'd better be good at this.

Registered Nurse Nora O'Brien, who had been here in Cooperstown since Sunday, and who had not shown up for her preliminary hearing on the various felony charges against her stemming for the New Orleans Tactical Unit raid on her little clinic in Algiers, balanced herself on the spinet piano stool in the corner. Her beloved Michael Green, M.D., whom the police had murdered in their raid, was resting now beside his little sister in a cemetery at Harrisburg, Pennsylvania. Frances Foster had told her this, and Frances had sent flowers for her, too. A small wreath of evergreens and roses with love from Nora. This had comforted Nora, for she had not wanted Michael Green to remain alone on that cold slab in the New Orleans morgue. Frances Foster also had told her about the call Frances got from Nora's young pipsqueak court-appointed attorney, Mr. Robert E. Lee Johnson, and about the little pipsqueak's earnest search for Nora. Well, he wouldn't find her. Nora twirled herself gently back and forth on the piano stool in the parlor of the house at Cooperstown. No indeed. None of them would ever find her again.

Frances Foster settled herself into the wing chair opposite Elizabeth. In a few hours, the dawn light would begin slipping over the horizon and before noon, her dear old friend Nancy Todd and Crofton School Dean Adele Pearson would be gone. They would return to Queens, New York and to Westport, Connecticut, Nancy Todd until August 12, when Frances would come for her, and Adele Pearson until the morning of August 11, when she would leave for Zurich, Switzerland. By Sunday afternoon, Elizabeth McKinley would be back in Washington, D.C., going about her usual Sunday afternoon round of household chores and errands and getting ready for a very normal workday on Monday morning. Frances Foster herself would be in East Hampton, packing and meeting with the realtor who would be selling the old Georgian house for her. But for right now, at just past two o'clock in the morning in Cooperstown, New York, her little band had this immediate work to do. "Tell us about the Roberto Quintero Salon," Frances said to Elizabeth.

Elizabeth McKinley pulled the schematic drawings of Roberto Quintero's Salon and The Chocolatier from her overnight bag; she spread them on the floor of the parlor, between the wing chairs and the sofa, where everyone could see them, and then in a quiet, even voice, and going slowly so that everyone would understand every detail, she began.

She had seen the second and third floors of Roberto Quintero's Salon on Thursday afternoon. She had been alone during her little tour, because Roberto himself had been out of town, and young Jonathan the hairdresser, busy with another customer right after her on Thursday, had urged her to look around by herself up there. Nobody would mind, Jonathan said.

The second floor included a fully equipped private salon area, far more luxurious than the main salon on the first floor, a bed-sitting room, a private bathroom, and a small kitchen in the rear. A narrow staircase leading to the third floor was wedged between the kitchen and the private salon. Looking over her shoulder all the while, fearful that someone from the salon would appear at the head of the stairs to question her, Elizabeth had crept up the staircase to the third floor. Her hand had trembled slightly on the staircase rail, and her heart had pounded as she reached the top of the stairs and slipped into the dark and dusty attic room; it was thick with stacks of old salon chairs and boxes of supplies. The fire stair that led to the roof was at the back of the attic; the fire door was a standard model, built to release from the inside. Elizabeth had opened the door. It had been a short distance to the roof of The Chocolatier next door; she had been able to see it on the third floor of the building housing the chocolate shop. She had been able to picture them carrying the inert body of First Lady Mary Holt Morgan across the narrow roof of Roberto Quintero's Salon to the building next door; and she had thanked God for fire codes.

Chapter Thirteen

They were on their knees, gathered in a circle around the schematic drawings that Elizabeth McKinley had spread out on the parlor room floor of the rented Victorian house in historic Cooperstown. Nora O'Brien, pointing to the drawing of the building housing The Chocolatier, was asking how they would explain their sudden appearance on the third floor when they came down the stairs from the roof, carrying the inert body of the First Lady in a chocolate carton.

Elizabeth picked up her red felt pen once again; she had been drawing, in thick red dashes, the path they would take through the high narrow wooden buildings in Georgetown on August 14. "We'll make a delivery to the chocolate shop from the back door first," she said. "We'll already be in the building; they won't know we've been on their roof. Or anywhere else."

Nora O'Brien nodded dubiously. More will be leaving than came in, she thought. Never mind, Nora. The First Lady will be in the chocolate crate, don't forget. The chocolate shop clerk won't see her. Nora leaned back on her knees. It was getting closer. She could feel a surge of excitement in her throat; she could feel the sweet juicy taste of revenge in her mouth. She watched as Elizabeth drew her red felt pen dashes across the drawings and then across a map of the District of Columbia and the Commonwealth of Virginia, all the way to the foothills of the

Appalachians, all the way to the little farmhouse back in the hills. Sweet, sweet, Nora thought, running her tongue across her wide mouth. Sweet it is.

The discussion in the parlor of the Victorian house in Cooperstown continued almost until dawn. The first morning light was just slanting in the windows when Elizabeth hauled herself upstairs to bed. She was asleep almost immediately. She did not hear the two cars start outside an hour later, did not hear the noise of the engines as they rumbled down the circular drive and were gone. Frances Foster's old friend Nancy Todd was on her way back to Queens, New York, on this early Saturday morning, and Crofton School Dean Adele Pearson was on her way to Albany, where she would be turning in her rental car and catching a commuter flight home to Connecticut and home to her duties at Crofton, which at the moment were focused on making ready for the September 1998 opening of the school year. Her preparations had taken on a new urgency in the last several days, because they were to be cut short by her journey to Geneva, Switzerland. It was a journey which terrified Adele Pearson, but one which even in her fear and trembling, she was determined to make; this was her opportunity to be brave, to be courageous and most of all to hold herself to her own standards. Thus it was that in spite of her trepidation, there was a part of Adele Pearson that felt almost giddy when she left Cooperstown on this sunny morning, almost as if she were a young girl again, starting out on a great adventure.

Nancy Todd, who would be seeing her daughter Christine this evening for dinner, was not giddy with any excitement. Instead, she was grimly determined, her jaw clenched until it ached, her thick body rigid with tension. She would be driving the van into Georgetown on August 14, and she would be driving it away as well, driving it away with their little bitch passenger, Mary Holt Morgan, President of the Rights for the Unborn League. Nancy had watched the First Lady on television over all these years; she had watched her throw her head back and smile her big toothy smile of self-righteousness and make her pretty speeches about saving the babies.

Whenever she saw Mary Holt Morgan on television, shoving her Human Life Amendment down the throats of the country, Nancy Todd was transported back to that day in February of 1967 when she struggled up the long staircase behind the building in Queens and felt the old doctor's ice cold instruments slide up her vagina. In spite of everything, including the stiff cash payment the old man had demanded, Nancy still was grateful to him; after all, he had done what she asked and she had saved herself for her infant daughter Christine, who had needed her. Nancy's round little face turned down when she thought of her daughter now; the infant who needed her had grown into an adult whom Nancy did not like very much. Christine Todd Blanchard was selfish, and she was so very sure of herself, so very sure she was right. In the midst of her grim determination, Nancy Todd smiled to herself as she drove south toward Queens on this bright Saturday morning; Christine would be so angry if she knew, wouldn't she. So very angry. Poor little Christine. Such a scandal in the family. Mother pulling something like this. Just to see Christine's pinched and horrified face would be almost enough to make up for getting caught, Nancy Todd thought to herself as she turned toward home.

By late morning, as Nancy approached Highway 87 near the town of Catskill, Nora and Frances, after napping for several hours, were fixing themselves a hearty breakfast in the kitchen of the historic house in Cooperstown. Next to the sink, Max the cat also partook of a hearty breakfast, his gray and white tail switching back and forth as he swallowed the tender morsels in his new yellow cat dish. Later in the day, Frances would be leaving for East Hampton, for she was packing up the house, putting every-

thing she would not be taking to Sweden with her in storage.
Frances Foster would be leaving East Hampton soon, and she
was never coming back.

Several hundred miles south of Cooperstown, New York, in
Washington, D.C., Rights for the Unborn League Executive Director Carlton Farnsworth, who had eaten a pasty yellow serving
of non-fat egg substitute for breakfast, which he had chased with
a Bloody Mary laced liberally with Tabasco sauce to get rid of the
egg substitute taste, was pacing impatiently back and forth in
front of his partner's mahogany desk. He was in the office on this
Saturday morning because his Special Security Assistant, Jack
Riley, had at last compiled at least a preliminary report on this
matter of the Foster woman and her daughter, whatever her name
had been. What Riley had told him during these last few minutes
had unsettled Farnsworth. Sprawling disrespectfully on
Farnsworth's burnished leather sofa, with his scuffed shoes resting insolently on the polished wood coffee table, Riley had told
him that the Foster woman appeared to be liquidating her consid-
erable fortune, as if she were raising money for something. And
Jack Riley told the Executive Director of the Rights for the Unborn League that Frances Foster had gone to school with First
Lady Mary Holt Morgan. These two disparate pieces of information might not have any connection to each other at all, but
Carlton Farnsworth did not like hearing about it. He was exceedingly respectful of two things in this world; money and position.
Taken together, these two things made powerful combinations;
they made people dangerous.

Riley, who had delivered his brief oral report on this matter,
and who now was smoking one of his Camel cigarettes, was
waiting for Carlton Farnsworth's response to this little preliminary report. He did not have to wait long.

Farnsworth turned now to Riley, smiling brightly at him. "How much money is she raising, do you think?" Farnsworth asked softly. At the bottom, money was far more important to Carlton than anybody's position. Carlton did like money almost more than anything. Yes, indeed.

Riley sucked reflectively on his Camel. "Oh, between ten and twenty million, give or take a few bucks," he said, the cigarette waggling between his teeth.

Those numbers brought Carlton Farnsworth up short. Twenty million. What was she doing with that kind of money anyway? An angry woman could do a lot of damage with twenty million dollars; she could do a lot of damage to the League. And there was this surprising business about being the First Lady's schoolmate. Farnsworth wondered how deep that old school tie went. "And she went to school with little Mary Holt," he mused, quietly, almost to himself, almost as if Jack Riley were not lounging on his expensive leather sofa a few feet away from him. Farnsworth looked again at Riley. "Were they friends at that school? Close friends?"

Riley was remembering Dean Adele Pearson of the Crofton School, wondering if she was a virgin, she with her high white forehead and her stiff back and her piano teacher voice. Farnsworth's question pulled him back from his little reverie about Adele Pearson, in which Riley was disrobing her, unbuttoning each button on her high-necked blouse, unbuttoning her all the way down. With an effort, Riley abandoned his pleasant reverie. "Foster and the First Lady were lab partners in a science class. In chemistry," Riley told him. "I haven't found any references to indicate a close relationship, either at Crofton School or later on. I'm still working on that."

Farnsworth considered this. "So they weren't that close," he said.

Jack Riley stubbed out his Camel cigarette in the belly of a Steuben glass swan on Farnsworth's coffee table. "No, I don't think so."

A part of Carlton Farnsworth was relieved to learn that the First Lady did not seem to be involved with Frances Foster, but another part, the part that wanted Mary Holt Morgan out of his damned hair for once, out of the spotlight that should be uniquely his as Executive Director of the Rights for the Unborn League, was just a little bit disappointed. Farnsworth took pains to conceal this little niggling bit of disappointment from Riley, whom he did not trust all that much. Farnsworth leaned one fleshy hip against his desk, staring at the life size oil painting of First Lady Morgan on the wall above the sofa, thinking about what Jack Riley had told him this morning. This business of the money worried him. It was a lot of money. What was Frances Foster going to do with all that money? Yes, she would have to be watched. Farnsworth dropped his gaze from the painting of the First Lady to Riley. "Find out what she's doing with the money. I want to know about the money." Farnsworth smiled at Riley, smiling his bright white smile. "Women can be very foolish with money, Jack. We have to look out for the women when they get their little hands on too much of it," Farnsworth said, smiling his wonderful smile, his clear blue eyes crinkling warmly at the corners.

On Sunday afternoon, as Jack Riley pored over his computer printouts of Frances Foster's life in his hotel room in Washington, Frances herself began to pack her own lifetime of possessions, along with those of the late Dr. and Mrs. Hugh Foster and the late Hillary Foster. A discreet For Sale notice had been placed on the front gate of her old Georgian house in East Hampton, and the real estate broker Frances had engaged had assured her that a sale would be imminent as soon as word filtered through the market that the Foster house in East Hampton was available. Movers were coming on Wednesday to crate and take away the contents of the house, but now she was packing her personal things, and some keepsakes to take with her to Sweden. Those items, along with some of her furniture, were to be shipped to Stockholm, where Frances Foster would be living soon.

Frances was wrapping her mother's heavy silver in tissue paper, tending to each piece separately and placing them all in a carton that also contained her grandmother's old cut glass crystal stemware. She would be happier in Stockholm with her things around her, she thought, holding up a soup spoon. And if she did not reach Stockholm? If something happened and she did not get there after August 14th? Frances squinted at the silver soup spoon. She had given her attorney, Matthew Adair, a set of sealed instructions, to be opened in the event of her death, which set out in precise language exactly what was to be done with her possessions.

Matthew had not been pleased to receive this sealed letter. "Can I assume this is a codicil to your will, Frances? You really need a new will, you know," he had said warily. He thought she was up to no good, no good at all, and he was helpless to stop her. If only she would talk to him about all of this.

But Frances didn't want to talk to Matthew Adair about anything right now; she didn't want him involved in any of this. He already sounded so very suspicious. "The letter will function as a codicil," Frances had said to him.

Matthew was liquidating her estate, as she had instructed, but he was registering his alarm at every step. Frances thought about poor old Matt Adair as she wrapped another silver soup spoon in tissue and put it in the carton beside her; he would just have to shut up and proceed with the liquidation, she thought. Maybe someday she would be able to tell him everything. But not now.

She was sitting, as usual, at her kitchen table, her long yellow legal pad on one side of her, the silverware in front of her, with the packing box in easy reach beside her chair. Absorbed as she was in her task, she did not hear the car coming slowly up the long drive to the Georgian house; she did not hear the car doors slam outside, or the footsteps of two men as they strode up the wide brick walkway to the front entrance of the Foster house.

The door chimes rang just as Frances was starting on the salad forks. Maybe it was the real estate broker, she thought, come with more papers for her to sign, or perhaps the broker had a customer already, a prospective buyer. In spite of her determination to sell, Frances felt an unexpected pang at the thought of someone else owning her old family home. Would they change everything? Well, it would be their house and they could change it if they wanted to, she thought. She put down the salad fork she had been wrapping in tissue paper and got up to answer the front door.

Opening the heavy wood door, Frances found herself facing two young men who were not prospective purchasers of the old Foster house; they were instead private detectives, up here in New York from New Orleans, all slicked up in their gray business suits and ready for a lengthy interview with Mrs. Foster regarding this worrisome matter of Registered Nurse Nora O'Brien, who had not shown up for her preliminary hearing earlier this week, and who they were very much concerned was, ah, attempting to remove herself from the long reach of the law and justice system and Judge Averill Higginbotham's courtroom in New Orleans. And did Mrs. Foster understand that the entire bail would be forfeited should this come to pass? That poor Mrs. Foster would lose her entire $25,000, which she had posted in good faith on behalf of this Nora O'Brien, who was in a lot of trouble, wasn't she.

The two young gentlemen, Robert Mayhew and Lawrence Sanderson, were on retainer to Robert E. Lee Johnson, Miss O'Brien's attorney, who was most anxious to locate Nora O'Brien. Of course there would be more money in this for the Messrs. Mayhew and Sanderson if they found her than if they did not. Gravely, they presented their respective identification cards to Frances Foster, who had not moved from her doorway as yet to invite them inside her very large and impressive home. Robert Mayhew, stepping forward just slightly, and assuming the role of spokesman during this awkward moment, decided that Mrs. Foster needed some kind of reassurance. "We are doing our very best to locate Miss O'Brien before she misses another hearing date, which would endanger your funds," he said, his hands clasped in front of him. Mayhew was slender, of medium height, and like his companion, he fairly gleamed with scrubbed and clean-shaven health and earnestness. In fact, Robert Mayhew and his companion Lawrence Sanderson resembled a pair of young missionaries far more than they looked like private investigators.

Frances Foster smiled at the two of them and handed their identification cards back to them. So they were looking for Nora all the way up here. She knew she should invite Mayhew and Sanderson into the house, but she couldn't stand to do it; their clean and earnest missionary look and their obvious determination to find Nora repulsed her utterly. Nora didn't deserve this. Frances realized that she had to say something. Anything. "I'm sorry," she said. "That is, ah, the painters are about to arrive, to paint the inside of the house, and I'm afraid everything is in chaos here," she continued breathlessly, blocking the doorway still more. "If you could come back another day. Perhaps next week?"

Mayhew smiled benignly at Frances, his full mouth closed all the while. The old woman was obviously going to be no help at all; she was clearly not even going to let them into her house. "Do you have any idea where Miss O'Brien might be?" he asked. He would get whatever Frances Foster knew out of her right here at her front door. The old biddy was probably the forgetful type anyway. He wondered how O'Brien had gotten all that money out of her. And then there was the bad business about her daughter. The nurse must have been very clever to get that bail out of the mother.

Frances Foster smiled back at young Mayhew. You slick little toad, she thought. You arrogant little weasel, you. Her mind was racing. She wanted these private detectives far, far away from New York right now. She could see how they were looking at her, how they thought she was a stupid old woman standing there in her old khaki trousers and her big faded blue shirt, how they thought she was just another rich old lady living on her annuities who had been taken advantage of by Nora O'Brien. Did they know about Hillary? Of course they did; they all did and they didn't care. She closed her eyes to keep them from seeing her hatred and disgust. They made her sick. She opened her eyes once again, opening them as if she had been thinking hard, combing her little pea brain for some grain of information that would help them find Nora. "I felt sorry for Miss O'Brien," she said, letting her voice trail off like a thin uncertain thread. "She did mention something about friends in Key West, Florida. I believe they were friends from nursing school." She pasted an inquiring smile on her face. "If that's any help to you."

Key West, Mayhew thought. A woman like the nurse would stick out in Key West, Florida, the cowboy town of the south, where outlaws of every stripe lived and where Robert Mayhew and Lawrence Sanderson would be pleased to travel if Robert E. Lee Johnson would be willing to pay for it. Mayhew decided the trip to New York had been worth it after all.

Frances Foster watched from her doorway as the two private detectives retreated down the long brick walkway to their car. She went inside after they drove down her driveway and out her front gate. But the car carrying Robert Mayhew and Lawrence Sanderson did not drive off; the car sat there right outside her gate, its motor idling. For more than fifteen minutes Frances watched them from her kitchen window, peering at the parked car and the shadowy figures of the two men inside. What were they doing? The minutes passed by so slowly, creeping by, as the car idled down by the gate. Frances' eyes grew tired watching them; it was so difficult to see what they might be doing out there. They seemed to be talking and she thought she saw one of their hands rise up, holding some papers, but from her kitchen window, she could not be sure.

Finally they were gone and Frances turned away from the window. There was a terrible clammy feeling in the pit of her stomach. She wanted to call Nora in Cooperstown, but just as she lifted the receiver from the hook, it occurred to her that her telephone call might be recorded somewhere, that someone might be monitoring her calls. She put the receiver down. From now on, she would use a pay phone to call Nora, she decided. Frances returned to packing the silver, going hurriedly through the flatware now, throwing the tissue around bunches of utensils and shoving them into the packing box. She felt the time going now, felt it slipping out from under her; she wanted to hurry.

In Washington, D.C. on this Sunday afternoon, Elizabeth McKinley felt the time slipping away, too; she felt it being wrenched from her fingers when her apartment building superintendent, Joaquin Garcia, making a special, somber visit to her apartment, told her that a man who called himself Jack Riley, who said he was a Special Security Assistant for the Rights for the Unborn League, had been looking for her. Garcia had looked sympathetically at Elizabeth, his liquid brown eyes soft. "Is trouble?" he asked awkwardly, his heavy bulk filling her doorway.

Elizabeth surmised instantly that the Rights for the Unborn League had taken her name from Hillary's things. The creeps. The bastards. She thanked Joaquin, and when he patted her on the shoulder sympathetically, she felt the surprising sting of tears in her eyes, blurring her vision, threatening to overflow. "It's OK," she said to him, thanking him, finally closing the door after she assured him that she was really OK, Mr. Garcia. But on Monday morning she did not go to work. Instead, she told them that she had been called away to Los Angeles on an unexpected family emergency, and no, she wasn't sure when she would be back.

On the following Wednesday morning in New Orleans, a hot and muggy August morning that showed signs of becoming a scorcher, and as the courthouse clock ticked perilously close to the noon hour, an impatient Judge Averill Higginbotham III crooked a stubby finger at Nora O'Brien's attorney, Robert E. Lee Johnson, summoning him to the bench. Leaning over, his hot and sweaty neck pressing painfully into his starched white shirt collar, Judge Higginbotham glared in disgust at young Johnson. It would appear that accused felon Nora O'Brien had defied his court after all. Well, he was not about to waffle on this one, not on this young lady, not on these very serious charges stemming from the murders of those babies in that filthy outlaw abortion clinic over in Algiers. "Where is your client, Mr. Johnson?" Judge Higginbotham asked peevishly.

Robert E. Lee Johnson swallowed hard. He was sweating bullets in his new navy blue suit. He didn't know where the hell she was! How could he. The frigging private detectives he had hired had taken his money and delivered zilch. Now they wanted to go to Key West. They could go to Hell for all he cared. He could see his chance to defend this case, his chance for some real serious publicity, some recognition, going right down the frigging drain here. If Nora O'Brien had crossed a state line, as Robert E. Lee Johnson was sure she had, then this whole thing could be bounced up to federal court. He would be replaced as the court-appointed attorney by one of the federal defenders; he would lose this whole thing. He looked up into the red and puffy face of Judge Averill Higginbotham III. "She doesn't seem to be here," he admitted finally.

Higginbotham sat up and pressed his full lips together into a thick flat line. Well she had her chance, didn't she. "Very well. I want a warrant from the bench for Miss O'Brien. Bailiff!" He handed the sheaf of paperwork on O'Brien to his bailiff and then looked back down at Johnson, who was still standing there. "That's all, counselor," Higginbotham said, dismissing him.

A hot and flushed Robert E. Lee Johnson turned and left the courtroom, his tail between his legs, and headed straight for the bar across the street from the courthouse, where he commenced to cool off with a pitcher of beer and a dish of dry roasted peanuts. A few hours later, soothed by a few more pitchers of beer, Johnson returned to his tiny, messy office down the street, where he placed a long distance telephone call to the home of Frances Foster in East Hampton, New York. Over his second pitcher of beer, Johnson had decided that he should tell Foster of this debacle himself; he should tell her that she had just flushed twenty-five grand right down the toilet. Bail had been revoked and Mrs. Foster's money now belonged to the Parish of Louisiana; she could just kiss that money goodbye.

There was no answer at the Foster place. No answering machine, no housekeeper, no nothing. Robert E. Lee Johnson grimaced and slammed the receiver down. Well shit, he thought. Maybe she had gone on vacation somewhere since the private detectives talked to her. It was August, after all. Normal people got to go on vacation in August.

In Washington, D.C., on this same August afternoon, Jack Riley was not on vacation. He was at the headquarters of the Rights for the Unborn League, and he had just completed a brief and unsatisfactory telephone conversation with an officer of the New Orleans Police Department, who had called to tell Riley that a warrant had been issued for the arrest of accused felon Nora O'Brien, now a fugitive.

Alone in the League library, Riley lit himself a Camel cigarette. If members of the New Orleans Police Department, and especially those in the Tactical Unit, knew what was good for them, they would just let the nurse stay lost. Riley had not been looking forward to witnessing Nora O'Brien's day in court; he did not think the New Orleans police would look all that great should its activities surrounding the raid on the little backyard clinic in Algiers be held up to the bright unyielding light of a courtroom examination. Still, he wondered where the nurse was, and he wondered if he should call the one person who might know, although he did not know whether she would tell him anything. Jack Riley picked up the telephone to call the home of Frances Foster. He was about to dial when it occurred to him that it might be a good time for a personal visit to her place in East Hampton. He had not been able to locate Elizabeth McKinley, whose office said she was in Los Angeles on personal business, but then she was not that important anyway. Frances Foster was so much more interesting. All that money was so very interesting, wasn't it. And it would be nice to get out of Washington for a few days too. He was tired of Carlton Farnsworth and his beady little blue eyes and his pouty little smile.

Chapter Fourteen

First Lady Mary Holt Morgan adjusted the collar of her yellow linen jacket, pulling it just a bit closer to the edge of her long white neck. The lovely yellow color of the jacket really did seem to bring out the glow in her complexion, didn't it. She stared at herself in the mirror, staring straight into her reflection in the heavily gilded hallway mirror in the family quarters of the White House. Her chin was sagging just a bit; she pressed her tongue to the roof of her mouth and watched the little sag disappear, watching it suck itself up into her throat. Whenever a camera fastened its glass eye on Mary Morgan, she remembered this little trick of rolling the back of her tongue to the roof of her mouth, and she remembered to hold her lips together very lightly, just so they barely kissed each other as they rubbed against her teeth; her mouth looked soft and full when she held her lips that way. The camera was so vicious, so harsh, really. It wasn't fair; it wasn't fair that they expected so much of her. Oh, the demands. The constant intrusions. Really, she might never have become President of the Rights for the Unborn League if she had known what a terrible price she would have to pay; it would almost have been easier to just be plain old First Lady Morgan, like Jackie Kennedy had been. Why, she hardly had time to take care of her personal needs anymore what with the constant traveling and the appearances for the League.

She smiled at her reflection in the mirror, opening her eyes wide, just like a young girl. Of course she wasn't so very much unlike Jackie, if you thought about it. They both were elegant women, from fine backgrounds, and really, Jackie had been the famous one, hadn't she. Why, Jack Kennedy used to say he just was there to carry her coat. It wasn't all that much different with Edward and herself. Why, if you took a poll, she probably would be the popular one, the one people actually loved, the one people truly cared about.

Well, today she was going to do a little something just for herself; she was going to spoil herself at Roberto's. Today was the full treatment: a facial and a tiny little facial peel, a touchup for her hair and a fresh styling. Mary smiled at herself once more in the mirror. Maybe she would have Roberto do a manicure and a pedicure too. Why not. She deserved it. These last few months since the ratification of the Human Life Amendment had been one long exhausting push; she wanted every single state on the record in favor of the Amendment. She had been getting these awful reports of illegal clinics operating, taking advantage of vulnerable and frightened young women. There had even been a report of a young mother being killed in an illegal clinic in Louisiana, on the very same night that she herself was in New Orleans, addressing this year's Rights for the Unborn League National Conclave. Thank God at least that clinic had been stopped; at least there would be no more murders of helpless babies and young mothers at that clinic.

Behind her, Mary Holt Morgan heard the soft footsteps of her Secret Service agent. She knew it was young Eugene Duffy, her favorite agent, and the one she always requested when she was on some personal business. Today, young Eugene, who was from that quaint old mining town, Wallace, Idaho, was scheduled to accompany her to Roberto Quintero's Salon on "K" Street in Georgetown. And she had her little deck of pinochle cards in her purse; she hoped Eugene was bright and shiny this morning, for she was looking forward to some spirited play. She patted her blonde hair and turned around. "Well! Are we ready?" Mary Holt Morgan asked, winking slyly at Eugene Duffy, who blushed pink to the roots of his thick brown hair.

Duffy shifted back and forth on the balls of his feet. She made him nervous when she did that. Her bulletproof limousine was outside, in the center of a short motorcade. There was a Secret Service car in front, leading, then her limo, and another car in the rear. It was easy duty today; no hostile crowds, no untried locations, no wide open spaces where some maniac could take a shot at her. "We're ready anytime you are," Duffy told the First Lady.

A few minutes later, the First Lady's motorcade moved smoothly out the White House gates, polished black metal and chrome and dark tinted windows glinting brightly in the hot August sunshine as the motorcade roared swift and sure for Roberto Quintero's Salon on "K" Street in Georgetown.

It was nearly 11:00 A.M. when Mary Morgan's motorcade rumbled to a stop in front of Quintero's Salon. Tiny Roberto opened his polished black door wide as the limousine door opened and Secret Service agent Duffy hauled himself out, unfolding his long legs in one smooth continuous motion. His hard eyes swept "K" Street once and then again while the front car in the motorcade disgorged its passengers—two more agents. One disappeared into the Salon, brushing past Robert Quintero as if he were a little fly; a second stayed in the street, posting himself in front of Quintero, right at the door. Duffy, who was blocking the open limousine door with his body, looked for a third time up and down "K" Street. The hot August heat already was shimmering on the pavement; water mirages already were floating up on the gray concrete, and the clotted Georgetown traffic was driving through them, slicing through the heat mirages like knives through butter. Duffy had been outside on the sidewalk for just over ninety seconds when the agent who had gone inside Quintero's Salon reappeared and nodded. Duffy turned to the First Lady, who had been sipping a cup of black Colombian coffee in the cool recesses of her limousine. "Mrs. Morgan? Mr. Quintero is ready for you," Duffy said. He reached one hand inside the limousine, and a moment later, the First Lady, grasping it, was out of her limo, walking the few steps to Robert Quintero's Salon, and then she was inside, the salon door closing firmly behind her.

Across the street from the salon, Elizabeth McKinley, dressed in her $750 I. Magnin suit, had been having a leisurely late breakfast, eating oat and cranberry scones with raspberry jam, sipping her strong coffee, and reading the morning edition of the *Washington Post*. She had finished her breakfast more than thirty minutes ago, and then she had lingered over her coffee, perusing the *Post* as if she had all the time in the world. But she did not have all the time in the world; she could not stand to wait that long. She was looking unseeing at the *Post*, all the while watching the polished black entrance door to Roberto Quintero's Salon, all the while hoping to God that her limousine would roll up within the next blink of her eye.

Elizabeth saw the black nose of the first car in the motorcade part its way through the "K" Street traffic; she saw the black limousine right behind it, and then the third car of the motorcade. She felt something fluttering in her chest as she watched the big shiny limousine pull up across the street, something trembling powerfully in her chest, something pounding. It was her heart pounding, so loud that she was afraid the waiter would hear it. She willed the pounding to stop as the limousine rolled to a halt. Folding her *Post* in half, she rose from her chair and walked deliberately to the rear of the restaurant, where there was a pay telephone. Her hands shook as she dialed the number. It rang only once before it was answered by Frances Foster. "She's here," Elizabeth said.

Frances answered the telephone at Elizabeth's apartment in the District of Columbia. "We're leaving right now," Frances said. She hung up and nodded to Nora O'Brien and Nancy Todd, who were standing beside her, rigidly expectant. Frances felt a surge of energy pour through her body, a surge of savage exhultation. Her eyes glittered with it as she turned to Nora and Nancy.

Two minutes later, a white van pulled out of the underground garage at Elizabeth's apartment building, heading for Georgetown. Magnetized signs on each side of the van declared that this was a delivery truck for the Von Roehm Chocolate Company, Wholesalers of Fine Chocolate and Confectionery Ingredients. Frances Foster rode in the front seat beside Nancy Todd, who was driving. They had rehearsed this drive, using Frances' old blue station wagon, and Nancy, her thick body planted in the driver's seat, had memorized the route through the District of Columbia. Elizabeth lived on the northeastern side of the District, almost at the border of Maryland near Chevy Chase.

Twenty minutes later, the Von Roehm Chocolate Company van was on Reservoir Road on the north boundary of Georgetown University. It turned off Reservoir Road and pulled into a crowded parking lot near the University administration building. Elizabeth was walking across the track field toward the parking lot as the van pulled up. A taxi had delivered her to the Georgetown University Hospital complex; after it disappeared from sight, Elizabeth had walked down the grassy hill below the main hospital building to the track field. A moment later, she was across the field and inside the van.

It was dark and cool inside the van. Nora, sitting on a jump seat behind the driver, handed Elizabeth a pair of black trousers, a black knit shirt, and a white cotton jacket with Von Roehm

Chocolate Company embroidered in bright red on the breast pocket. It was Elizabeth's uniform, purchased, like the others all of the women wore, from Sully's Uniform Emporium in Baltimore. They had paid extra for the rush job, and Sully himself had taken care of them; Sully, an Armenian who never allowed himself to be called anything but Sully, was always ready to do a rush job for a customer who paid a premium. Especially when that customer paid in hard cash.

Elizabeth stuffed her I. Magnin suit into a plastic bag and threw it under the jump seat. Shrugging into the Von Roehm Chocolate Company uniform, she looked quickly around the interior of the van; she wanted to be sure everything was there. Beside her, Nora was examining, once again, the small black medical kit on her lap, which contained a package of loaded syringes along with emergency first aid materials. Squeezed into the jump seat, Nora counted the syringes once more. There were eight of them. Nora was just closing the medical kit when she heard Frances clear her throat.

Turning to them, turning to Elizabeth and Nora in the back of the van and Nancy Todd beside her in the driver's seat, Frances raised one hand up and began to rub her forehead with it. Frances was prepared to go forward; she was, in fact, prepared to do nothing else. Her personal luggage and household goods already were on their way to Sweden and her estate had been almost completely liquidated, in spite of her attorney's objections. She looked long at them, at each one of them, at her dear old stalwart friend Nancy Todd, at Nora O'Brien, whom she had known only for these few weeks, but who felt almost like a younger sister to her now, and at Elizabeth McKinley, whom she had known as a child growing up but who she did not know so very well anymore. I am the only one who has lost a child to the Amendment, she thought; I'm the only one who has nothing more to lose. She saw that they had turned to her, that it was very still inside the van, very quiet; there was just the noise of the cars outside as they came and went from the Georgetown University parking lot and the sound of distant doors opening and closing and very faintly, the steady rumble of traffic on Reservoir Road. "Nobody has to go through with this," Frances said finally. "If anyone wants out, well," she paused, "that's fine, it's not a problem."

Each one of them looked back at Frances: Nancy Todd, whose memory of a long staircase in Queens and of ice cold instruments scraping her unwanted fetus from her womb were as sharp and brittle and painful today as on that winter day in 1967; accused felon and Registered Nurse Nora O'Brien, whose beloved Mike Green was gone forever to the little cemetery in Harrisburg, Pennsylvania, and whose little backyard clinic in Algiers was no more; and Elizabeth McKinley, whose fine free careless youth had died with her best friend Hillary Foster in Algiers. No, they said to Frances; there is no going back now, they said, as the August sun beat down and the hour crawled toward noon.

First Lady Mary Holt Morgan leaned back in her private salon chair and shook her wet golden hair. It felt so good to have Roberto shampoo her; he shampooed her hair so perfectly. It felt just like a massage when Roberto shampooed. Absently, she reached up and felt the back of her neck, feeling for the smooth spot where the hair was gone; she so hoped it would grow back someday, but it never had. She had finally broken herself of her little hair pulling habit, but not soon enough, it seemed. Never mind. Roberto never let it show. Mary Holt Morgan closed her eyes and let her head fall all the way back, until the skin on her pretty white neck was stretched taut. Oh, it felt so good! She could hear Roberto, behind her, setting his cutting tools out on a little cloth. They were blissfully alone, the two of them. Agent Eugene Duffy was in the sitting room across the hall, reading a magazine, and her two other Secret Service agents in this morning's squad were posted on the first floor, at the front and back entrances to Roberto's Salon, bored with this day's duty. Mary Holt Morgan smiled a warm satisfied smile. "Ah, Roberto dear, you don't know how good it feels to have you taking care of me," she purred, stretching like a cat in the salon chair.

Tiny Roberto Quintero, who had created himself from nothing, from just an ordinary salon school beginning in Kansas City, reached out and began to massage Mary Morgan's wet scalp, his strong fingers pressing into her flesh. She was his most important customer; unfortunately, Mary Holt Morgan knew this, too. "You need this little bit of time just for yourself, for your renewal," Roberto said softly, his fingers working strong and sure.

The Von Roehm Chocolate Company van idled slowly up "K" Street in Georgetown, threading its way through the traffic. At the southern end of "K" Street, the van turned left at the intersection, slowed almost to a stop, and rumbled slowly into the alley behind the Georgetown street. In the front seat, Frances switched on her new stopwatch. Beside her, Nancy, her thick fingers glued to the van steering wheel, maneuvered the van up the alley toward the bright green back door of The Chocolatier 100 yards away. She could see a slender, well-built man in a dark suit lounging at the back door of the place next door; it was a Secret Service agent and the place next door was Roberto Quintero's Salon. The van inched closer. Fifty yards. Twenty-five.

At ten yards, Elizabeth McKinley and Nora O'Brien picked up their automatic pistols, long silencers attached to the barrels like cigars. Nora slipped six hypodermic needles into the pocket of her Von Roehm Chocolate Company jacket, and Frances picked up a clipboard. As the van rolled to a stop, Frances took a long deep breath, grasped her clipboard importantly in one arm, and opened the passenger door of the van.

Secret Service agent Harry Hughes watched the white van as it rolled toward the back door of The Chocolatier. It was getting close to noon, and Harry was hungry; the sweet smells drifting from The Chocolatier were making his mouth water. When the van stopped, Harry stiffened automatically, his practiced gaze sweeping the van. As he watched, his right hand inches from the revolver in his belt, a white-haired woman in her sixties opened the front passenger door and got out. She looked up and smiled and waved at Harry as she walked to the rear of the van and opened the double doors. Two more women were in there; it's an all-woman crew, agent Harry Hughes thought, relaxing, smiling benignly at them. The two women inside the van lowered a hand truck to the pavement and then they muscled a large carton bearing the Von Roehm Chocolate Company label onto the hand truck. They looked up briefly at Harry as they trundled the hand truck to the service entrance of The Chocolatier, the woman with the clipboard striding along behind them.

Elizabeth McKinley pressed one gloved finger on the back door buzzer of The Chocolatier. In a moment, a disembodied voice, raw with static, answered. "Delivery from Von Roehm Chocolate Company," Elizabeth said into the little voice box beside the buzzer. A few seconds later, she heard the automatic latch click open and she opened the bright yellow back door. The puzzled face of a young clerk greeted her. Elizabeth recognized this face; it was the same young clerk she had seen in the store two weeks ago. Did she recognize Elizabeth? Elizabeth saw a quizzical look cross the young woman's face. My hair is different and I'm not wearing makeup, Elizabeth thought; please don't remember me. "We have a special order to deliver," Elizabeth said. She felt Frances Foster brush by her and go into The Chocolatier, her clipboard thrust out in front of her.

The clerk backed away as Frances advanced. "I believe we are to take the delivery upstairs," Frances announced smoothly, writ-

ing something on her clipboard and then motioning Elizabeth and
Nora up the narrow staircase to the second floor of The Chocolatier. "This may take a little time," Frances told the clerk. "The
boss said we were to take back any stale ingredients, no charge of
course. Von Roehm's provides only the best." Her gray eyes
twinkled at the clerk, who smiled back.

At that moment, the little bell in the front of the store began to
peal sweetly, as the front door opened and two customers strolled
inside. The young clerk looked once more at Elizabeth and Nora,
who had taken the carton from the hand truck and were carrying
it up the stairs. Then she turned toward her customers. Frances,
watching her, smiled once more and started up the staircase behind Elizabeth and Nora.

The second floor kitchen was all steel and polished chrome and
antiseptically clean, polished countertops. The three women
paused for a moment, standing close together at a stainless steel
sink. Frances Foster's stopwatch clicked past 11:35.

The staircase to the third floor was narrow, and boxes were
stacked against some of the risers; the three women picked their
way up the staircase. The third floor was choked with equipment
and supplies; the fire stair was against the back wall.

They were running now, moving swiftly, taking the fire stairs
two at a time. Now the fire door. Elizabeth pressed down hard.
The door opened. Brilliant noontime sunshine poured down on
them, blinding them with its brilliance. Adjusting their eyes to
the brightness, they saw that they were on a black tarred roof,
and off to the right, less than fifteen feet away on the other side of
a low wall, was the roof of Roberto Quintero's Salon.

The warm tar stuck to their feet. In the bright sunlight on the
rooftop, they could see buildings all over the narrow streets of
Georgetown. Roofgardens bloomed on some buildings, and the
traffic noise floated up toward them, the honking horns, the

sound of car motors accelerating, the distant whine of a siren mingling with their harsh breathing and their heaving chests.

As they reached the low wall separating the two buildings, Elizabeth turned to Nora and Frances. "Here we go," she whispered fiercely.

For a brief second, just for part of a second, Frances wondered once more if they should call this thing off, if they were wrong after all. No, she thought. No more Hillarys.

In one more movement, they were over the low wall and treading softly toward Quintero's fire door, ducking low, trying to be invisible on the fearfully exposed rooftop.

Elizabeth yanked the door, pulling on the door edge with her fingers. When she had toured Roberto Quintero's private salon, she had taped over the lock; now she prayed that it was taped over still. The door was heavy and unmoving. Elizabeth swore under her breath. She felt Nora beside her, saw Nora's strong hands above hers on the door, pulling, pulling. Please God open, Elizabeth thought.

Very slowly, the heavy metal fire door gave way, very slowly as they pulled on it with their fingertips wedged against the door-jamb. "There!" whispered Elizabeth.

In another three seconds, they were inside, the fire door closed silently behind them, breathing hard as they stood on the fire door landing, hearing their harsh breaths, fearing their breathing could be heard for a long distance. The fire stairs were dusty. Creeping down them in black darkness, trying not to make a sound as they moved tread by tread down to Roberto Quintero's third floor storeroom. Elizabeth McKinley and Nora O'Brien and Frances Foster felt themselves stepping downward into a black hole. But they had memorized this; they stepped softly and surely down to the third floor.

In the darkness, Elizabeth motioned toward the staircase leading to the second floor. Suddenly the floor began to creak with their footsteps. They froze, their eyes wide in the darkness. They began again. Slowly. A sound floated up from the second floor. What was it? Music. Music had begun to play. Frances Foster recognized Mozart; it was the theme from *Elvira Madigan*. She smiled broadly, her teeth gleaming in the darkness. Roberto Quintero was playing Mozart for the First Lady. How nice of him; how wonderful of Roberto, Frances thought, pulling her automatic pistol from the deep pocket of her Von Roehm's Chocolate Company jacket and flipping the safety off.

First Lady Mary Holt Morgan lay back in the salon chair, her eyes closed, listening to the violins play her beloved Mozart. Roberto was busy behind her, applying the new gold toner to her hair. In a few minutes now, she could get up and go into the sitting room, where she could listen to more Mozart and play pinochle with Eugene Duffy, who was, at that moment, reading an article about male impotency in the latest issue of one of Roberto's magazines, and he was thanking God he didn't have any problems in that area.

Chapter Fifteen

Elizabeth McKinley felt sweat trickling down her armpits; she felt it covering her face beneath the tight nylon stocking mask, coating her eyelids, sticking to her. It was so hot on the staircase, so close and hot, the air so thick and wet in her throat. Down below Elizabeth and Nora O'Brien and Frances Foster, on the second floor of Roberto Quintero's Salon, violins were playing Mozart; the sound grew louder and louder as they inched down the staircase. They nearly were at the bottom now, where the door was slightly ajar and light from the hallway slanted onto the landing. Now they heard a low hum of conversation, a snatch of voices that blended with the violins sounds coming from the private salon room near the staircase landing.

Very slowly, Elizabeth inched open the door, flattening herself against a wall that separated the hallway from the salon room. She felt Frances next to her; Nora was behind Frances on the shadowed landing.

Their guns were drawn. Holding them with clean white gloves, they raised up their three long black gun barrels toward the doorway, pointing them toward the gleam of light.

First Lady Mary Holt Morgan lay back in her salon chair, her eyes blissfully closed, waiting for Roberto Quintero to begin her facial. She could hear him shuffling around back there, getting his equipment together.

Roberto heard a soft little noise in the hallway, a little shuffling sound. He looked up, his soft brown eyes shifting slowly over to the hallway, where the sound was coming from. What he saw was a terrible dark horror coming toward him, coming into his private salon. He saw a young woman with a nylon stocking stretched tight over her face, distorting her features into a terrible mask. She was holding a gun, a long-barreled gun pointed straight at his heart. Two more women behind her. The big one coming toward him like a terrible big cat in a stocking mask. "*Quien es*," he whispered, his dark eyes wide, his face draining of blood. But he dared not speak more; he could not. Roberto wanted to live. Now a gun was pushed against his side, pressing painfully there. Terror gripped him; helplessness. Then he felt something jabbing into his arm, jabbing deeply, stabbing him, and something went over his face. He panted for breath, breathing deeply through a wet cloth pressed against his mouth and nose, sucking in the sickly sweet fumes. "Ahhh," he whispered, sinking slowly. I want to live, he thought as the dark cloud of unconsciousness swept over him.

"Roberto?" Mary Morgan said, twisting in her chair at the noise behind her. Now a thick cloth went over her face; she felt strong hands on her, holding her. The cloth was smothering her. Cry out Mary! Eugene! She kicked helplessly against the soft salon chair as the Mozart played on and the deep fumes of chloroform entered her lungs. Something jabbed her in the arm, hurting her. Sleepy. Dark. Eugene. Her head fell back against the salon chair, the cloth still against her face, and she struggled no more.

In a moment, Mary Holt Morgan was in Nora O'Brien's arms, a little rag doll going quietly up the stairs, just like a sleeping child going up to bed. Nora and Elizabeth went up the stairs, Frances following them, wiping the surfaces they had touched clean with a cloth, closing the door to the staircase behind them as Nora and Elizabeth ascended above her. Now Frances saw the fire door open on Roberto Quintero's rooftop. The bright noonday sun poured down on them as they stepped outside onto the rooftop.

In the sitting room adjacent to Roberto Quintero's private salon, Eugene Duffy finished the article on impotence and began to thumb through the rest of the magazine as the Mozart violins neared a crescendo. They should be taking a break in there pretty soon, he thought. He wondered how long it would be. It was almost noon and he was hungry; he thought he heard some activity in there a moment ago, but now it was quiet again. He considered looking in on her; but he remembered her orders to them. He was to stay just outside the salon door; he was not to come in there unless she called to him. So the First Lady was vain, he thought. So what. They all are. He would give it a few more minutes. Maybe they would put something else on the stereo besides that damned violin music.

Elizabeth McKinley pulled open the fire door of The Chocolatier, kicking a rubber door wedge out of the way. They were panting with exertion, their chests heaving, as they closed the fire door and ascended into darkness once more, into the dim third floor storeroom of The Chocolatier. The Von Roehm Chocolate Company crate was open.

Nora O'Brien pressed the First Lady's wrist, checking for a pulse. A little slow. The powerful anesthetic was responsible for that. Mary Holt Morgan would sleep like a baby for several hours now, sleeping the long dreamless sleep of the unconscious. Very gently, Nora folded her into the chocolate crate, wrapping her in a blanket, her head resting on one arm as she curled into the fetal position. Nora looked up at Frances and Elizabeth. "She won't wake up," Nora said. "Not for a long time," Nora said, closing the chocolate carton. They peeled the nylon stocking masks from their faces; the masks were soaking wet with perspiration. Unaccountably, Nora thought of her mother just then. Eileen O'Brien was about the same size as the First Lady. About the same age, too. Nora pushed the thought away. She would think about her mother later.

Now they came down the staircase at The Chocolatier, Nora and Elizabeth awkwardly balancing the chocolate crate between them, Frances in front of them, carrying her clipboard as they descended once again. Frances lifted her chin as she stepped down the last step and onto the landing; her heart was beating fast, fluttering like a trapped bird's heart, like an animal caught in a trap. She wanted to be in the van outside, driving away from here. She felt her gun bulge in her pocket and she pressed the gun barrel against her thigh; the gun was heavy. Could she use the gun now? Could she raise it and fire it into the face of the chocolate shop clerk if she had to do it to escape now? She felt Nora and Elizabeth right behind her on the staircase. Yes, Frances thought. Yes I will if I have to.

The chocolate shop clerk looked up as the three women emerged onto the first floor and loaded the crate onto their handtruck at the bottom of the stairs. Unconcerned, the clerk turned back to a customer who had just ordered a full pound of walnut pralines. It wasn't her business what the owner of this place ordered, the clerk thought. She just wanted to get through another day at The Chocolatier. She was going to an outdoor concert at the Elipse tonight, and she was hoping the cleaners had been able to get that stain out of her pink dress because she wanted to wear it to the concert. You never knew who you might meet at an outdoor concert.

Frances felt a surge of relief pound through her body. Goodbye little clerk, she thought. Goodbye to you. Frances opened the yellow back door, holding it open for Nora and Elizabeth, who rolled the handtruck over the threshold and out into the brilliant sunshine.

Outside, in the hot noontime sun, Secret Service agent Harry Hughes, lounging at his post at the back door of Roberto Quintero's Salon, watched the little all-woman crew load a chocolate crate into their van. He nodded genially as the women waved goodbye, watching idly as the Von Roehm van rumbled down the alleyway, turned onto the main street and disappeared from sight.

Nancy Todd, her chubby fingers gripping like iron on the steering wheel, guided the van down the street, her face rigid with concentration, her blue eyes fastened on the row of cars ahead of them. Why couldn't they go faster? Jesus! She allowed herself to look once at Frances, who was pulling off her Von Roehm Chocolate Company jacket. "How much time do we have?" Nancy asked urgently.

Frances threw the jacket behind the seat and grabbed her old oversized blue shirt. She didn't know how much time they had. There had been a Secret Service agent in the sitting room; a single look into the private salon and the hunt would begin. "A few minutes if we're lucky," she said grimly. She buttoned up the old blue shirt and turned to Nora and Elizabeth. The van rocked slightly as Nancy pulled off the main street onto an alleyway three blocks from "K" Street. Nora and Elizabeth already were out of their Von Roehm Chocolate Company uniforms; both had changed into bluejeans and loose shirts. "This is the first stop," Frances said to them. Her hand was on the passenger door handle. Nancy had barely rolled the van to a stop when Frances was out of the van, tearing the magnetized Von Roehm Chocolate Company sign from the truck. Elizabeth, opening the side door on the other side, pulled the other company sign off. In less than five seconds, they were away.

Nancy gunned the motor of the white van; they were less than three minutes from the Georgetown University parking lot. Nancy could feel the seconds grinding by slowly, like a truck going up a long steep grade, taking forever to get to the top of the hill.

Secret Service agent Eugene Duffy stood up; the sitting room was cramped and he needed a good stretch. It was time for lunch, too. They were sure taking their time in there. He turned to listen for sounds coming from the salon; the Mozart tape had run through and he should be able to hear them now. Eugene looked toward the closed door to the salon. He couldn't hear anything in there; he couldn't hear anything at all. There was no sound coming from the salon. A quizzical look passed across his face. No sound. That was odd. He walked over to the salon door and opened it.

There was a dark figure slumped in the salon chair. In one long second, Duffy absorbed the still tableau. It was Quintero's inert body in the salon chair, and the First Lady was not there. In one more agonizing second, a terrible desperation arose in Duffy's throat. Maybe Quintero was asleep and she was in the bathroom? No. In two long steps, he reached Quintero. He pushed at the hair stylist's shoulder; Quintero's head bobbed up and down from the pushing, just like the head of a rag doll. The salon owner was unconscious. Duffy looked around the salon room. One more place to check; one little stupid hope. He ran to the hallway and barged into the little private bathroom, not stopping to knock; there was no one there. Duffy ran down the staircase to the first floor, taking the steps two at a time, his gun drawn, the safety off, desperation and fury rising like bile in his throat.

Nancy Todd jerked the van into second gear; the back wheels spit gravel as the van turned sharply into the parking lot at George Washington University Hospital. The parking lot was full; she cruised along one row of parked cars, then another. Midway through the third row, she pulled the van to a stop; she was stopped behind the dusty chrome bumpers of Frances Foster's old blue station wagon. There was a University parking ticket on the windshield. In less than one minute, they were out of the van, shoving the chocolate carton into the rear cargo door of the big station wagon, stuffing the plastic bags of Von Roehm Chocolate Company uniforms into the back seat. And Nancy was walking away from them, strolling through the University hospital parking lot and into the main entrance of the hospital complex, her eyes blurred with tears. She wanted to go on, to go with them all the way, but this was as far as Frances would let her go. Much earlier, in Cooperstown, she had argued with Frances to no avail about this. No, Frances had told her. You have your family, your life in New York. Go back now while you can. I'll be in touch, Frances told her. It's OK Nancy.

And now there had not even been time to say goodbye; there had just been a quick squeeze of Frances' hands, a parting whisper of good luck to Nora and Elizabeth, who looked so young and strong. The glass entrance doors parted automatically as Nancy Todd entered the hospital complex, where she went into the gift shop and purchased an arrangement of silk flowers to take home to New York. When she emerged from the complex five minutes later, the blue station wagon was gone, and the white van was sitting in its place. Nancy did not look over at the van as she walked to a taxi stand. She was on her way to Union Station, where she would board an afternoon train to New York. She would be home in time for dinner tonight in Queens, New York.

Secret Service agents Harry Hughes and Eugene Duffy were shaking the unconscious Roberto Quintero and slapping him across the face. Quintero's silent tongue lolled from between his lips, flapping there. It was no use; Quintero was out cold. "Shit," whispered Hughes, who was the senior member of the First Lady's detail today. They had searched the building in vain for First

Lady Mary Holt Morgan. A disaster of stunning proportions was shaping up; the First Lady had been abducted from under their very noses. Duffy was engulfed in rage and frustration. He was responsible for this; they got her on his watch. Four minutes had gone by since Duffy opened the door to the private salon; Eugene Duffy wished he were dead.

Hughes let go of the unconscious Quintero. "Get him downstairs into the limo," he yelled to Duffy. He would take care of Roberto Quintero later. Hughes remembered the Von Roehm Chocolate Company truck; he remembered the women wheeling the chocolate carton out the back door of The Chocolatier. Those women had her! He raced downstairs, hurtling down the stairs and out through the salon to The Chocolatier, where he confronted the startled clerk, his gun drawn, murder written all over his face.

Two minutes later, the terrified little clerk found herself in the long black limousine of First Lady Mary Holt Morgan, sitting next to Roberto Quintero, who was slumped next to her, his head against her shoulder, a rivulet of spittle running down his chin. Hughes was sitting next to her, his big black gun fastened on her face, and the limousine was careening through Georgetown, the traffic parting before it. In the front seat, Duffy was on the secure black telephone, whispering urgently to the Chief of the Secret Service, who until three minutes ago had been calmly eating a ham and cheese sandwich in the White House mess. In another three minutes, after activating roadblocks on every exit out of the District of Columbia, and after issuing a top priority alert for a white van belonging to the Von Roehm Chocolate Company, the Chief of the Secret Service would go upstairs and inform President Edward Morgan that his wife Mary had been abducted, apparently by four women in a fucking chocolate truck.

Elizabeth McKinley turned the blue station wagon onto Virginia Avenue, driving southeast toward Constitution. For the noon hour, traffic was light. Congress was not in session, and the capital was slumbering in the dog days of summer. Frances Foster was beside her in the front seat, and Nora O'Brien was in the back seat. Behind Nora, inside the chocolate carton in the rear of the station wagon, First Lady Mary Holt Morgan lay unconscious, curled up in the fetal position, her breathing shallow and drawn out, her eyelids fluttering over unseeing eyes. Elizabeth reached the intersection at Constitution Avenue; the traffic surged, sweeping the station wagon onto the broad avenue. How much time did they have left, Elizabeth thought. Roberto Quintero had surely been found by now. Not much time, she thought. She turned off Constitution, heading south now toward the Tidal Basin and the Potomac River. She hoped to God the *Reliance* would be waiting for them; she was certain roads and bridges out of the District of Columbia would be blocked soon. She fingered her gun, which lay beside her on the front seat, and she wondered if the First Lady was going to suffocate in that little box back there. Wouldn't it be funny if she suffocated in the dark back there, Elizabeth thought, running her free hand up and down the gun barrel.

Frances looked anxiously out the window as the station wagon turned down 17th Street, cruising past the Washington Monument. The Tidal Basin was just ahead; in a few more minutes they would be along the Potomac and she would see the *Reliance* bobbing in the water, its white hull shining. Crowds of tourists choked the walkways along 17th, their faces hot and red in the sun. The station wagon turned onto East Basin Drive, sweeping around the perimeter of the Tidal Basin. In another five minutes, perhaps in another four, they would be at the moorage on the Potomac; they would be safe aboard the *Reliance*. Frances leaned back against the car seat. Suddenly she was tired; suddenly the tension of the past weeks, the tension of this moment, filled her with the bone-weary ache of exhaustion. She willed herself to hold on; there was more than two hours of traveling ahead of them, two hours in the hot sun, two hours of traveling on open ground with her old schoolmate Mary Holt. Would Mary sleep for two long hours? Frances worried about the anesthetic; she did not want Mary to sleep forever. She twisted in her seat, turning back to Nora, who was readying another hypodermic needle. "Can she get her breath in there Nora? She's breathing all right inside there, isn't she?" Frances asked.

Nora reached back and opened the cover of the carton. Heaving herself up against the seat, she looked in, just as if she were looking at a sleeping kitten in there. "She's fine. I want to give her another shot right before we board the *Reliance*," Nora said. "How much longer?"

Frances glanced out the window. They were past the Tidal Basin; she could see East Potomac Park across the river. "Two minutes," she said. The traffic buzzed around them. Were there roadblocks above them on the George Washington Bridge? Were the roadblocks in place already? If they were lucky, they would never find out, Frances thought.

Just over two minutes had gone by when Elizabeth pulled the station wagon into the public parking lot at the Potomac Marina. There was a spot near the public landing, and Elizabeth eased the station wagon into it and turned off the engine. Frances would carry their duffel down to the boat; Elizabeth and Nora were to transport their precious little box of human cargo. Elizabeth reached up and pulled the car registration from the dashboard; the glove compartment was already empty. They would leave nothing behind, not even the license plate, which would be snapped off at the last moment. Frances Foster's heart began to beat faster; the terrible exhausted feeling was swept away by the sight of the *Reliance* rocking gently in the slow current of the Potomac River, waiting for them.

No one was waiting for Jack Riley when he pulled up to the closed gates of Frances Foster's old family home in East Hampton, New York, that afternoon. The gates were locked shut; no one answered when he pressed the buzzer beside the gates. There was something empty about the place, something deserted. Riley ground out his Camel cigarette beneath his heel. Well, well, he thought. Gates were made to be opened, or to be gone around. There were dense hedgerows on each side of the gates; the hedges were dark green and thick with vegetation even in August. Riley looked around once more; he was alone there on the wide street in front of Frances Foster's gate, alone on the outside looking in, just as he had been all of his life. But not this time, he thought, smiling to himself. With one smooth athletic thrust, he reached for the top of the gate, pulled himself up and propelled himself over. He landed with a soft thud on the other side, the soles of his feet bouncing lightly on the gravel.

Five minutes later, and with the aid of a small steel file, Riley was inside Frances Foster's old Georgian house. He was panting slightly from the exertion, but the panting stopped as his dark brown eyes swept the living room. It was empty. There was not a stick of furniture in there. Not even a piece of paper. He stood stock still in the middle of the living room; his dark eyes, darkening even more now in the cold blood of anger, roved back and forth across the empty room. The bitch was gone. "Well shit," Jack Riley said to the emptiness. His voice was hollow in the vacant house, the sound echoing against the still walls. Riley turned and ran swiftly from room to room. First through the main floor, then up the wide staircase to the second floor, and on to the attic rooms on the third floor. There was nothing left in the house except the dust bolls his swiftly moving feet stirred up, nothing except the old shadowed imprints of furnishings that were not there anymore.

Riley's eyes narrowed as he searched through the house like a ghost. Where was she? Where had Frances Foster gone with all that money? Even now, even in the empty house, he could smell the money. Damn her!

Frances Foster eased the *Reliance* through the swift current of the Potomac River, one hand on the wheel, her white hair blowing out behind her. Nora O'Brien and Elizabeth McKinley were in the galley below decks, the unconscious form of First Lady Mary Holt Morgan stretched out between them, her golden hair spread out like a fan on the cushions. The *Reliance* rocked to and fro in the current, its engines roaring on full throttle down the Potomac. They already had passed beneath the Woodrow Wilson Memorial Bridge, steaming under Highway 95, the beltway that encircled Washington and its surrounding suburbs. The *Reliance* slowed as Frances throttled back, easing toward the little harbor near Belle Haven, Virginia. The marina was just ahead. Frances let out a long breath; she would miss the *Reliance*.

On the floating dock at the marina, Helene Dupré, her long steel gray hair drawn into a braid down her back, dark glasses covering her hazel eyes, raised a long arm to her head to shade the sun still more. She could see the *Reliance* coming slowly toward the dock. Frances was right on time. Helene hoped their little bundle was on board the *Reliance*; she hoped fervently that her old friend Frances Foster was at the wheel and that all was well below decks. Helene had been aboard the *Reliance* many times over the years, once for a memorable three week trip up along the Bay of Fundy between Nova Scotia and New Brunswick, Canada. Had it been twenty years since that trip with Frances and her little girl Hillary? Yes. And now the *Reliance* was on another journey altogether; Helene Dupré and Frances

Foster were on another kind of voyage this time. Helene Dupré
was not afraid. She refused to even acknowledge that such an
emotion could be within her. Not after all these years of running
her little place in Connecticut by herself.

Helene knew all about varmints; they plagued her sheep farm
in rural Connecticut. It was why she kept her .22 loaded and
ready to go right on the kitchen table where she could get at it
quick. So here she was helping Frannie go after another kind of
varmint. Once she got Frannie and the others loaded into the
pickup truck she had parked in the first space next to the dock,
Helene would take over the *Reliance*, going on alone, piloting
the vessel to a yacht brokerage at Oyster Bay. Helene would miss
Frances Foster and the *Reliance* and the old house at East Hampton. But at sixty-four, she knew damned well that nothing stays
the same. The damned Rights for the Unborn League had made
sure of that, hadn't they. The damned self-righteous weasels.
Frannie would show them, Helene thought. Good for Frannie.
And when it was over, she would visit Frannie in Sweden, and
take them some good wool for sweaters. It was cold over there.

Helene Dupré threw a line over the bow of the *Reliance* as it
nudged against the dock. She grinned at Frances in the pilot
house as she pulled the line taut. Frannie is going to make it, she
thought, grinning once more. Frannie will show them.

President Edward Morgan listened calmly as Secret Service
Harry Hughes told him what they knew so far. Edward Morgan
wanted to hear it direct from Harry. Young Eugene Duffy was
standing beside Harry, and James Peterson, Chief of the Secret
Service, was next to them both. They had found the Von Roehm
Chocolate Company van in the parking lot at George Washington
University Hospital. The van was empty, of course, and the Von
Roehm Chocolate Company did not exist. The Secret Service
was crawling over the two buildings in Georgetown, but Presi-

dent Morgan should know that nothing had been found in either building. The hairdresser, Quintero, was still out cold, but the little clerk from the chocolate shop was wide awake and trying hard to help them. She had already given them a pretty good description of the women. Quintero and the clerk were both over in the old Executive Office Building, down in the basement. They weren't going anywhere. The lid was nailed shut on this, and with any luck, they could keep it that way.

Edward Morgan's eyes narrowed. His wife had many enemies. Maybe even more than he did. He wasn't even sure what she had been up to lately, and while he would not admit this to the Chief of the Secret Service, he had even wondered whether she was fooling around on him. But that didn't matter now. What mattered was getting her back and keeping a lid on this. Morgan turned to James Peterson. "Do you think a foreign power is behind this, Jim?" Edward Morgan dreaded the thought of an international incident. Especially if they killed her. He felt a sudden rush of emotion; it was like a powerful wave washing over him. All these years together. He clenched his jaw together until it hurt.

The long professional career of James Peterson, first with the Bureau of Alcohol, Tobacco and Firearms, and then as a Secret Service agent and now finally as Chief, had prepared him for the worst. But the worst had always been losing the President. There had never been a serious attempt on a First Lady. Threats, yes. Incidents, yes. But never this. And by women. If it weren't for the women, Jim Peterson would point his strong fingers at the Libyans. But the women had looked like Americans, and the older one, the one who seemed to be in charge, had clearly been an American from the east coast of the United States, probably from the northeast. "It doesn't look like a foreign job, Mr. President. We're virtually certain the women are Americans. We have roadblocks up. There is a chance we can contain them in the District."

President Edward Morgan shook his head slowly. Too much time had gone by now. She had been missing for more than an hour. Whoever had her had gotten away clean. A part of Edward Morgan was relieved that his wife's kidnappers were women. Somehow, he believed she might be safer with women. But what did they want? They would want money of course, but Edward Morgan knew that more than money was on the table here; more than money was always on the table. The FBI Director was on his way to the White House now, along with the Chairman of the Joint Chiefs and the Director of the Central Intelligence Agency. One advantage still was theirs: the press didn't know. Edward Morgan was determined that they would not find out; he did not want every two-bit terrorist group around the globe taking responsibility for his wife's kidnapping. "I want the task force on this based here," Morgan said, pointing a thick finger at the Aubusson carpet. "In the family quarters. This is where they'll call. And I want the lid on!" he added, his voice shaking now with rage. Who were these women that they dared to kidnap the First Lady of the United States? He would see them shot if they hurt her!

Less than an hour later, James Peterson called the assembled task force together. They were in the Lincoln bedroom, where a bank of secure telephones, a computer system, and an institutional coffee pot had been set up. The coffee was brewing, filling the Lincoln bedroom with the smell. It was just after 2:00 P.M. on August 14, and the whirring air conditioners did not cool the stifling heat in the room. Peterson distributed a computer-enhanced drawing of the woman who they believed had been in charge of the kidnapping. She was in her sixties, and she looked just like a suburban matron who should have been playing a quiet little game of bridge somewhere.

James Peterson heard the unmistakable tread of President Edward Morgan coming down the hall toward the Lincoln bedroom. President Morgan was flat-footed, and his footsteps always sounded like pancakes slapping against the carpet. The President was going to lead the task force himself.

Chapter Sixteen

Elizabeth McKinley brought the pickup truck to a shuddering halt in the rough clearing beside the old farmhouse outside of Middletown, Virginia. They were deep in the enveloping folds of the Appalachian foothills now, deep in the limestone heart of those sheltering mountains, alone at last with First Lady Mary Holt Morgan, President of the Rights for the Unborn League. Frances Foster was beside Elizabeth in the front seat, shading her eyes from the bright afternoon sun. And in the bed of the pickup, sheltered by a fiberglass canopy, Mary Holt Morgan lay beside Nora O'Brien, who was checking the First Lady's blood pressure once more. Nora had ridden all the way from the marina in the back of the pickup, crouched beside the First Lady, who slept on, stretched out on a thick blanket. The First Lady's forehead was damp with perspiration; it had been hot under the canopy in the back of the pickup truck, and damp tendrils of her golden hair were wet on her flushed face. Elizabeth sighed and leaned her head back against the upholstery. Her neck ached; she wanted to rest there, just for a minute before they went in. They had not been followed; she knew that now. She peered out at the old shingled farmhouse that Middletown realtor Thomas B. Tuttle had leased to Missus Frances Foster two weeks ago. The windows along the second story of the house were in shadow now, the afternoon sun blocked by a massive oak tree that crowded against the east side of the old saltbox house. But even in the shadows, Elizabeth could see thick plywood sheets nailed to the inside of two windows at the corner of the house; the plywood sheets would be the bars on First Lady Mary Holt Morgan's prison. Elizabeth heard Frances beside her, opening the passenger door.

More than an hour passed before Mary Holt Morgan felt the first stirrings of consciousness, before she felt the warm wet fog that had wrapped her in a dreamless sleep begin to lift. Her head felt thick, like there was cotton there; she felt cotton in her mouth, dry and sour-tasting. Her eyelids fluttered; they felt so heavy, like lead, so hard to lift. It seemed so dark here. Had Roberto turned out the lights? Had she slept after his massage? She felt something rough on the bed beside her. Her fingers rubbed against it. What was that. Something smelled funny here. A musty old smell. With an effort, she forced her eyes open. "Roberto?" she murmured. She was so tired, wasn't she; she was worn out. She closed her eyes once more.

Frances and Nora were standing in front of Mary Holt Morgan, watching her waking from her long sleep. The First Lady was on a narrow cot in an upstairs bedroom of the old saltbox. Elizabeth was downstairs, in the living room, where she was stationed at a front window that looked out on the clearing in front of the saltbox and onto the rutted dirt track that led out to the main road. Her fingers were wrapped tightly around her automatic pistol.

First Lady Mary Holt Morgan began moving her fingers against the canvas side of the cot and her eyelids fluttered open once again. The upstairs bedroom was very dark; only the light from the hallway illuminated it. Frances raised her long black barrel and pointed it at the First Lady's head. Now, Frances thought. Now she gets to make her first phone call; now she starts to pay us back. Frances felt something hot in her chest, like a hot red ball there; it was hatred so powerful it nearly took her breath away. Its strength frightened her, so fierce was her hatred, so murderous. It occurred to Frances that she could squeeze the trigger on the automatic pistol she was holding right now; she could squeeze and fire and the object of her hatred would be gone from this life, gone forever. No, Frances thought. Oh no. She reached her other hand out to Nora O'Brien; now she needed Nora. The pistol trembled in her hand. Frances felt Nora move closer; now their shoulders were touching. She felt Nora's hand on her arm, just resting there. It gave her strength somehow, just feeling Nora next to her like that. Frances could go on now; she could look down at the figure of Mary Holt Morgan stirring on the cot, asking for Roberto Quintero, who was not here, and she could go on. "Roberto is gone, Mary. You're with us now," Frances said.

Nora moved swifly to the side of the cot, grabbed the First Lady's wrist, and snapped a handcuff on it. She pulled the First Lady's arm down and fastened the other handcuff to the exposed aluminum rail of the cot. There you are, sweetheart, Nora thought. Now you're snug and safe right here. Safer than Mike Green had been in Algiers, she thought. Mike Green never had a chance to ask your police anything, did he. No. You killed him before he had a chance to cry out for mercy, didn't you. Dr. Michael Green's face floated before her; his thick brown hair with its dumb little cowlick, his small calloused fingers, his gentle voice asking her how many would there be tonight, how many were coming to their little clinic. But Mike Green was gone. He was dead and Mary Holt Morgan was alive. She was their pricey ticket to safety and a safe new clinic in Sweden, wasn't she. Pricey little bitch. We'll take good care of her, Nora thought. She reached for the First Lady's handcuffed wrist and counted her pulse. It was a good strong pulse. Using the flat of her hand,

Nora reached up and briskly slapped Mary Holt Morgan across the face.

The First Lady's eyes flew open and her head jerked toward them. "What?" Now she felt the sensations of full consciousness rolling through her body, pitching her awake. She looked up and saw two women standing there above her in this dim room and she felt something pulling on her wrist when she tried to raise her arm; it kept her arm imprisoned down there.

"Wake up, Mary," Frances insisted. She reached down and grabbed the First Lady's shoulders, pulling her to a sitting position on the sofa. "Wake up." Frances' angry gray eyes bored into the startled white face of her old schoolmate. "You will do exactly what I tell you to do or I'll kill you right now. Right here." Frances raised her automatic pistol and pointed at the First Lady's face, aiming it at the middle of Mary Morgan's high white forehead.

Mary Holt Morgan drew a ragged breath. So these people kidnapped her; that was obvious now. How long had she been unconscious? Where was she? She prayed to God that she was still in the United States. "You'll never get away with this," she whispered fiercely, her white teeth bared at them. Where was the Secret Service, for God's sake? Mary felt the hot throb of fear race through her body, pounding in every part of her. "You'll get the death penalty for this!" she hissed at them.

Frances Foster looked at the First Lady, at the murderous rage on her white face, at the flinty blue eyes staring up at her in the dim light. "Don't tempt me, Mary," Frances said tautly. She pushed the pistol closer to the First Lady, shoving the thin black barrel against her forehead.

Mary felt the gun barrel pressing against her skin. Please Lord help me, she thought desperately. Who are these people? She shrank back from the terrible gun barrel, from the smell of oil on smooth steel. Play for time, she thought. Be smart now; you want to live through this. "What do you want me to do?" she whispered to them.

At a gesture from Frances, Nora walked to the door and picked up an electronic telephone. A thin cord ran from the telephone all the way down the staircase and outside the saltbox to the pickup truck parked in the clearing. It was late in the afternoon now, almost 5:00 P.M., and the First Lady was going to call home, to her dear husband, President Edward Morgan, who was surely waiting to hear from her.

When the private telephone rang in the family quarters, President Edward Morgan picked it up himself, lifting the extension in the Lincoln bedroom, which now was crowded with men and equipment. He felt a vast relief wash over him when her voice came over the line, echoing as if she were talking through a tunnel. She began talking immediately, in a kind of sing-song voice, as if she were reading something aloud.

"I am safe. Please prepare electronic bank transfers for $100 million. Fifty million from the White House. Fifty million from the Rights for the Unborn League," the First Lady pleaded, her voice rising. "Edward—"

The line went dead in Morgan's ear. He looked up at Secret Service Chief James Peterson. "Did you get that?"

Peterson was already deep in thought. The Rights for the Unborn League, he thought. Well isn't this a pretty picture. This was almost worse than some two-bit foreign crowd. So the pro-abortion people had her. Good Christ, that was half the country. Peterson looked into the pasty face of President Edward Morgan; he saw terror there. "We picked up everything. Not enough time for a good location," Peterson said gently. "We may be able to break it out in a computer search; at least we can get a regional radius on it," Peterson said.

Edward Morgan pulled himself up to his full height of six feet two-and-a-half inches. "Do it, then. And get Carlton Farnsworth over here," he said to Peterson. Morgan turned to Albert Arntsen, the Director of the Central Intelligence Agency, who was standing beside him. "Al, I'll need a check from you people. I haven't got that much in the White House contingency fund, thanks to the fucking boys on the Hill." Congress had, over the last few years, clamped down on the President's famed ability to cover a large variety of special political expenses. Until now, it had been just an annoyance, like a fly buzzing around the dinner table, irritating him. But at this moment, Edward Morgan hated the Congress for strapping him like this.

Albert Arntsen, who had been CIA Director for five years now, and who carried secrets within his small, slight body that stretched back over nearly twenty-five years of political and bureaucratic warfare in the District of Columbia, would have no trouble finding $50 million. That was peanuts for Albert Arntsen; it was a drop in the bucket. "I'll take care of the White House funds," Arntsen said. The CIA Director paused. He could see that his old friend Eddie Morgan was going to collapse on this one; he could already see the unconditional surrender. Albert Arntsen did not like losing, not when he had such truly magnificent files on the pro-abortion groups out there. Very tentatively, Arntsen leaned toward the President. "We'll start a search based on our current information on pro-abortion groups," he said, speaking in his customary low monotone, which could not be heard from a distance of more than a few feet.

President Edward Morgan whirled on the CIA Director, towering over Albert Arntsen. "Now hear this! Don't do anything to make this worse," Morgan yelled. "Nothing!" Edward Morgan loomed threateningly over Arntsen, his jaw working furiously. The CIA Director stood his ground, silently absorbing the President's anger. The others crowded into the Lincoln bedroom—

Secret Service Chief Jim Peterson, FBI Director Clayton Mandel, Gen. Robert Lander, Chairman of the Joint Chiefs, and three trusted computer technicians—fell quiet, and their eyes dropped to the floor as the silence between President Edward Morgan and the CIA Director stretched out like a rubber band. It was Edward Morgan who broke the silence at last. "You know what I mean, Al," he said finally. "I want her back."

Albert Arntsen nodded slowly. He understood. A man has his priorities in this life; nobody understood that better than Al Arntsen, who had stopped trying to change his own after his fourth wife walked out on him.

President Edward Morgan swallowed hard. After they got her back, after it was all over, then he would turn his old pal Al Arntsen loose on these people, whoever they were. He remembered the demand for $50 million from the Rights for the Unborn League. Edward Morgan had never been comfortable with his wife's involvement in the League. She should have been with him; she should have been right here at his side instead of going off on her own like that, as if being First Lady of the United States wasn't enough for her. And now look where it had gotten them all.

Frances Foster opened the door to the little upstairs bedroom, flinging it open all the way; light from the hallway outside flooded the room and the cot where First Lady Mary Holt Morgan was sitting up now, her wrist handcuffed to the cot. Frances watched as Mary Morgan blinked in the bright light. The plywood they had nailed over the windows had kept the upstairs bedroom in the old saltbox artificially dark all this time. Frances stepped close to the cot and looked down at the First Lady. She was smaller than Frances remembered from the old days when they were lab partners at the Crofton School, but the cold blue eyes were the same, and the straight line of her closed mouth was the same, too. Mary Holt Morgan was still the little perfectionist, wasn't she. Still the self-righteous one. "You don't remember me, do you," Frances said.

Mary Morgan raised her eyes to Frances Foster's face. She saw a woman about her own age. She searched her memory. But there were so many people to remember; she couldn't remember them all. And this woman wanted $100 million from her husband and from the Rights for the Unborn League. She knew the White House would get the money, but the League extortion enraged her; how dare these women steal from the League! Robbing the money from her very own organization, from the people who had contributed all that money to keep the League going. Now that was simply obscene. Her lips tightened into an even straighter line. Mary Holt Morgan never doubted that she would survive this. Except for the one moment when this horrible woman standing in front of her had pressed that gun barrel against her forehead, Mary Morgan had simply steeled herself to endure this terror; she simply said her silent prayers and knew the Lord was going to take care of her in her hour of need. She stared up at Frances. She didn't know her at all. But she knew these women were pro-abortion fanatics, didn't she. "No. I don't remember you," Mary Morgan said.

Frances moved closer; she was just a few feet away from the figure on the cot now. Nora was standing in the shadows by the boarded up windows. Frances could feel Nora watching her. "I'm Frannie Foster. From Crofton School. A long time ago," Frances reminded her.

The First Lady started to rise from the cot and then sank back down. "Frannie? My God." Her mind raced. Frannie Foster from the Crofton School. It was so long ago; it was another world. Frannie Foster. The name jabbed at her memory. She forced herself to remember back. But she had been so miserable then; and there was something awful back there, something terrible that she never wanted to remember.

Frances watched Mary Holt Morgan's expression change; she watched as a ripple of terror stirred the First Lady's frigid face. "Something happened to you at the Crofton School, didn't it. Something you've kept secret all these years," Frances said. Very slowly, Frances Foster drew a yellowed piece of paper from her pocket; it was a page from her father's journal.

First Lady Mary Holt Morgan's eyes were very wide now, wide with fear. She felt her heart pounding fast, and she felt heat rising to her head, just as if all the blood in her body were racing to her head, as if her head were going to explode with the heat. "I don't know what you mean," she whispered.

Frances unfolded the paper, opening it completely, and held it in front of the First Lady. "My father kept a journal," Frances said. "You remember my father. Dr. Hugh Foster. Dr. Foster who performed your abortion. You were carrying a seventeen-week fetus. A second trimester fetus. It's all here, written in his journal." She held the paper away from the First Lady, just out of her reach.

The room was very still; outside, the late afternoon sun was sinking behind the leafy birch trees and the shadows from the trees that fell across the clearing were beginning to lengthen. A fly buzzed along the ceiling in the bedroom where the First Lady sat like a statue on the cot. Across the room, Nora watched the First Lady's rigid expression begin to crumble; Nora had seen this before, so many times before on so many young women. She had seen the beginnings of it on Hillary Foster that night, that familiar expression of terror and grief mingled with relief. But Hillary Foster was dead and Mary Holt Morgan was alive. The First Lady started to speak; her mouth opened as if she were going to say something, to answer Frances, but then she closed it again, drawing her lower lip inward and biting on it with her white even teeth.

Frances Foster held the yellowed paper aloft. "The members of the Rights for the Unborn League who worship you and send you their money wouldn't be pleased if they knew about this, would they," Frances said. "They wouldn't like to know that you had betrayed them. That you are a liar and a hypocrite. That you outlaw for others what you provide for yourself."

The First Lady closed her eyes and turned away. "It wasn't like that. You don't understand." Her head pounded and she felt the sting of tears in her eyes. "It broke my heart. I've never forgiven myself for what happened." She didn't like to remember what had happened back then; she had just pushed it far away, far back into a little corner of her memory, where it had rested until now, small and still and secret. God damn that doctor for keeping records! How could that little man do that after her mother paid him all that money. Even now, nearly a half-century later, she remembered that night in his office. He had been so nice to her, patting her on the shoulder and telling her she was going to be just fine, it was all right Mary. Only it had never been all right. Not ever. But at least it had been her secret; at least nobody ever knew about her shame.

Nora O'Brien moved out of the shadows by the boarded up windows across the room, and for the first time, she spoke to the First Lady. "You should have forgiven yourself. It would have been better for all of us if you had," Nora said. But Nora could not be sympathetic now; it was too late for any damned sympathy.

The First Lady saw what they wanted now; she saw that they would betray her if they didn't get the money. Mary Holt Morgan looked up at the yellowed paper Frances Foster was holding and she saw her wonderful life, her leadership of the Rights for the Unborn League, her public appearances, the adoration of all those people, the love they had for her, dissolving into a horrible swirl of nasty ugly publicity and scorn. Oh God, she would rather die than face that; she didn't think she could stand to face such a thing. But they wouldn't expose her, would they. They would take the money and go away. Everything would be all right then; everything would be just like it was before. "I'll never tell anyone what happened or anything else. I'll make sure you get the money!" she said urgently.

Frances Foster looked down at the First Lady. She felt revulsion rise like bile in her throat; the First Lady disgusted her. "We thought you would," Frances snarled. She thought of her father, her dear beloved father, who risked everything one night for a woman like Mary Holt Morgan. Now it would mean something after all. And now her daughter Hillary's death would mean something too.

On the floor below the darkened little bedroom where Mary Holt Morgan was bargaining for her life, Elizabeth McKinley was in the living room of the old saltbox house, staring fixedly out the window toward the dirt track that led out of the clearing. From far away, she could hear the unmistakable sound of an engine, a motor laboring, and the sound was growing closer. Someone was coming. Elizabeth dropped her hand from the windowsill and raced upstairs to Frances and Nora, her fingers gripping her automatic pistol. They would have to shut the First Lady up right now, Elizabeth thought as her running feet reached the top of the staircase. She was panting for breath as Frances came out of the little bedroom, closing the door behind her. "Frances, somebody is coming! For God's sake shut that bitch up," Elizabeth said.

Frances leaned against the closed door. Nora was inside with the First Lady. She tried to listen, straining to hear what was coming. There it was. She could hear the sound of a motor; it sounded loud now, terribly loud and near. Dear God, she thought. OK, Frances, she told herself sternly. You just get a grip on yourself right now. She turned to Elizabeth. "It's probably nobody important. Go back downstairs. I'll be down in a minute." Frances jerked her head toward the closed door. "Don't worry about her. Nora will take care of it." She looked once more at Elizabeth. There was something in Elizabeth's face, something dangerous there, a kind of terrible wildness in her eyes that frightened Frances. She wondered suddenly if Elizabeth were about to do something foolish. She reached out to her, grabbing her by the arm. "Put the gun away. We don't want anyone to see these guns, Elizabeth," Frances warned. She saw a clouded expression pass over Elizabeth McKinley's face; it resembled the expression of a sleepwalker. Then it was gone and Elizabeth was nodding silently, agreeing with Frances. Frances released her grip and Elizabeth turned and ran back down the stairs. Frances looked at her retreating figure for another second and then she opened the bedroom door and went back inside to Nora and the First Lady. In less than a minute, as the motor noise grew louder and whoever was coming up the farm road grew closer, Nora O'Brien was standing over the still and frightened form of Mary Morgan, Nora's automatic pistol just a few inches from Mary Morgan's sweating forehead, and Frances was on her way downstairs, to meet whatever it was that was coming toward them.

Less that a quarter of a mile away from the farmhouse, a battered yellow pickup truck rocked and lurched on the rutted road leading to the farmhouse. Inside the pickup, Middletown realtor Thomas B. Tuttle ground the gearshift on his old reliable pickup into second gear. Lord this old road was a bad one! It had been a long slow afternoon down at the office in Middletown today, and Thomas B. Tuttle had decided that this would be a fine day to drive on up to the old Fletcher place, the farm he had rented to that nice lady from New York, Missus Foster. He figured she just might be there by now, and hey, she might need some help up there! Tuttle could direct her to some fine local fellas who could be depended on to cut wood and clean the place up for her. God knew the Fletcher place needed a cleaning up, didn't it. Tuttle sucked ferociously on the cigarette clamped in his mouth as the pickup jounced over a dried-up mud hole in the farm road. Good thing it wasn't much farther now, he thought. The old pickup didn't like this jouncing and it was getting late, too. He didn't want to be on this little old road after dark. No sir. Tuttle bit down on the cigarette and gripped the steering wheel as the truck rounded the last curve and chugged into the farmhouse clearing.

Hey, look at that nice little red pickup there, Thomas Tuttle thought. Why it looks almost brand new. It surely does. He straightened up his bony shoulders and clamped the good old gray fedora on his head. That red pickup must belong to Missus Foster, he thought. He grinned to himself. It was nice to rent the place to a quality person like Missus Foster, he thought, squinting out the window now at the front porch of the saltbox house. There she was now, right there on the front porch. She was waving at him, too. She recognized him right off, didn't she. He pulled his yellow pickup right in behind her red one and hopped out. She was coming right down off the porch to greet him. Wasn't that nice, he thought. He doffed his fedora respectfully and smiled warmly at the nice woman. "Missus Foster. I just thought I'd drop by and see how you were doing," Tuttle greeted her when she reached him in the front yard.

Frances Foster shuddered inwardly as she advanced on realtor Thomas B. Tuttle. They had to get rid of him right now. "Mr. Tuttle. How nice," she said, extending her hand to him, wishing his brightly smiling face away from them, wishing Tuttle and his yellow pickup truck away from the farmhouse and the clearing and back to Middletown. Obviously, he wanted to come inside. She couldn't let him. "We're just in the middle of cleaning up the old place," she said brightly. "I'd invite you in, but really, it would be such an imposition on you."

Tuttle looked past her to the saltbox. It did look like Missus Foster and whoever was in there with her were hard at work, didn't it. His gaze lifted to the second story. He squinted up at it. Those two end windows looked boarded up from the inside didn't they. That was odd. For the first time, Thomas B. Tuttle grew uncomfortable. Renters shouldn't go and board up windows like that. Not even renters like Missus Foster. Tuttle's smile began to fade; he hoped he hadn't been wrong about her.

Frances saw where Tuttle was staring. He had seen the boarded up windows. She smiled brightly once more. "I'm afraid we're having to paint one of the upstairs bedrooms. The walls were—. Well," she said, sighing gently. "We simply couldn't leave them like that. So filthy," she said.

Thomas Tuttle heaved an almost visible sigh of relief. Of course. Missus Foster was painting the place. Why hadn't he thought of that. He tried to remember that upstairs bedroom, what it had looked like up there, but he couldn't recall it exactly.

Five minutes later, after an earnest discussion with Missus Foster regarding the availability of local help for her painting and cleaning and so forth, Thomas B. Tuttle climbed back into his yellow pickup truck and drove away, his truck bouncing over the ruts in the old road. Missus Foster had invited him to a picnic a week from Sunday out at the old place. Wasn't that nice of her, he thought to himself. And of course he could handle the hiring of any local help for her. Not to worry there!

Chapter Seventeen

The telephone was jangling in Jack Riley's hotel room when he arrived early that evening after a long drive to Washington from Frances Foster's big Georgian house at East Hampton. Riley was hot and sweaty and he wanted a cool shower and a hot drink. He looked for a moment at the ringing telephone, thinking about whether to answer it. They could leave a damned message, he thought. He could get a message after he cooled off. But the telephone did not stop ringing; it rang on and on insistently. Well shit, he thought, striding across the thick hotel room carpet to the bedside telephone. Whoever it was didn't want to wait, did they.

Riley heard Carlton Farnsworth's voice trumpeting through the telephone even before the receiver reached his ear. Farnsworth was shouting, asking Riley where the hell he had been and didn't Riley know he should check in at the League! Farnsworth calmed down after about fifteen seconds of this tirade, and then he delivered his message. "The First Lady has been kidnapped and they want $100 million for her, including $50 million from the League," he rasped into the telephone. Farnsworth went on for another two minutes, filling Riley in on the kidnapping. "The President thinks it's pro-abortionists. People who hate the League. So if you know anything, if you can do anything, get on it," Farnsworth finished.

Riley shifted the telephone receiver to his other ear and reached for his new bottle of Bushmills whiskey. A hundred million. Now that was real money. And he could hear the desperate notes in old Carlton's voice, couldn't he. Fifty million dollars from the League itself. Surely the League would compensate their Special Security Agent if he could get their money back. Sure they would. "I may be able to help," he said slowly. "A finders fee would accelerate my efforts, Carlton. A ten percent finders fee on the League money." He could hear the sharp intake of breath at the other end of the phone and he smiled as he waited for Carlton Farnsworth to answer him, smiling to himself as he poured a shot of Bushmills and drank it down.

Farnsworth, who was at Rights for the Unborn League Headquarters, and who when he finished with this call would begin assembling $50 million in bank drafts which he would take to the White House with him a very short time from now, smiled a terrible little smile. He should get rid of Jack Riley. In fact, he should take care of that little matter just as soon as this other one was taken care of. He wanted to fire Mr. Riley right now, but the thought of recovering their $50 million, minus Riley's extortion of a $5 million finder's fee, prevented Farnsworth from doing that. Instead, he said yes to the finder's fee, and he allowed himself to hope that Jack Riley knew something he didn't. Someone should know something. He didn't ask Riley what it was; he knew Riley wouldn't tell him anyway. Jack Riley was like that.

After Riley finished his conversation with Farnsworth, he pulled a wrinkled business card from his pocket, turning it over and over in his hand. It was the only thing he had brought back to Washington from Frances Foster's empty house at East Hampton, and he had found it on the floor of the empty garage. The geometric marks of a running car tire marched across the card, and a corner had been torn away, but Riley still could read what was on there. He smiled to himself and picked up the telephone once again, this time to dial a number. He was calling the Middletown, Virginia, office of Thomas B. Tuttle, proprietor of Tuttle Realty. Mr. Tuttle's business card declared that his was a twenty-four-hour a day office. Jack Riley hoped it was, because he was almost certain that Frances Foster was with the First Lady tonight, and he was hoping that this dirty little business card was going to turn out to be worth five million dollars.

Tuttle was in his Middletown office when Riley called. It had been nearly dark by the time he got back from the old Fletcher farm and parked the yellow pickup in front of his office, and he had considered just going on home tonight and picking up his messages in the morning. But Thomas B. Tuttle was not one to let any little blades of grass grow under his feet, was he. No indeed. If he went home, why it would be just his luck to miss a hot call waiting at the old office, he thought as he hauled himself up the three steps to his office door and went inside.

In a very short time, Tuttle was rewarded for his diligence by a call from Washington. It was a fella named Jack Riley, and he was looking for Frances Foster. He thought she might be in the Middletown neighborhood, he said. He was Frances Foster's younger brother and his big sister Frances had been talking about acquiring some property down that way, Mr. Riley said. In fact, Mr. Riley himself was thinking he might just be interested in doing a little serious shopping himself.

Tom Tuttle's chest puffed out and he stood up straight. "I just arrived here at my office from visiting with your dear sister at a charming old farm she has rented for the summer, Mister Riley. In fact, I will be returning there a week from Sunday for a picnic dinner," Tuttle announced over the telephone to Jack Riley. His nicotine-stained teeth gleamed yellow in the overhead light. He was already running over his real estate inventory in his mind, thinking of properties that might just fit this nice Jack Riley fella.

In his hotel room in Washington, Riley smiled a wide juicy smile. Maybe he was going to be in luck here. "I hope my sister isn't all alone out there," Riley said.

"Oh no! There was people there with her," Thomas B. Tuttle said. He knitted his bushy eyebrows together thoughtfully. Of course he hadn't actually seen anybody else had he, except for that other lady he had glimpsed in the window downstairs. But Mr. Riley didn't need to know that, did he. "Yes, they were hard at work painting one of the upstairs bedrooms. Had the windows all boarded up and everything for the painting," Tuttle said. "The old place needs some work, I'm afraid."

Jack Riley balanced the telephone receiver on his shoulder and lit himself a Camel cigarette. Boarded up windows. He sucked on the Camel, drawing the stinging smoke down his throat. Boarded up windows in an upstairs room would give Frances Foster and whoever was with her their own private jail cell, wouldn't it. He licked his lips. Frances Foster had liquidated her estate, sold everything, and now she was holed up at a dirt farm outside of Middletown, Virginia. He would bet his last nickel that the First Lady was locked in that upstairs bedroom. The kidnapping was more than eight hours old now; he did not have much time.

Fifteen minutes later, Jack Riley was in his rented car, headed for the George Washington Bridge. A map of the Commonwealth of Virginia was on the seat beside him and his dark brown eyes were fastened on the roadway. It would be full dark in another ninety minutes. Riley wanted to be on Highway 66 and closing in on the Appalachian foothills by then. He pushed the accelerator to the floor as a surge of adrenalin pounded through his body. So he would meet First Lady Mary Holt Morgan, she whose motorcade had nearly killed him on the night of Carlton Farnsworth's plantation house party a couple of weeks ago. She had made him feel small that night, like a pile of dirt to be squashed under the hard wheels of her motorcade. But Jack Riley didn't care now how she had made him feel that night; now she was worth five million dollars to him, wasn't she, and that was all that mattered.

Frances Foster turned up the knob on the gas lantern. The bright white light from the hissing lantern shone on Mary Morgan's pinched and drawn face. It was 9:00 P.M. Time for their second call to President Edward Morgan, who had better have the electronic cash transfers ready. Frances hung the lantern from a heavy nail driven into the wall and picked up the electronic telephone. In seven hours, the International Bank of Zurich would open in Switzerland. On this Friday morning, if all went well, the International Bank of Zurich would be receiving two electronic cash transfers from the United States, which were to be deposited in a brand new numbered account. Frances brought the telephone to the cot where First Lady Mary Holt Morgan was sitting up, her back resting against the wall.

The First Lady looked up at Frances through dull and reddened eyes. It seemed like such a long time ago that she had been in Roberto's Salon, such a long time ago that he had been massaging her temples with his wonderful fingers and telling her she deserved to spoil herself. A lifetime ago.

President Edward Morgan picked up the private White House telephone on the first ring, nodding to the computer technician, who switched on his recorder and activated the computerized search apparatus. Morgan drew his full mouth into a hard line. He didn't think the computerized search program would work, but they had to try it. He had already tied CIA Director Albert Arntsen's expert hands, at least until they got her back. Edward Morgan refused to think of any other alternatives that fell short of getting his wife back. Carlton Farnsworth, Executive Director

of the Rights for the Unborn League, had come and gone now.
President Morgan had gotten the $50 million out of Farnsworth,
but the League Executive Director had whined about the money
and urged the President to hold up on the ransom. Edward Morgan would not forget this disloyalty, and he would not forgive it
either; he would settle Carlton Farnsworth's hash later. Her voice
came over the telephone now, sounding once again like she was
reading something from a long ways off, echoing in the
receiver.

"There is not much time. You are to transmit the $100 million
to account number 7653241, at the International Bank of Zurich
in Switzerland, as soon as the bank opens in the morning," Mary
Morgan said in her echoing sing-song voice. She stopped suddenly, and for the space of a second or two, there was no sound at
all on the telephone line.

Now President Edward Morgan heard something in the background, someone else talking. It sounded like a woman talking;
now there was a scuffling sound. Morgan strained to hear more.
"We'll send the money. We have the money!" President Morgan
said. He looked desperately at the computer technician, who was
nodding silently and twirling a finger at him, silently urging him
to keep her on the telephone line. "Mary, are you all right? Have
they hurt you?" He heard her draw a ragged breath.

"SEND THE MONEY OR I WILL BE SHOT TO DEATH!"

The line went dead in Edward Morgan's hand. He cursed and
slammed the telephone receiver down. "Damn them all to Hell!"
Morgan turned to the computer technician, who was slowly shaking his head as he scanned his computer screen. It had not been
enough time. Those portable telephones were hard to trace outside the District of Columbia calling area. But now that they
knew the kidnappers were using a car telephone; at least they
knew something, even if it was not very much. It was not enough
for President Edward Morgan. He turned to Albert Arntsen, his

CIA Director, who was standing beside him. "Al, start that work you want to do on the pro-abortion groups," Morgan said quietly. It was time to turn Albert Arntsen loose.

Arntsen nodded and rubbed his hands together, as if he were washing them. "I'll have the boys get right on it, Mr. President." Arntsen did not tell President Morgan that one CIA section, the one that reported to him directly, had been working the kidnapping for the last three hours. The President didn't need to know these things; he was better off not knowing them.

Nora O'Brien knocked the portable telephone from First Lady Mary Holt Morgan's shaking fingers and sent it hurtling across the upstairs room, into the darkness outside the arc of the gas lantern. She stared down at the white face of the First Lady, who shrank back against the wall, pressing herself against it as if she were trying to dissolve herself into the old lathe and plaster wall and disappear from Nora's sight. "You'll say what we tell you and no more," Nora warned her.

Nora wanted to strike the First Lady's white face; she wanted to punch it until it was purple and swollen and bloody, like the faces of the women and children Nora had cared for at Charity Hospital, the ones she would care for no more. Nora's hands were balled into fists at her sides; she felt something surging through her body, something that wanted to hit and hit the white-faced woman on the cot, something that was almost uncontrollable, almost unearthly in its power. But that would make her just like them, wouldn't it. Nora O'Brien would be no better than all the rest of them out there, the ones outside the old saltbox farmhouse, if she gave in to this thing inside of her, would she. No, she wouldn't. Very gradually, Nora's fists opened and she straightened her fingers out, flexing them as if they were stiff from holding something for a long time. Now she heard Frances Foster behind her. Frances had picked up the portable telephone and she was watching Nora, but she was not coming any closer. Nora realized that Frances did not need to come any closer because she was not afraid of what Nora might do; she was not afraid that Nora would lose control and give in to something terrible inside of her. Frances trusted her, didn't she. More than Nora trusted herself. It was almost like Frances loved her, wasn't it, almost as if Frances had a kind of loving trust in Nora that Nora had not felt from another human being since the death of Michael Green, M.D., in the little backyard clinic in Algiers.

Nora felt relief wash over her like a bath of warm water and just for a moment, she closed her eyes. When she opened them, the First Lady was sitting up straight once again. "I'm going to give Mary a shot now to help her sleep," Nora said. She heard Frances Foster's murmur of assent behind her as she pulled the First Lady's limp arm from her side and began to roll up her sleeve.

Mary Morgan did not fight Nora; instead she held her arm out like a child would hold it out. She wanted to sleep now. She wanted to go to sleep and dream a nice dream that would take her far away from here. Edward has the money, she thought. He'll take care of this and I'll be going home soon and all this will be over with. She felt the prick of a needle in her arm, and a few minutes later, she felt the sweet threads of sleep begin to wrap themselves around her, soft threads like soft silk sheltering her, carrying her away.

Frances and Nora closed and locked the door to the little upstairs bedroom, and carrying the gas lantern, they went downstairs, where Elizabeth was waiting for them. The First Lady would be out for at least four hours, perhaps longer. In just over six hours, in Switzerland, the International Bank of Zurich would be open for Friday morning's business. There were six hours left now before it all would be over, before they could leave the old

farmhouse and First Lady Mary Holt Morgan and the Rights for
the Unborn League.

The hours had passed by too quickly for Rights for the Unborn
League Special Security Assistant Jack Riley, who had driven
across Virginia to the foothills of the Appalachian Mountains
with the accelerator to the floor. He was off Highway 66 now,
driving on a winding secondary road that led out of Middletown,
Virginia. The twisting, turning two-lane road was carrying him
up into the hills. He was driving too fast on the sharply curving
road; he knew that, and the black darkness that was descending
on the rolling hills around him was making his high speed even
more dangerous. He didn't care. He cared about the five million
dollars. Nothing would get in the way now. They were up there
somewhere and Jack Riley would find them. He would find
Frances Foster and the First Lady, who he was certain now was
locked in a boarded up bedroom on the second floor of the farmhouse. He would risk the high speed on this lousy road. He remembered the little plastic statue his dead grandfather had bolted
in the wheelhouse of his old shrimp boat. What was the statue?
Now he remembered. It was a saint; the fishermen's saint that
bobbed in the wheelhouse. His grandfather's saint would protect
Jack Riley now.

Riley jerked the wheel of the rented car as the road dropped in
front of him, curving down into a swale. He let up on the accelerator and then floored it again as the car swooped down to the
bottom of the swale and began to follow the road up the other
side. Riley didn't see the little dirt side road at the bottom of the
swale; he didn't see the Frederick County police car until its red
and blue lights went on behind him and its siren began to wail.
He didn't have time for this; he didn't have time for some local
cop. For a brief moment, Jack Riley considered trying to outrun
the local cop, but it was no good. The rental car didn't have the

juice and Riley knew it. He lifted his foot off the accelerator and prepared to stop.

Frederick County Sheriff's Deputy Jason Wheeler pulled in behind the dusty red Ford and squinted at the license plate. No telling what was out here on this stretch of road these days; the county road had become a thoroughfare for drug dealers in the past few years and Jason Wheeler was not taking any chances. The car had out of state plates, too. Wheeler read the license plate number to dispatch and sat back to wait. He did not have to wait long. Ten seconds later, his police radio sputtered to life once again, this time with the information that the Maryland vehicle was suspected of being used by a cocaine ring in Baltimore. Wheeler was to wait for a backup, the dispatcher said.

Now young Jason Wheeler, who had been on the police force for nearly a year, licked his dry lips and pulled his service issue .38 caliber revolver from his brand new holster. There was a shotgun in a slot beside him and he pulled that out too. Then he opened the door of his patrol car, got out, and positioned himself behind it, his .38 drawn and pointed at the dusty red Ford. Wheeler had heard the ward room stories about these drug runners, about how they carried automatic machine guns in their cars, about how they didn't care who they shot, about how they killed for no reason at all. Jason Wheeler was ready for the bastards.

Very slowly, he reached for his bullhorn, which was fastened to the dashboard of his patrol car. He had to bend over slightly to get at it, and just for a second, he had to take his eyes off the red car, so he could get his free hand on the bullhorn. He was trembling inside, and his heart was pounding hard against his chest. He felt a sheen of sweat on his face and his sharply pressed shirt collar felt tight all of a sudden, real tight on his neck. He longed to loosen the tight collar, but he could not. Jason Wheeler's hand was inches away from the bullhorn when the car door on the driver's side of the red car opened and a man got out. The man was in a hurry; he was striding toward Jason Wheeler, reaching his hand inside his jacket, right at chest height where a shoulder holster would be. Jason shouted at him to stop but he kept coming; he was calling something to Jason, but Jason didn't hear him. He just saw the headlights gleam on something the man pulled from his jacket, and something told him the gleam came from a gun. Jason shouted once more, and then he squeezed the trigger of his .38, squeezing off one shot.

Now the man dropped down, like he had been punched in the side or something and he was out of breath. But the man reached into his jacket once again and Jason Wheeler saw a revolver in the man's hand now, plain as day, and Jason squeezed off another round before the bastard could raise the gun and fire at him. The second shot went in at chest level and Jason Wheeler saw a dark stain spreading over the man's jacket as the man crumpled to the ground, the hand with the gun in it stretched out beside him, his fingers curled around it, his index finger on the trigger. Jason Wheeler stared at the crumpled figure. The figure twitched a couple of times, and then it lay still on the blacktop pavement, the gun still clutched in its hand. Jason Wheeler lowered his service revolver and his body began to shake like one of those spindly little trees shakes in a high wind. And he began to cry.

On the pavement, blood spurting out of his body from a hole torn in the main artery to his heart and more blood pouring from the wound in his side, Jack Riley's last thought was of the little plastic statue in his grandfather's wheelhouse, of the shrimp boat bobbing in the warm waters of the Gulf of Mexico, of his grandfather beside him. He didn't care about Frances Foster and the First Lady now; he didn't care about the money anymore.

Chapter Eighteen

Six hours and fifteen minutes after Jason Wheeler pulled himself together long enough to radio dispatch once again, this time to tell dispatch that something terrible had happened on the dark and lonely two-lane road outside of Middletown, Virginia, and now a man was dead out there, the International Bank of Zurich, in Switzerland, received two sizable and identical cash transfers from Washington, D.C., for $50 million each. The $100 million transfer from the United States was promptly deposited to account number 7653241. Immediately after this deposit was made, Swiss banker Michele Campeau, who handled these personal matters for International Bank customers, disappeared into his thickly carpeted office, closing the heavy door behind him. A moment later, Michele Campeau placed a discreet telephone call to a guest at one of Zurich's small but very fine hotels, which happened to be about six blocks from the International Bank office. Speaking softly into the receiver, Michele Campeau delivered his message, received a thank you, and rang off.

In her Zurich hotel room, Adele Pearson hung up the telephone, breathing a long grateful sigh of relief. The money was there! She felt herself shaking once again, as she had at odd moments during the long night of waiting. She had been awake most of the night, staring at the ceiling above her bed, praying to God that everything was all right and that the money would come in the morning and then she could go home to her safe little house in Westport, Connecticut, and return to her beloved post as Dean of the Crofton School and no one would ever know the part she had played in the abduction of First Lady Mary Holt Morgan, Crofton School alumna. With a trembling hand, Adele Pearson now moved to fulfill the last part of her bargain with Frances Foster. Picking up the telephone receiver once again, she asked for the overseas operator, for she wanted to place a call to the United States.

Across the gray waters of the Atlantic, Nancy Todd paced off the distance between her telephone and the little bay window that overlooked a littered neighborhood park on the other side of the street from her row house in Queens, New York. It was 4:30 A.M. in Queens, and Nancy had been up all night, pacing her living room, her stocky body moving restlessly back and forth over the worn carpet. Except for trips she made to the cramped kitchen for more black coffee, Nancy's eyes never left the telephone. Still, when it finally rang, jangling suddenly in the early morning stillness, her whole body quivered as if in surprise, as if the sound were a fire alarm instead of a ringing telephone. Now she raced the few steps to the telephone and jerked the receiver to her ear. "Yes!" she answered breathlessly.

From across the wide Atlantic came the voice of Adele Pearson, clear and strong. "Jane came home this morning," Adele said.

Nancy Todd's heart surged with excitement. It was the coded message she wanted to hear. The $100 million was safely in the numbered account in Switzerland. Jane was home. "Thank you," she breathed into the phone.

High in the Appalachian foothills, a pink dawn was beginning to glow on the eastern horizon; it was nearly a new day now, nearly daylight when the electronic telephone beside Frances

Foster buzzed softly with an incoming call. Frances was sitting on the staircase, the phone beside her, when the call came from Nancy Todd in Queens, New York.

They had won.

But there was no time now to celebrate; they would celebrate later. Upstairs, in the little bedroom with the boarded-up windows, First Lady Mary Holt Morgan slept on, dead to the world. Frances heaved herself up and went to Nora, who was inside the little bedroom with the First Lady. They would give the First Lady one more shot now, an injection that would prolong her deep sleep for another four hours, long enough for Frances Foster and Nora O'Brien and Elizabeth McKinley to drive Frances' new red pickup truck over the summit of the Appalachians and down the other side and on to the Kanawha Airport at Charleston, West Virginia, where they would board a Delta Airlines flight for Mexico City. On Saturday night, they would leave Mexico City for the long flight to Sweden. Frances paused for a moment outside the door to the little bedroom. Elizabeth McKinley was downstairs, watching at the living room window, and Nora was at the First Lady's bedside, standing guard over her. The old saltbox house was as still as death in this last hour before morning; it was still as only the end of a long night can be still. Frances thought of her daughter Hillary now; she thought of her as she had last seen her, laying white and still and cold as marble on the steel slab in the New Orleans morgue. Frances knew now that the pain and loss would never go away, that it always would be with her, that she would feel the pain even as she drew her last breath on this earth. But it would mean something now; Hillary's death would not have been for nothing. Frances drew a long breath, almost a sigh, and then she opened the door to the little boarded-up bedroom and went inside to Nora.

It was just before 5:00 A.M. when the red pickup truck pulled away from the old saltbox house, leaving the clearing behind.

Inside the saltbox, the First Lady was alone now, sleeping soundly on the little cot, her blanket tucked neatly under her feet, one arm thrown over her face. She was snoring softly.

President Edward Morgan stared across the Chippendale dining table at his wife, who looked back at him and then looked away. It was Monday morning, and Mary had been home since Saturday afternoon, when she called from a pay telephone outside of Middletown, Virginia, and told them to come and get her. In the intervening period, they had learned nothing about her abductors. Nothing at all. She kept telling them she didn't remember anything, and Albert Arntsen, President Morgan's wily CIA Director, had not turned up anything either. At least the press didn't get in on this, Morgan thought. At least they didn't have the media to contend with.

But there was something else, wasn't there. Morgan's wide mouth twisted into a scowl. Something had come in to the White House this morning, and Al Arntsen, who had intercepted this particular message, had now delivered it to his old pal Eddie Morgan, who wasn't going to like this one. Morgan put his coffee cup down and picked up a thin envelope that was beside his saucer. He had read what was inside the envelope an hour ago, but now he wanted to see what was in there again. And he wanted his wife to see it. Flicking a stray piece of lint from his immaculate jacket, Edward Morgan reached for the envelope. He withdrew a single piece of paper, a copy of something, and he read it again. Then he tossed it across the lustrous mahogany table to his wife, who was watching him. "The women who kidnapped you sent this to me," he said. His eyes narrowed now as he looked at her pinched face. He didn't know her at all, did he. "You should have told me about your abortion." The paper was a copy from a page in the late Dr. Hugh Foster's journal of so long ago, long before he met her. Whose kid had it been? She would never tell him; he knew that. Maybe she didn't know whose it was, Morgan thought. Well, he had already called Al Arntsen and his boys off. There would be no hunt for those women now; they could spend their $100 million and go to Hell. What else could they do? He had a re-election campaign coming up. He couldn't afford a scandal about his wife's fooling around and getting caught at it before she ever met him. Damn her!

First Lady Mary Holt Morgan looked only once at the piece of paper that her husband threw across the table; she looked long enough to see what it was and then she closed her eyes. So they had betrayed her after all; they had taken the money and then they had betrayed her. Oh how she hated them. Now she looked across the table at her husband. She had borne him two children. She had been a good wife to him, hadn't she, and now he was looking at her with that sickly contempuous look of his, that superior look on his face that she despised so much. She prayed for strength. "I tried to make up for it. For the abortion," she whispered. "The League has saved so many babies." Oh, if she could make him understand how much the League meant to her!

Edward Morgan's voice shot across the table like gunfire. "You're resigning from the League as of right now. You're going to be where you should have been all along, young lady. You're going to be here at my side as First Lady and I'm going to win that election!" He threw his napkin on the table and stalked from the room, his face red with pent-up anger. She would toe the mark from now on, by God. It was about time.

Mary Morgan watched him go, sitting rigid in her dining chair. The bastard, she thought. She picked up the piece of paper that bore the copy of Dr. Hugh Foster's journal and she crumpled into a tiny ball, rolling it round and round until it was small and hard. She had been so tired lately. Maybe it was time to let go at the League, to let a successor take the reins. After all, she had been wanting more time to herself, hadn't she. And she wanted to do some writing, too. They had been after her to do that. Why, the story of her founding of the Rights for the Unborn League, her struggle for the Amendment, could probably be made into a movie. And the producers would want her to help, of course. That would be after the election, naturally. She would have to spend a great deal of time in Los Angeles, probably. She pictured herself at the premier of her movie, sweeping through the crowds, the spotlights waving, her golden hair gleaming as she floated into the theater past the adoring crowds. Mary picked up her coffee cup and sipped thoughtfully. Yes. Perhaps it was time to move on, to broaden her horizons.

It was winter now in Stockholm, Sweden, and frigid air from the Arctic Circle had swept down through Scandanavia this winter, delivering the coldest temperatures in many years. But it was warm and comfortable inside this modern glass and steel building that stood in one of the cluster of satellite cities on the edge of greater Stockholm. Frances Foster wiped her wet hands on a cloth. Their clinic was a success. In fact, their success threatened to overwhelm their resources. With salaries and rent and other expenses, like air fare and hotels for their low-income clients from the United States, their expenses were outstripping their income, which came principally from funds in their numbered account at the International Bank of Zurich. Frances had long ago spent her own bank account down to the nubbin, in spite of the enraged and quite expensive overseas telephone protests of her dear friend and attorney Matthew Adair, who knew just about everything now. He knew about the abduction of the First Lady, which had never made the papers, and he knew about Hillary, too. He supported all of their efforts, too. But he thought Frances should spend the Zurich money first. Frances, however, considered the Zurich money to be the clinic endowment fund.

Two weeks ago, a newspaper reporter from Chicago had been in to see Frances Foster, the American Women's Clinic administrator, and Nora O'Brien, the director of nursing services for low-income women, which included a referral service in the United States, transportation, lodging and medical care. Now her dear friend Nancy Todd had called from Queens, New York, to tell her that the American Women's Clinic was in all the papers. Frances put the towel she had been using to dry her hands back on the rack in the little bathroom in her office. Would the Rights for the Unborn League try to stop them? Let them try! But she worried about the reaction. She didn't want their clients harassed; she didn't want vicious ugly letters coming to the clinic. She just wanted the clinic to do its work in the world, to have its place in the sun. She heard the buzz of her telephone in her office. A moment later, she picked it up. It was Nora. She was on her way to the office and she had Elizabeth with her.

Frances had barely had time to settle herself in her chair when the door opened and Nora came in, followed by Elizabeth. They were carrying two bags.

Nora threw her bag on the sofa opposite Frances' desk. "It's mail," she said. "From the United States. I guess that newspaper reporter did this." She reached into the bag, pulled out an envelope and tore it open. "Probably hate mail," Nora said sadly as she opened the letter and began to read.

The letter was from Norfolk, Virginia. "Dear American Women's Clinic," the letter writer said. "I am a Navy wife and we have three children now. I'm pretty happy. But ten years ago I needed an abortion and thank God my mother helped me get it. (My husband doesn't know.) I just wanted to write to you and tell you to keep up the good work. I hope this fifty dollars will help. (I put it on my Mastercharge and my husband doesn't know, either.) Sign me Sandy in Norfolk." Fifty dollars in cash was stapled to the letter.

Nora rocked back against the sofa and turned to Elizabeth. "You open the next one," she said.

Elizabeth McKinley dropped her mail sack beside Nora's and pulled out a letter. She had changed in the six months since the three of them had arrived in Stockholm on that August morning. They had flown all night, flying across the Atlantic, leaving their lives in the United States behind. There was a new purpose in her step now, a new gentleness in her manner. Elizabeth was home. Carefully, using a fingernail, she sliced open one of the letters.

Two fifty-dollar bills fell to the sofa from the opened envelope. The tissue-thin paper inside had been folded carefully three times. When she opened it, Elizabeth saw that it had been written by someone who was very old. The spidery handwriting was shaky and feeble. "Dear ladies," it began. "I am eighty-three years old and I have six children. Three of them are still living. I decided that six children were enough for one woman, and when I got pregnant with another one, I had an abortion. They were illegal then, too. I'll never forget that night. The pain and the terrible bleeding. I thought I would never stop bleeding. Lots of women had abortions back then. We didn't have much in the way of birth control and there was a lot of ignorance. You take this money for your clinic and God bless." The letter was signed by Amanda True, Denver, Colorado.

Now all three of them began opening the letters, the hundreds of letters from the United States. They were from women, most of them, and they were filled with love and support and money. Money in cash and cashier's checks and personal checks and money orders. And now Frances and Nora and Elizabeth, their arms around one another, were hugging one another and laughing and crying and opening the letters just like bright and shining little children open holiday packages. It was only after the knocking on Frances' office door became loud and insistent that they stopped to see who it was out there, Frances wiping the tears from her face as she called out to whoever it was to come in.

The door opened slowly, tentatively, and a tiny woman, short and stout, her gray hair permed into little curls, her black coat drawn firmly around her round body, stepped cautiously into Frances' office.

On the sofa, Nora's brown eyes widened in surprise, and her wide Irish face was suffused in a bright pink flush as she struggled to her feet and went to the door to greet her mother.

"Nora, dear," Mrs. Eileen O'Brien said to her daughter. "I read about you in the newspaper and so I came to see you," she said softly. Her blue eyes were bright with tears as she looked up at Nora.

Nora O'Brien stood stock still in Frances' office. How could her mother understand? Once more, the regret came back to Nora that she was not like the rest of them, not like the other four O'Brien children who were right there in Chicago and happily married, all of them but Nora. She had not talked to any of them since last year, since long before the incident in the little back-yard clinic in Algiers, where Michael Green, M.D., and Hillary Foster had died. No. They would never understand, would they. "Mother," she said.

Now the little wrinkled hand slipped into Nora's broad hefty one, holding it warm and soft. "Your father sends his love, dear," Eileen O'Brien said.

Her mother was so small. So much smaller than Nora remembered. Had it been three years since Nora had seen her mother? Yes. It was more than three years. It was three years ago Christmas since Nora had been home to the South Side of Chicago. Now her mother was here. "How is he doing?" she said. Patrick O'Brien had a bad heart.

"He's doing fine," she said. She stopped and looked up at her daughter. "He misses you."

Nora felt a stab of guilt. It had been so long and now her mother was here, so far from home, so unexpected. She didn't know what to say, how to make her mother understand, her Catholic mother who went to mass every day and who lit the votive candles for Mary. But she wanted to try. Her mother had come all this way and now Nora desperately wanted her to understand. "We're helping women who have no other place to get help," she said tentatively.

Eileen O'Brien moved closer to her daughter. "I know that, dear."

Nora bent her head toward her mother. Across from them, Frances Foster and Elizabeth McKinley sat transfixed on the sofa, witness to this exchange between mother and daughter.

"Some of them would surely die without our help," Nora said.

Now Eileen O'Brien's plump little arm went around Nora and she was patting her daughter gently on the back, and somehow, in spite of her small size, she was drawing Nora closer to her, enveloping her daughter as if she were a child again. "I know, dear. How do you think I stopped at five children," she whispered. "We all had them, Nora. All of us. The midwife took care of us then."

Nora felt a great weight lifting from her chest, a great heavy weight she had not even known was there. She felt the sting of tears rising in her eyes. "The Church," she said faintly.

"The priests didn't get pregnant, Nora."